The Apple of My Eye

Mary Ellen Bramwell

The final approval for this literary material is granted by the author.

Second printing

This is a work of fiction. Names, characters, businesses, places, events and incidents are either the products of the author's imagination or used in a fictitious manner. Any resemblance to actual persons, living or dead, or actual events is purely coincidental.

ISBN: 978-1-61296-405-8

PUBLISHED BY BLACK ROSE WRITING

www.blackrosewriting.com

Printed in the United States of America

Suggested retail price $16.95

The Apple of My Eye is printed in Adobe Caslon Pro

ACKNOWLEDGMENTS

The journey that produced this book would have been incomplete without the help of a number of people. First, I need to thank my daughter, Amy Barnes. Her early reading of this manuscript, and brutal editing of it, made it a much better book. She had a way of getting to the heart of what worked and what didn't. Without her input, literally this book would not exist. Also, I want to thank my parents, Kent and Janyce Harrison, for their numerous readings of the book in its various forms. Their edits and suggestions were very helpful.

Many other people contributed in various ways: My great-grandmother, Martha Fereday Harrison, who was always sweet and kind despite a hard life, Phyllis Bestor, Rachel Horn, Robin Horn, Paula Kriz (my early sounding board), Kristen Gough, and the Black Rose Writing team. Special mention needs to be made of the Solon Branch of the Cuyahoga County Public Library. Within its walls, the early pages of this book were written.

Lastly, I want to thank my family, especially my husband, Allen. He took over the running of the household to free up my time so I could write. He believed in me before I believed in myself.

To Janyce Maxfield Harrison,

my earliest and most ardent cheerleader

The Apple of My Eye

PART 1 – DARKNESS GATHERS

BEGINNINGS

I'm not sure which came first, the phone call or the sense of being strangled in my sleep. The choking sensation, as if all breathing on my part must cease, is still vivid in my mind. The feeling engulfs me and I am lying in bed all over again. I feel my throat constricting, intense pressure bearing down on me that I cannot escape. I push away at nothing. I flail and scream, but no sound escapes as my throat is squeezed shut, not by some actual physical hands clasped around my neck but from some nameless danger lurking just as real around me. I gasp for air, seeking somehow to gulp in one long breath that might see me through until I can breathe again. But that breath won't come, and I feel certain that I will perish in an instant, without even a cry on my part.

I look around, but all is immense darkness, a dank cavern that must soon swallow my soul. Thoughts race through my mind. *Can't ... breathe!! Air ... air?* My thoughts, frantic and disjointed, fade to *Why?*

... *What?* as my mind starts to shut down. Stretching out my arms, I reach for ... what? I know not. My fingertips long to touch something, anything, but all is emptiness. There is no hope, no light, no life. . .

Then a breath, a flicker, and just as suddenly as it came, the strange sensation dissipates, leaving me sucking in deep breaths, surprised to be alive. *What is happening to me?* I wonder in panic. *Where did that come from?* I continue to take in large, gasping gulps of air, almost choking on the attempt. Light is now just visible around the edges of the window where moonlight sneaks past the curtain into my bedroom. As my breathing begins to slow and the terror recedes, I puzzle over what has happened. Was I dreaming? The sensation felt so real. I look around me, and in the dim light I can discern shapes but no colors, as if they have been drained from the palette of my life. I feel, more than I see, that I am alone.

It's at that moment that the phone on my nightstand rings, or it could have happened earlier. I really don't know for sure now that I look back. I remember it in this order, but why would I have a sense of dying before the phone call? That makes no sense. Even now, when so much is clear to me, I can't reason it out. I try to switch the order in my mind, to take back even a small tidbit of control, but something in me won't allow it. It's as if even my own mind is fighting against me. Or maybe it was quite simply a sense of what was to come. But I'm getting ahead of myself. The phone needs to be answered.

It rings several times before I dare to answer it. Phone calls in the middle of the night are either wrong numbers or calls that take your life in the wrong direction. How I wish this had been a wrong number.

"Hello, this is Brea," slurring out Bree – ah, as if I still lack the oxygen to speak.

The voice on the other end is indistinct, or maybe I just imagine it so, refusing to understand what is happening.

"Mrs. Cass? Mrs. Brea Cass?" finally registers in my ear. "I'm sorry; there's been an accident. Your husband is on his way to Summerhill General Hospital. We don't know if he's going to make it. You might want to get there as quickly as you can."

And that's it — no explanation, no consoling words. Although I can't, for the life of me, think of any words that would have consoled me that wouldn't have been lies. In the end, lies would not have helped; they never do.

I had become so strong in recent years, so comfortable with my life, but suddenly, I found my knees buckling beneath me, unsure of my very footing, unable to think clearly or even make a simple decision. All control was now an illusion as I began to gasp for actual breath, fighting the rising fear overtaking me.

Strange thoughts flood your mind in moments of crisis. *Should I just go in my pajamas? Should I put on my makeup? Should I wake the baby to take him with me or find someone to watch him? He's teething and he'll be so cranky,* as if any of that matters now. It has been six months since this moment and no one remembers how I looked. I don't even know whether Noah was cranky the next day or not. I honestly don't remember Noah even being present, although he certainly was. I know he was cared for, but I don't know if I did it or someone else did. I only remember that life had changed, and I was sure it would never be right again, that it would always appear to me as gray. I also assumed, wrongly, that I would never again in my life eat an apple.

But I must not linger on that thought for now if my story is ever to be told, and tell it I must. For this is how I made order out of chaos, because for Noah's sake, that's what I knew I had to do.

PAUL

Paul was a senior the year I entered college. He was everything I was not: confident, charismatic, funny, and everyone's favorite. He couldn't enter a room without charging the electricity in the air. Everyone would turn in his direction as if drawn to him in some otherworldly way. The strong ones would engage him in conversation. Most would simply follow him with their eyes or hang on every word like obedient puppy dogs.

I was one of the quiet puppy dogs. I had never seen anything quite like him before. I immediately recognized his appeal. His good looks were a perfect match for the character he presented. At first, he seemed arrogant. I heard many accounts of him jokingly introducing himself with, "My name's Paul, but you can call me Apollo." Not many people have the audacity to equate themselves with Greek and Roman gods, but Paul could get away with it. He would even add,

"You know the god of truth and light." I'm still not sure why no one took exception to it, but such was Paul and his following.

Only one thing surprised me. With a bit of chagrin, I have to admit that I had stereotyped the handsome type to be synonymous with a barely average intelligence. Paul surprised me. He was smart, and at the time, I would only admit to myself that we were equals there.

Growing up intelligent and female created difficulties for me. I learned at an early age that outscoring all the boys in math didn't make them like me better and often produced the opposite result. My good friends accepted my intelligence, but the boys I was attracted to were often intimidated by me. So, I had learned to underachieve in classroom discussions and overachieve on homework and tests to make up for it. Most of my teachers caught on and tried to talk me out of such behavior, but what teenager listens to reason?

Entering college, however, I thought I might make a fresh start and do the best I knew how on all fronts. But Paul frightened me. What if I scared him off by being his equal in this one arena? I shouldn't have worried. Eventually he found me out and tenderly chastised me for robbing the world of my knowledge and abilities. However, that conversation didn't happen for some time.

It had all started when I entered my first class that freshman year of college, CS 101- Introduction to Computer Science. Wanting to appear attentive yet not too eager, I slipped into a middle seat. Hopefully its location would not draw attention to me. Of course I was fifteen minutes early, so when the professor entered five minutes later, and I was the only one present ... it became apparent that my seat choice was irrelevant.

Professor Haynesworth immediately addressed me with, "Good morning, young lady. It's good to see that *someone* is interested in my class today." He smiled, and the lines at the corners of his eyes smiled with him. He reminded me of my grandfather. He was pleasingly plump, and he wore a somewhat wrinkled suit that, rather than detract from his appearance, projected an image of sagely wisdom. His tie, a conservative regimental stripe, hung almost straight down his front. His mother must have passed along good genes because it appeared he hadn't lost a hair from his head, although it was pearly white with silver highlights. Unruly, yet stately, it added to his mystique.

He pulled out lecture notes and began to write on the whiteboard in blue and green ink. I smiled to realize red, synonymous to me with blood and homework corrections, would remain capped. Finishing his introductory notes on the board, he turned to me again. "So what brings you to the Midwest? I don't believe you're from around here, am I correct?"

Startled, yet pleased that he would take notice of me, I stammered, "No, I'm not. I'm from back East, but I liked this school's computer science department, and they offered me a scholarship." For some reason I added, "But I guess I really came because when I visited last year, this just felt like home." I was surprised at my openness with someone I had just barely met. For that matter, we had yet to be introduced, but something about his manner said I could trust this man.

This first impression, as first impressions go, was surprisingly accurate. Haynesworth was a man with no guile. What you saw was what you got. In the coming months and years, I would find him always to be impeccably honest, and as such, always assumed the same in others. It was refreshing to be viewed that way. I worked hard to always deserve it.

The memories of that day, etched into my mind, centered more on the next person to enter the classroom since it was the first time I laid eyes on Paul. He walked in the door behind me and brushed past my seat, walking down the aisle to the front of the room.
"Professor, how's it going today?" he asked, with a ready smile.

"Ah, Paul. Thanks for coming. I want to introduce you to the class today. I'm sure the newer students will need your assistance as the semester progresses. We have one young student, so far, but I'm sure the others will find their way here in a minute or two."

Paul turned to take me in and smiled in my direction. I melted. He was tall, like my father, probably six feet or so. He was trim yet fit with broad shoulders, a perfect image of someone that could and would protect me. He had wavy auburn hair and eyes that seem to draw me in. I couldn't make out the color of his eyes from my "middle" seat, and I found myself wishing I had chosen the front row. His clothes were neat and clean, no crumpled t-shirt, but a button down shirt that seemed neither too dressy nor too casual on his muscular torso. I was surprised to find my heart beating faster, yet I felt helpless to slow it down. Nervously twisting my fingers through my long hair, I ended up with blonde strands caught in my jewelry.

He seemed aware of the effect he had on me, and, I came to understand later, he well knew the influence he had on others. He looked at me and winked before turning back to speak with the professor.

Trying hard to hide my smile, I looked down and started to rummage through my backpack for a pencil, a phone, any kind of distraction. As I did so, I noticed other students had started to trickle into the lecture hall. By the time class started, thirty students were spread out around me.

Professor Haynesworth began his introduction to the class, but I struggled to focus. I couldn't take my eyes off Paul seated near the front of the class. He stood when he was introduced as the teaching assistant for the class. As I watched, he flashed his smile at everyone, especially pausing on my female classmates. I felt foolish. I should have known that I was nothing special, just the opposite sex, just one of many objects of his attentions.

I should have had an easier time listening to the lecture after that, but I felt like a rudderless ship, tossed about by the conflicting emotions this momentary encounter sparked. I was confused that such intense feelings could appear so suddenly. I no longer watched Paul, but I couldn't concentrate on the professor's words either. Eager for the class to be over, I just wanted to escape and plant my feet on solid ground.

When class ended, I quickly gathered my things, spilling pencils and books in my rush. Flustered, I started scooping up my belongings, trying to keep tears from forming at the corners of my eyes. Just when things seemed like they couldn't get worse, Paul appeared at my elbow, reaching down to help gather my things.

I looked at him not knowing what to think and certainly not wanting to be the fool again. He handed the last pencil to me and said,

"May dropped papers be the worst thing that happens to you all semester long."

Taking away my embarrassment and making me smile at the same time was not what I had expected. It was also not what I wanted. How dare he make me smile!

He looked me directly in the eye, and I saw how his blue eyes complimented his auburn hair, but then chastised myself for noticing. Never dropping his gaze, he stretched out his hand towards me. Opening his fingers, I could see he held a small, rosy colored apple. "Here, maybe this will help," was all he said, as he placed it in my hand. I was too dumbfounded to even mutter a thank you before he was gone.

. . .

After that first classroom introduction, I was determined not to care. Clearly, he was the catch of the day, and I had no real chance. But even more, I recognized the type. I would be like a shiny, new toy that soon loses its luster.

The apples, I suppose, won me over in the end. Throughout the semester Paul always flashed me a smile, along with all the other girls in the class, but he reserved the apples for me alone. The type and size varied, and over the course of the next few months, I tasted more varieties than I knew existed. I can't say that I understood this quirky behavior, but I didn't linger on it. His magnetism always melted away my desire to dislike him.

By then I had heard all about Paul Cass. He had a reputation. Whomever he wanted, he got. Despite not wanting to be another prize ribbon for his trophy case, I found myself entranced. The apples were the only thing that didn't figure in. No matter who I talked to or what conversations I overheard, and there were plenty about "Apollo, the god of truth and light," apples were never part of the equation. Tales were abundant about his numerous girlfriends and his unending charm, but no one ever mentioned apples.

THE CLOCK TOWER

The day of my CS 101 final dawned crisp yet clear. Walking to class bundled in my coat and boots, a thrill of excitement mixed with relief washed over me. I would see Paul one more time, one last time. How does one comprehend such conflicting emotions? I had always looked forward to seeing him in class, but then I would kick myself for feeling that way as soon as he smiled at another girl. *You know better than this!* would be my silent self-recrimination. I felt weak, that as long as I could see him I would never completely get over him, and get over what anyway? I had never been one of his girls. He hardly spoke to me, other than some simple words as he handed me an apple, such as, "Enjoy the fruits of your labors," or "An apple a day, you know…"

I had created in my mind a relationship that just wasn't there. It would be a relief never to see him again, to dump the boyfriend I never had. This I wanted to be the "final" moment of infatuation, no more torturing myself with his looks that bewitched me, no more thinking about him as I lay in bed trying to sleep but unable to let rest my thoughts of him. This would really be final.

And it was, in a way. It was the final end of my misconceptions.

When I finished my test, I stood and walked to the front of the class to lay my paper on top of the stack of completed exams. As I did so, I was surprised to find Paul by my side. "Brea, please meet me in ten minutes under the clock tower. I'll make it worth your time."

Bewildered, I lifted my gaze to his. Was I not free yet? Was this just another manipulation? I wasn't sure what to think.

Sensing my hesitation, he simply pled, "Please?" It was at once plaintive and sincere, and the raw and honest nature of it caught me off guard. Nodding consent, I turned and left the room.

True to his word, ten minutes later he joined me under the clock tower. He was uncharacteristically and visibly nervous.

"Brea, I just needed to talk to you. I would like to get to know you better. I'm so sorry I haven't talked to you before this." His words started gushing forth as if a dam had broken and they could no longer be held back. "I've wanted to see you outside of class, but I didn't think it was appropriate while I was your TA. Professor Haynesworth agreed with me, that it wouldn't be right, but he also assured me that you were worth waiting for." Looking down, he stammered, "I probably shouldn't have given you the apples. It's just that after that first day, I didn't want to stop." Raising his eyes to mine, he simply added, "You're the apple of my eye."

When I recall this moment for others, it always comes out sounding cheesy, but it never felt that way to me, not then and certainly not now. It felt like the most romantic thing ever said to me or anyone else on the planet. I would have done anything for him in that moment.

All barriers collapsed and I burst forth with the smile I had been suppressing all semester. "Apollo, I don't know what to say." Then I burst out in embarrassed laughter for using a name he had never mentioned in class.

He smiled but got a funny look in his eye. Then a twinkle appeared as he asked, "Now why would you call me that?"

"I ..." was all I could stammer out, before just shrugging my shoulders and painting a mock surprised look on my face.

To his credit, he let it go. "So, Brea, I wonder if we might go about this a little more properly, now that class is over. Would you like to have dinner with me? Say tomorrow? Unless you're already heading home for the holidays?"

"Sure," was my only response. I was heading home, but a friend was driving me. I figured I could convince her to postpone for a day.

"Around five? Is that too early? And where do I pick you up?"

Arrangements were set, and I literally floated back to my dorm room. I almost forgot to go to my last final later that day I was in such a daze.

. . .

Paul came for me at ten to five, but I was ready. He greeted me with an apple. He didn't need to repeat the earlier sentiment; the expression in his eyes said it all as he gently placed the apple into my open palm. His hand lingered this time, as it never had during the semester. He looked at me with what felt like too honest a look; he seemed to read into my soul. His power over me was almost frightening. He immediately sensed that his intensity had disturbed me. Breaking his trance with a smile and a wink put me at ease, repairing the moment.

I don't remember what we ate for dinner, you think I would for a first date, but I do remember the conversation as if it were yesterday. We talked the whole way to the restaurant as if we had known each other all our lives. Paul was every bit as charming as I had feared.

All too soon dinner was over and I was reluctant to end the evening. Paul apparently felt the same way, for when we left the restaurant, he asked if I would like to stroll around campus. It was a mild winter evening, but I was grateful when he offered to put his arm around me, fearing at the time it might also be a mistake. Was I ready for this? Was he? I knew so little about him.

All concerns dissipated, however, as I became intoxicated by the sound of his voice and the protective feel of his arm around my shoulder. I leaned my head against him as we wandered the sidewalks of campus gazing at the stars and talking about our plans and our futures. I felt like I belonged right there in his embrace.

We didn't return until two in the morning. We stopped outside my apartment and I leaned back against the brick of the building, looking up into his eyes. He placed his hand on the wall behind me, returning the intensity of my look. Bending down he gently kissed my lips. He took my breath away as I returned his kiss while his free hand came down to find mine and our fingers laced together.

He surprised me by pulling his lips away from mine, but he still held on to my hand. He looked down at our joined fingers, hesitating as if he didn't trust himself. Then gradually he lifted his eyes to mine, slowly backing away until, still connected, our arms stretched between us. His look was serious, and I didn't know what it meant. He dropped my hand, stared through me for a moment longer, and was gone without a word.

. . .

I barely slept that night, but my friend and I were trying to get an early start, so I arose early anyway. As we were loading the last of our things into the car, I was surprised to hear Paul's voice behind me. I hadn't seen him approach.

"Good morning, Brea. I just wanted to wish you a safe journey."

I was so happy to hear his voice that I surprised myself by twirling around and giving him a big bear hug. He wrapped his arms around me and picked me up off the ground. My heart beat faster, and I realized I didn't want to go home. I wanted to stay here forever in his arms.

Paul finally set me down. "Brea, hey call me and let me know you got there safely, okay?"

"Sure, although it might be late."

"That's okay." Then reaching into his pocket, he pulled out two apples. With a grin and a wink, he said, "You know, just in case you're hungry during your long drive home." And then he was gone.

I made it safely home for the holidays, and almost before I greeted my parents, I was on the phone with Paul, telling him of my safe arrival. My parents looked at me with raised eyebrows and slight smiles as Paul and I talked for over an hour.

. . .

Over the next few days, I could think of nothing but Paul. We talked to each other every day, sometimes multiple times a day. My mother smiled knowingly while rolling her eyes each time my phone rang. I found myself trading my infatuation for something else; I just wasn't sure what it was yet.

I felt guilty for having left him behind at school when he confided to me that his parents had both been killed a few years earlier in a car accident. I hadn't realized he had no other place to call home. He assured me he was fine. "I am at home, and now I'm thinking more and more about finding a little bigger apartment to call home. You know, just in case." I'm sure he could hear my smile.

It turned out that once we were "together" we didn't want to be apart. With my parent's consent (and curiosity), Paul flew out to see me for New Year's. He spent the day stealing glances at me while conversing with my father about football. He complimented my mother's cooking and lingered over old family photos lining the walls. Before he left the next day, my parents were as smitten as I.

AN ECHO IN MY EAR

I headed to the hospital in disarray. Before leaving home, I had awakened my neighbor, Martha, a sweet great grandmother who loved Noah. Martha would have happily watched him at our place, I realized, right after scooping Noah up out of his crib. Instead, I roused her, dumping Noah in her lap with a hastily packed diaper bag and a key to our door so she could get whatever she needed. I had no idea how long I would be gone.

Driving through town in the dark night felt wrong. Since having Noah, I was rarely out this late. Nothing looked the same. Usually I loved this town. It was the right mix of small and large, big enough to have all the amenities someone might want, but small enough to feel cozy. The university was close, but not so close that the parties spilled out onto our streets. Paul had taken a job here after his graduation so that I could finish school.

Tonight nothing appeared welcoming or inviting. In the midnight hours all the colors on buildings and signs looked washed out, fading to merely gray or pale white. I felt certain that if I looked in a mirror even my blue eyes would look gray. I wondered for a moment if I were dreaming, but the thought of dreaming brought back to mind the strange sensations of earlier, and I took a deep breath just to make sure I could.

Paul, Paul, please be okay. Please be okay! I pled silently in my mind, too scared and too much in shock to let the tears loose that threatened to drown me. I drove past quiet homes lurking in the darkness. I wondered how anyone could be sleeping at a moment like this, but I knew their lives were not hanging on what was happening at the hospital a few miles away. They could not feel my anguish nor see the concern in my eyes. They would wake up in the morning as if nothing had happened and make their breakfasts and go to work or school or take care of their children as if the day were like any other. But it wouldn't be, and I knew it, regardless of what greeted me ahead.

The hospital, ablaze with light, was in sharp contrast to the rest of the bleary town. A large neon EMERGENCY sign assaulted the dark night while echoing my fears. I almost pulled up directly to the emergency entrance, only stopping myself at the last minute as I realized I was expected to take the time to park my car and walk to the entrance, as if I had all the time in the world.

Hospitals are not warm and welcoming places. Noises abound - the rattle and swish of curtains being pulled around patients for a mock sense of privacy, the constant pad of feet in hallways, beeps of machines and the pumping of blood pressure cuffs. And then the voices, saying things you don't want to hear, things you should never hear, some meant for your hearing while others overheard in moments solemn, thoughtful, noisy, but not noisy enough.

I started with the emergency room desk. "I'm looking for my husband, Paul Cass. Do you know where he is?" The receptionist looked harried and tired. The waiting room was full, indicating it had not been a slow night. She half-heartedly looked through her computer and flipped some notes on her desk. Without saying anything, she got up and went back into the recesses of the emergency room.

Hollering loud enough for all in the waiting room to hear she called, "Hey, Jules, was that DOA named Paul something or other?"

"Paul Cass," came the echoing reply.

OF LIONS AND ELEPHANTS

Memories after that moment are mixtures of haze with snippets of clarity. I remember there was a police officer who came and found me in the waiting room. Gently he led me to a quiet place. I'm fairly certain he gave me the official word that Paul had died in the ambulance on his way to the hospital, but since I already knew, what did the words matter. I do recall he used the word "hero," although it made no sense at the time. I believe he asked me some questions, but I don't even know if I answered them or not. At some point, a friend of mine was called to come drive me home. Amy delivered me back to my place either in my car or hers, I couldn't tell you which. I only know that later my car was parked neatly in my garage as if I hadn't taken a slight detour to the hospital, altering forever the path my life would take.

With my mind in a fog it surprises me that I remember the remainder of that night, my first night truly alone, with absolute clarity. How can you describe feeling so totally alone, with no hope for change? Paul had been working nights lately, so I had slept alone in our bed, been alone until he would come in around three AM. He would climb quietly into bed so as not to disturb me, but the smell that was only him would intrude upon my dreams, and I would open my eyes and smile, knowing he was there. Some nights the exhaustion of being a mom overwhelmed me, and I would smile at him and then drift peacefully back to sleep. Other nights we would talk about his day and mine, and I would snuggle into his protective embrace, willing sleep away for just a few more private moments.

But that first night, he never came home. I knew in my head that he wouldn't come, that he never could again, but my heart kept calling to him. Surely he would hear me and come. It would be like *The Princess Bride*, my favorite old movie, when Wesley says to Buttercup, "Death cannot stop true love." Paul would find a way and come to me!

My body was bone tired from a night like no other, but I couldn't sleep. *How can I go on? How can I move even one step forward?* I wondered. I could not understand what had just happened. How does someone go from being here to being gone? It just doesn't seem possible. There has to be a warning somehow, a way to prepare. With a grip of fear I thought of my experience at the beginning of this night (could it still be the same night?) and of how I felt before the phone call. Was that my warning?

I wrestled all night long like a lion taking down an elephant alone. No matter which side I attacked, I couldn't gain a purchase. Looking from every angle I could imagine, all I could see appeared gray and rough. I couldn't sink my teeth into the tough hide of the reality of my life. I have never known such despair. My mind was blind to everything but my indescribable grief. It was bigger than my soul, and I felt it would crush me before morning.

Surely if I just let the grief in, it would run throughout my body, and the elephant would win. I would fade away and die, be gone, feel nothing, but all I felt was a crushing weight that would not kill me. I did not wish to die, but living felt cruel and impossible.

The tears did not come until I thought of Noah. For his sake, I could not die. I had to live, and living meant dealing with pain like I had never known before. And so the tears came, slowly trickling at first, and then in rushing torrents soaking my face and my pillow and our bed, a bed meant for two, now home to only one. I sobbed in great body shaking sobs that echoed throughout the hollow house. I cried for Noah, who would not long remember the father who bounced him on his knee, who tickled him, who kissed him and threw him in the air to the sound of baby giggles. I cried for Noah, and I cried for me. I cried my eyes from pink to red to swollen. I cried and while I did, the lion in me decided I could not slay the elephant. The elephant would live, but so must I. Just how was I to survive?

A SECOND CHANCE

Starting my second semester of college was very different from starting my first. I wasn't worried about classes or roommates. I had only one thought and that was Paul. As soon as I returned from the holidays, Paul picked me up and we went to his apartment to watch old movies and eat popcorn.

He cringed when I chose *The Princess Bride*, but I told him how much I loved watching it with my parents. I was pleasantly surprised when he sat through the whole thing, and I subsequently vowed to watch a guy movie with him the next time.

That evening was followed by many others. We watched more action flicks than I knew existed, and we played card games and board games, sometimes with friends but mostly with just the two of us. Often we sat together in silence, each of us intently working on our respective homework assignments, content to be side by side.

One weekend, after a particularly grueling week, Paul invited me out to a nice restaurant for dinner. When he picked me up, he seemed to be in a more serious mood than usual.

After we were seated in the restaurant, Paul regarded me thoughtfully, then asked, "Why did you give me a chance?" We had talked so much lately, but he had never been so direct, and we had never talked about why and how we had actually gotten together.

I wasn't sure how to respond. "What do you mean? I was taken with you from the moment I met you, but I didn't think I meant anything to you." Pausing, I looked at him. Did I dare ask what I really wanted to know? With a sense of calm, I realized I had no qualms asking him anything I wanted. "Paul, why did you ask me out? Why did you pick me? It's clear you can have anyone you want."

He blushed slightly but didn't back away from my questions. "Brea, you intrigued me. That first day I met you I thought you were beautiful. Then you smiled, and you could have melted glaciers. Those things definitely caught my eye, but that's not what kept my attention." Then he sheepishly added, "I guess you pegged me right, I do pretty much get whoever I want. That's the whole point. I couldn't get you. I worked my charms on you, but you didn't seem to care. The only thing you reacted to was the apples.

"I'd never met anyone like you, someone I couldn't get to like me right away. I guess I just had to know why. The thought that someone else might capture your heart when I couldn't was something that just didn't sit well with me." He shrugged his shoulders while smiling sheepishly.

"You know, I even talked to Professor Haynesworth about it. You know what he said?"

"I haven't a clue. What?" I was curious now.

"He told me if I really wanted to impress you, I should stop trying to impress you. How's that for crummy advice?" He laughed. "He also said that instead of hoping you were watching me, I should watch you." He paused and shrugged his shoulders. "I guess I didn't really have a choice. I took his advice. Let me tell you, that was an eye-opening experience. I've never seen anyone like you."

That should have made me nervous, but it didn't. His honesty was comforting. "I must have done something right, but I'm not sure what," I replied.

"Stop doing that. You're dismissing yourself, and you know better than that. I'm pretty sure down deep you know you are one amazing person. Don't hide that. You are strong, don't ever forget that."

No one had spoken quite so bluntly to me before. All I could do was smile; I wasn't about to deny anything now.

"Brea," he continued, "you have a fierce strength. I mean, if you could hold off on your feelings for me, that's a heart of steel." His eyes were smiling and I could tell he was teasing me, easing up on the gentle but firm reprimand of a moment before.

"You have no idea!" I laughed out loud. "I think my major for last semester was 'Just try not to fall for Paul Cass!'"

We both laughed and then naturally reached across the table to clasp each other's hands, as if to make real what we both had feared was just a dream.

"You really do intrigue me, Brea. You have the looks, but I've never seen you use them to get ahead. You could have flashed a smile and skated through without much work at all, or simply have gotten others to do most of the work for you, but you didn't. Instead, you worked harder than anyone. That reminds me of lessons my mom tried to teach me," he said with a chuckle, yet a wistful look, too.

"Yeah? There must me a story behind that."

"What?" His thoughts were still elsewhere. "It's just, my mom and ..." he trailed off.

"I'm sorry. It must be hard having your parents gone. I didn't mean to bring it up. I didn't think, I ..."

He cut in with, "No, it's okay, Brea. I just don't like talking about my parents." Then his demeanor quickly shifted, and he was once again in control of the situation. "But you don't get to change the topic that easily. We were talking about you, and how you totally bewitched me." He flashed me his infamous smile.

I laughed at his apparent dramatics. "Oh, really?"

His smile dimmed and his eyes took me in completely. "Brea, I really did watch you," he said in all seriousness. "I have learned to read your face. I can tell when you understand something right away, and I can tell when you don't. But when you don't, you get determined rather than frustrated. You work that much harder to learn and understand, and then you turn to all those around you to make sure they understand as well. I know Haynesworth doesn't grade on a curve, but if he did, I'm sure you still would have helped everyone else get a leg up. You are very impressive, Brea."

He got quiet and looked down at his hands. When he finally raised his eyes to mine, they were moist. "Brea, I spent all last semester falling in love with you. I hope you will come to feel the same way about me."

Just when I thought he couldn't surprise me further, he just had. I was taken with Paul to be sure, but I wasn't ready to call it love. I didn't really know Paul, and yet he knew me better than I knew myself.

After his declaration of love, he backed off, letting me digest those feelings. The conversation didn't lag, though, and while we talked, I thought. Any remaining concerns I had about Paul were gone. I started to fall hard and fast.

Neither of us was surprised, although we should have been, that our talk soon turned to "our" futures and what "we" would do. It just seemed the most natural thing in the world.

APPLE PIE

That second semester passed in the flurry of attending class, homework, and studying. Any free time was spent with Paul. Often when we studied together, I found it hard to concentrate. Even when Paul was deep in a book I would find myself watching him, noticing the way he ran his hands through his hair or the quick flick of a motion he would use to turn a page.

In so many ways I didn't know him. I didn't know what his childhood was like, where he went to school, or what he did in high school. I figured memories involving his parents were still painful reminders of his loss. When he was ready, he would tell me those things.

In the meantime, I was learning his mannerisms and the cadence of his voice, what foods he liked and the music he listened to, as well as what he would sing along to. Each thing I learned made me feel more a part of his life, as if we were connected or were meant to be.

I remember finals vividly. I was exhausted when they were over. Paul was in his last semester of school and his finals were a mixture of exams and senior projects, some of which had taken weeks to prepare. We agreed when everything was completed and turned in we would meet at a small, grassy hill at the edge of campus.

I arrived first and promptly fell asleep on the warm grass. The next thing I remember was the soft touch of Paul's hand as he brushed my hair back from my face and gently kissed my cheek. "Brea?" he whispered.

"Yes, Apollo," I mumbled back sleepily before I even realized what I was saying.

He gently lifted up my head and placed his jacket under it for a pillow. Then he ran his fingers through my hair until I woke up completely. I felt at ease and safe. "I love you, Paul."

He smiled. "I've been hoping to hear those words. Come here," he said, while carefully helping me to a sitting position. He reached into his backpack, then turned to face me. Opening his hand, he revealed a small apple. As he brought it to me, I could see it was not a real apple, but a small, red, apple-shaped jewel case. He placed it gently in my palm.

Inside I discovered a beautiful diamond ring with one large stone in the middle encircled by smaller diamonds and rubies. I gasped and looked up into his eyes.

"Brea, would you be my wife?"

I squealed with delight and started giggling so heartily that I almost forgot to say, "Yes." When I did, Paul let out his breath, as if he had been afraid I was going to say, "No," instead. I threw myself into his arms, knocking him to the ground. We stayed there, lying on the ground in each other's arms, softly talking about our lives together until it was dark.

. . .

Paul and I were married at the end of the summer. Paul was determined to give me more time since I was so young, but in the end, we saw no reason to wait. Paul, being an only child, was eager to belong to a family again. Mine welcomed him with open arms. Our wedding was small but beautiful, with most of our guests being from my family. Professor Haynesworth, feeling like the cupid in our story, insisted on standing in as a surrogate father for Paul.

It was a little unusual, but we served apple pie. It was a day I will never forget.

MY GROWING LIST OF WORDS

I made it through the next day, the first full day without Paul, mostly because there was so much to do. My parents were flying in, and someone went to pick them up at the airport. My minister came by to talk about funeral arrangements, and the morgue (what an awful sounding word) wanted to know where to send the body. Even the thought of that question gave me chills. Amy and Martha were with me all day. One would play with Noah while the other dealt with the phone calls and the questions.

More than one reporter called, and even a brazen few rang the bell. "She has no comment at this time. She is busy dealing with her grief. We would thank you for respecting her privacy at this difficult time," was the line I heard repeatedly.

I moved to hide out in my den, the office that Paul insisted should be mine. Our big house was meant for the large family Paul and I planned on having, which now only served to mock me. My own private den served to shut out the expanse of a house I no longer wanted.

My thoughts kept going back to the choking sensation from the night before. If it was a warning of some kind, could I have done something to prevent all this? Could I have called Paul and warned him somehow? Logic told me there wouldn't have been time, but logic couldn't explain any of what was happening, could it?

I needed to be more aware of such things, any possible warnings. That was the problem, I concluded; I hadn't been aware enough. My nightmare was just beginning, I knew, but if I was acutely aware, maybe I could change some outcomes, I rationalized. Maybe I could bring a small piece of Paul back into my life. I almost deluded myself into thinking I could undo what had already been done.

As I pondered these things in my den, I focused what energy I had on the sounds and sensations around me. As I did so, a heightened sense of awareness engulfed me. Everything was deathly quiet. Straining for any evidence of life, I could faintly hear from the direction of the kitchen a small sound, probably Martha drying a dish and returning it to the cupboard. It must have been a small plate, maybe two, by the sound of the clink and the noise of a cupboard door. Martha was a frequent guest in my home. After sharing a bite to eat, if there were too few dishes to fill the dishwasher, she would insist on washing them by hand, not wanting to leave any cleaning left undone. Now she was replacing a glass in the cupboard, and a second. She and Amy must have had a bite to eat. Although I wasn't conscious of Noah or Amy being nearby they must have been, and as I wondered where they were, I fell into a dark and thankfully dreamless sleep.

I awoke to the sound of voices, welcome sounding voices, Mom and Dad. The familiarity of the sound for a brief moment transported me to a different time and place, bringing to mind little snippets of memories.

. . .

I remember the night before my wedding. I was excited and nervous, and I started to cry. Only I wasn't sure if they were tears of joy or tears from stress and anxiety, and not knowing which made me cry harder. Mom came into my room. She opened her mouth to speak, and then shut it without actually forming a word. Instead, she sat down on my bed next to where I lay. Gently she started to play with my hair, using her hand to brush it behind my ear. When she finally spoke, the words were melodies to my heart. "Brea, I have treasured you from the moment you were born. It wouldn't be fair to other parents to say that I loved you more than they loved their children, but I think you would be hard pressed to find a child more loved than you. After so many miscarriages, Dad and I were both very grateful to finally have a child of our own. Someday, you will understand the fierceness of a mother's love. But Brea, despite all that, after tomorrow you are no longer mine, at least not mine alone. You and Paul will belong to each other, and I will have to be content playing second fiddle. Actually, I wouldn't want it any other way."

Her efforts at comfort only made me cry more, but at least now I knew they were tears of joy. I wiped my eyes with a tissue, just as Dad poked his head into my doorway.

"Hey, what's this? Why wasn't I invited to the cry fest? You think because I'm a man that I can't cry with the best of them? It's just not true. In fact, the other day when I got the bill for that dress of yours, the one you'll be wearing for a few hours only, I'll tell you, I almost cried. And then there was the caterer. When we were sampling the food, she thought I was crying because of the onion, but no, that wasn't it. I was thinking it would be easier to rent out a Wendy's and treat everyone to everything on the menu - and cheaper too!"

I was laughing now, even while the tears still wet my cheeks. My dad's eyes were smiling and the comfort of his voice enveloped me. I sat up in bed and reached to embrace my mother beside me. Dad soon knelt at the bedside by the two of us, looking over us with a protective smile.

. . .

The sound of their voices always filled me with wonder. Now as I heard them, I wanted to rush into their arms, but I stopped to listen to them, to get accustomed to the reason they were here.

"Does she know yet how he died?" Mom asked.

"I'm pretty sure they told her, but I don't think she actually heard anything that was said to her last night," Amy's voice responded. "Paul is being hailed as a hero, but he just swapped his life for that of an old man already dying of cancer. I don't mean to sound cold and uncaring, but Paul had his whole life ahead of him. It just doesn't seem fair. I can't explain that to her. I wouldn't even know where to begin, and it's not like the old man's terminal condition isn't going to be common knowledge sooner or later. I don't know how she'll deal with that."

Then my father's deep voice could be heard saying, "What's done is done. The bottom line is Paul did the right thing regardless of the outcome. He saved a man's life for heaven's sake. Dying a hero is better than dying a coward in my book."

"You're right. I'm probably selling Brea short. She'll come out of this. She's just so young to be a widow."

From my hidden perch I thought, *Widow – another nasty word to add to my list along with "morgue," and "casket," and "corpse."* I didn't realize until she said it that I was a widow. Martha was the only other widow I knew, and her husband died of old age. Nothing about this was right. Nothing made sense. And what in the world did Paul do?

DADDY'S LITTLE GIRL

Leaving my shelter, I made my way to the warmth of my kitchen. Mom and Dad rushed to me, embracing me in turn. Mom held me tight for several moments, and I could feel her tears on the nape of my neck. I was torn between gratitude and anger. I was so glad she was here, but I didn't want her tears. I wasn't crying right now, and her tears made me feel like *I* needed to comfort *her*. I knew anger was the wrong emotion to have, but if I let go of the anger – anger at my mother's tears, anger at being the object of their pity, anger at Paul for dying and leaving me, anger at him for not finding his way back to me – if I let go of all this, I would collapse, having no strength to even stand, and I must admit defeat.

Taking control of a situation where control was only an illusion, I accused, "So, how exactly did Paul die? And don't leave out any details, like the terminal old man."

Amy gasped at my tone and the sudden realization that I had

overheard her earlier comments. Tears welled in her eyes, but she could not bring herself to speak.

My father, wiser than I, gently put his arm around my shoulder and guided me out of the kitchen into the great room. Paul and I had decorated this room together. The walls were cream colored, a nice backdrop to the artwork that graced the walls. I couldn't look at the paintings and prints that reminded me so much of Paul. We had either picked them out together or they were gifts from Paul to me, on birthdays and anniversaries or just because he loved me. I wouldn't look at those pictures, but I couldn't escape the sun shining through the large windows we both adored. They invited light into a room that was normally cheerful, made even more so by the dancing rays I usually welcomed.

My father guided me to the leather couch in the middle of the room, Paul's favorite spot in the house. I could tell my father wanted to talk to me, but my thoughts made it hard to concentrate on him and what he might say. Always patient, he waited until my eyes registered awareness before beginning, hoping that I would hear and listen.

"Brea?"

Reluctant to answer, I wiggled my toes in the plush taupe carpet at my feet before acknowledging him with a small nod.

"Brea, Paul was at an all-night grocery. Two men entered the store, we presume to rob the place. Paul, the storeowner, and an old man were the only ones in the store at the time. It appears the old man was there to buy some food for his cat. According to reports, the old man turned to the intruders and challenged them by asking what they thought they were doing. At least one of the thieves had a gun and he turned it on the old man. Paul reacted by jumping in front of him, taking the bullet in the chest. I'm sorry. It nicked his heart. He really had no chance."

Somehow, my dad's straightforward answer softened my anger. He hadn't actually mentioned the old man's cancer, but we both were aware that I already knew, so it wasn't important anymore. I looked up at his rugged yet gentle face, the face that had seen me through scraped knees, bruised egos, and broken hearts. I buried my head in his shoulder and sobbed.

Dad just sat on the couch with me, letting my grief soak his shirt.

He held me tight, but didn't patronize me with words of comfort that couldn't possibly be true. How long I cried I don't know, but my anger seemed to wash away with the tears.

"Dad, I don't know what to do. How do I move forward without him? I don't think I can do it without Paul. He was everything to me."

"I don't think anyone expects you to know how to do it yet. Right now, you just need to deal with one day at a time. Just worry about you and Noah, and I'm just talking about basic things like making sure you eat meals every day. That should be enough of a goal for right now.

"Brea, I hate to ask, but what are your finances like? Will you be okay for a while? If not, you know your mom and I will help you."

"No, Dad, I'm okay with finances. We bought the house free and clear with Paul's inheritance money from his parents, so I don't have to worry about a house payment. I'll have to do some checking on our investments with the bank, but we should be okay for the time being at least." I winced when I slipped and used the word "we" knowing that it wasn't three of us anymore, just Noah and me.

He felt my shudder, "What is it?" he whispered gently.

It was a minute before I could speak, and even then, all I could get out was, "We?" in a choked whisper.

Dad knew exactly what I meant and held me to him ever tighter. My composure broke and tears coursed down my cheeks.

"I know, honey. I'm so sorry. We'll work on details another time. Just cry. There's nothing wrong with crying. I'll hold you as long as you want."

· · ·

The rest of that day was a blur. I don't think I left that couch, sitting by my dad, for hours. I was aware of Mom's hovering concern, but both my parents seemed intuitively to know that I needed Dad. I needed his strength and the security of his presence, especially since he was once again the only man in my life. I felt like a little girl again, wrapped in the protective arms of my daddy. He was going to make all things better. He had to, because I had no idea how to do it on my own.

AMY

It was odd entering my sophomore year as a married woman, but it was such a relief as well. When I had seriously started to notice boys in middle school and was aware that they were noticing me, I wasn't sure how to act. All the emotions and turmoil of puberty threw me into a tailspin. The first boy to have the courage to talk to me (and me him) was Tucker. He was cute, with a dimple in his chin. We shared a math class right before lunch, so we walked to lunch together, sitting side by side while we ate. It was an idyllic two weeks.

Then I made a fatal mistake in math class. Our teacher, Mr. Georges, asked me to demonstrate on the board the solution to one of our homework problems. I did so correctly, never realizing that most everyone else had gotten the problem wrong. Tucker gave me a look of betrayal and walked off to lunch without me. It was the first time, but unfortunately not the last, that I regretted displaying my intelligence.

For some reason, I discovered over the next few years it was okay to be good at English, but boys seemed threatened when I excelled in math or science. To be fair, not all the boys were taken aback by my brains, but at that age, even one negative reaction was enough for me to hide my test scores.

Despite my determination when I got to college not to bury my talents, years of doing just that made it difficult to start new habits. Being married helped, since I wasn't trying to impress any of the men in my classes. At home, I had the best catch of my life, but that alone was not enough.

Once afternoon, after returning from classes and studying, I walked in to find Paul busy in the kitchen making dinner, a real dinner. "Hey, what's up? Did I forget that it was my birthday or something?"

Paul smiled and chuckled at me. "No, but I do have a surprise for you, even if it isn't your birthday."

Thinking the meal was what he was referring to, I said, "What are you making me?"

"Nope, that's not it. I am making a lovely meal, but that's not the surprise. You're just going to have to wait."

I watched him make a fancy chicken dish with a name I couldn't pronounce, but any questions I asked he quickly rebuffed with a simple, "You'll just have to wait and see." The only thing I could tell for sure was that he was making way too much food for the two of us, but not until I watched him setting the table for four did I even know how many guests were coming.

At 6:30 sharp, a knock sounded on our apartment door. I rushed to open it, but Paul swept past me and got there first. From the hallway, I heard the always welcome voice of Professor Haynesworth. What a wonderful surprise! But who was he bringing with him?

The door opened up to reveal only the professor. "Is someone coming with you?" I asked in confusion.

"No, I'm afraid not, Brea. You're stuck with me."

Embarrassed, I tried to back pedal. "No, I didn't mean that. It's just that the table is set for four. I thought ..."

He cut me off with, "I know, dear. Allow an old man to tease a little. There is another guest coming, but she's not with me."

So the professor was in on it as well. I gave them each a dirty look while they just laughed at my dismay. Paul decided to release me. "Brea, Haynesworth is here to keep me company and out of your way while you meet your new best friend, after me that is."

He wasn't helping to clarify anything much yet, but I looked at him expectantly, hoping he would explain. He hesitated, but then relented when I smiled plaintively at him.

"Okay. We have a new intern at work. Her name is Amy, and she is just what you need."

"I didn't know I needed ...," I started to protest.

"Let me finish, Brea," as he smiled lovingly at me. "Amy is just like you in so many ways. You are going to love her. She is also completely at ease in her own skin. If she has a better idea than what's out there, she speaks up. She has good comments and suggestions, even though she's just an intern." He placed his hands on either side of my face and looking right into my eyes, softly added, "You are so bright, Brea. I think of you and your quick mind every time she says something. I just wish I wasn't the only one who knew that about you. Amy is not afraid to shine. I want you to feel that same way."

I started to tear up as what he said sunk in. I felt rebuked and loved all at the same time. Paul knew just what to do. He took me in his arms and whispered in my ear, "Brea, I love you. You are an amazing, intelligent, strong woman. I don't deserve you. I just want everyone else to know what a lucky guy I am." Then he added, "And I want you to put your fellow classmates to shame."

I started to laugh in the midst of my tears. Professor Haynesworth spoke, now that it appeared safe. "Brea, Paul doesn't quite have it right. There are a few others who know how smart you are, like me, for instance. But I agree with Paul; there is nothing wrong with allowing others to see that as well. Ultimately, they'll figure it out anyway when you're the one they all end up going to for help with assignments. Why not save them the trouble of searching you out." Then he smiled kindly at me.

I felt a little ganged up on, but I guessed that was okay. If anything, it was a bit embarrassing. These two meant the world to me, so I supposed I could get over myself. I knew they meant well.

Amy arrived a few minutes later. She was everything Paul had indicated she would be – eventually.

She knocked on the door, and then before we could even answer it, she opened it herself. *Self-assured is right*, was my first thought.

"Hi, Brea. Paul's told me so much about you. I was thrilled when he invited me to dinner."

I wasn't warming to her yet; I even gave a sideways glance to Paul. How could he tell this woman so much about me and not even mention her in passing to me?

Paul just shrugged and smiled, then urged me with his eyes to stick it out. I turned back to my "new best friend" with a heavy dose of skepticism. "Well, he told me nothing about you. So, I guess you're going to have to fill me in." As soon as the words left my mouth, I realized they could easily be seen as an insult. While I decided whether to feel smug or guilty, Amy looked at me a little surprised but then appeared to immediately move past it.

"Well, there's not much to tell, quite frankly. I'm really very average."

This self-dismissive remark didn't sound like the self-confident woman I was expecting. I began to wonder exactly who she was. Her statement, basically a non-statement about her life, made me curious. I forgot all about looking down my nose at her, too intrigued was I by the woman herself.

I watched as Amy turned to the professor and exchanged some pleasantries. I couldn't tell if they had met before this moment. Neither one was shy or withdrawn.

Paul ushered everyone into the kitchen for some cheese and crackers while he put the finishing touches on dinner. I stood frozen in place as if watching from outside the room. Amy walked down the hallway like she had been here a million times. She wasn't arrogant, acting like she owned the place, just comfortable, as if this was where her best friend lived.

When I didn't move, it was Amy, not Paul, who turned to see why. "Brea, are you all right?" she asked brightly.

I wasn't sure how to respond. I must have had a quizzical look on my face, because Amy mirrored a puzzled look back at me. Then she walked back down the hall to where I was standing. Haynesworth and

Paul had disappeared, leaving the two of us alone. What should I think of this woman? She looked to be in her early twenties, with short, curly brown hair. She was cute, although not pretty, but she radiated something. I was trying to put my finger on just what it was.

She broke the silence with, "Paul tells me you're studying computer science?"

I nodded, still a little tongue-tied.

"I love computers." I noticed as she talked she put her arm through mine and started to gently guide me towards the kitchen. "I'm studying business, but I've taken a fair number of computer courses. I'm considering it as a minor, so I can easily see the appeal. When did you decide to focus on C.S.?"

I felt the need to respond to the direct question, and before I knew it, we were talking freely about our likes and dislikes, our strengths and weaknesses. Somewhere during the evening, we ate dinner and dessert, but I was oblivious to the food even as I was eating it. Amy entranced me. She had the ability to tell me about her accomplishments and abilities without once sounding like she was bragging or making me feel inferior.

However, Amy actually talked very little about herself. She asked me question after question, drawing things from me that I hadn't even gotten around to telling Paul, such as my chess championship wins and my college entrance test scores. In retrospect, I'm not sure how such things came up, but it didn't strike me as odd at the time.

The evening was over too soon. As Haynesworth and Amy got ready to leave, Amy pulled me aside. "Brea, you are every bit as amazing as Paul claims. You can prove your intelligence with accomplishments and test scores if you want, but in reality, it's much more than that. You have a sense about you of what you want in life, and you clearly love life itself. I have had a truly enjoyable evening." Then she added with a whisper, "Don't let on to Paul, but dinner was great, too. I do not cook, so I appreciate it all the more." She winked and then walked out the door.

For the second time that night, I stood frozen in thought in the hallway, thinking about Amy. She described me as liking life, but I think what made her stand out is that she liked people, including herself. It was contagious. It felt impossible not to like her, but also not to like myself when I was in her presence.

I turned to Paul, only to find him staring at me with a sly grin on his face. He was suppressing, "I told you so," with every fiber of his being.

I had to laugh. "You were right. If you weren't already my best friend, she would be."

He reached out to me, drawing me close. "Can you believe you were actually annoyed with me earlier this evening?" His eyes were twinkling.

"There'll be no stopping you now, will there?" I asked, laughing. I reached up and kissed him, as if to silence any comeback, but all was forgiven and forgotten as my heart beat faster, completely smitten with this loving, caring man I had married.

REBIRTH

I don't know if Paul ever regretted introducing me to Amy. If he did, he never let on. Under her tutelage I became more comfortable with myself, more willing to speak my mind in all situations. I suppose in retrospect he approved, because even though Amy taught me to find my voice, it was Paul who made me feel like I had something to say.

I remember walking across campus with Paul. It was my senior year and the first real fall day of the year, not according to some date on the calendar but from the surprising chill in the air. I had donned a thin jacket, but a short time into our walk I realized I was not prepared for the weather. Paul put his arm around me, trying to warm me, but my bones would not warm.

"Brea, do you want to go inside to warm up?"

"Yes, but we're just heading to the library. I'll survive until then," I responded as I nestled further into his arms.

He surprised me by stopping mid-stride and turning me about to face him. "Brea, what do you want to do after you graduate? I've moved up enough in management with my work at the hotel that I can find a job just about anywhere. I'll follow you wherever you want to go. So, what do you want?"

I was shivering slightly, but inside I was solid. "You know, I've been thinking about that. I love what I do, but I want to start a family. We've talked about it, but never with a timeline. I'm ready Paul. Are you? You don't talk about your parents and growing up so I don't always know whether you want a family in theory or one in reality."

It was not the answer he was expecting. For once, he was tongue-tied.

"You think about it, Paul, and after your shift at work we can talk about it again."

"No, it's okay. We can talk about it now. You just caught me by surprise, and I suppose you pegged me right. I do like the idea in theory but somehow never thought about the reality of being a parent. It scares me to death."

He read the disappointment in my eyes. "Brea, I'm not finished. You have taught me much about goodness. You are strong yet always kind. That's the kind of children I would like to raise, and if you're willing to help me, I think I'd like to give it a try."

I threw my arms around him. "Paul, I love you so much! I want lots of kids!" I felt him shudder then stiffen in surprise. "Oops. I'm sorry; my timing on that one probably wasn't the best." I pulled back in apology.

"No," he responded feebly, "I probably could have used a little more time to warm up to the idea of a first one before thinking about 'lots,' but if you're game, I'm game."

His trembling voice didn't fill me with a lot of confidence, but I knew Paul enough to know that once he agreed to a course of action, he would not deviate from it. I smiled up at him. "You know, I don't really want to go to the library so much anymore. Let's go grab some lunch before you need to head to work. I feel like celebrating, and I think maybe you need something to revive you. It'll work for both of us."

He just nodded in response.

We changed directions towards a favorite bistro of ours. It was no surprise to see Professor Haynesworth by the door as we arrived, since he had introduced the place to us.

"What a pleasant turn of events to see the two of you. And Brea," he said turning to me, "you look brighter than a summer sunrise. What's up?"

I turned to look at Paul and burst out in embarrassed laughter. I didn't think we were ready to announce to the world what we had discussed, especially since Paul was still warming to the idea, but how should I respond? He answered for me.

"Professor, you encouraged me to chase this woman who will forever be two steps in front of me. This is not an announcement, but she is going to be the mother of my children, and I am scared to pieces by the thought, but equally delighted. She will be amazing, and hopefully she'll help me be passable."

His straightforward response touched me. I was still looking up at him when I heard the Professor congratulate the two of us.

"It appears that I intruded on a private moment," he responded. "Wait here just a moment," and with that he disappeared inside the little restaurant while we exchanged puzzled glances with each other.

He returned a few moments later. "Fred, the owner, has a small, private room at the back. It's not open to the general public. You will be dining there today, my treat."

. . .

A few months later, Haynesworth was the first to share in our good news. Amy was next, and only then did we call my parents to tell them they were going to be grandparents.

WHO WANTS TO BE A HERO'S WIFE?

Dad didn't actually make things better. I mean, how can you? Paul was still gone, and my dad couldn't undo that. But just as he had done when I was a child, he helped me get up from my fall and brush off my skinned knees. He started with the newspaper, a staple in my childhood home. When I was a little girl, I would read the comics at his feet while he read the front page. As I sat there, he would point out interesting articles to me until I was hooked on the whole thing. Even though the internet was an information source for me now, I still loved the feel and the nostalgia of the newspaper.

It was different to be on the other side of the articles. The phone calls were constant from reporters, so the next day my father finally released the following statement:

Paul Cass was a loving husband and father. He will be greatly missed. Although we are saddened by his sudden loss, we are not surprised by his heroic actions. Paul has always been a leader among men, someone to whom many looked for guidance and direction. With this tragic violence, our family and our community have lost a great human being.

After that they left us alone for a time. The newspaper articles abounded, but our input was no longer requested or needed.

Even if the media was finally leaving me alone, my father wouldn't. He handed the newspaper to me. "You need to know what's going on in the world. Read the article about Paul, and then read whatever you like after that," he admonished.

I found the statement my father released buried inside a larger article, an article that explained what had happened to my Paul, telling me details that the police had probably already told me, but I had been too shell shocked to even hear.

... Sometime around midnight, according to the storeowner, who wanted to remain anonymous, two men wearing ski masks entered his small, all-night grocery store. Paul Cass had come in a few minutes earlier and an elderly gentleman, Frank Walker, was already at the checkout counter. He was buying a couple of cans of cat food and a bag of Cheetos. The owner said, "The old man, Mr. Walker, was tellin' me about his cat and how finicky the old thing's gotten, kinda like himself, he said. I guess he was lonely and couldn't sleep. He comes in a lot late at night. You see, his wife passed a few years ago, and I been seein' him a lot since then. I opened the register to give him his change, but he just kept on talkin'."

At that point, what had been a quiet evening suddenly turned chaotic inside the little grocery. According to police reports, the men entered the store and one of them pulled a gun on the storeowner, telling him to lie face down on the floor. His accomplice reached across the counter to grab cash out of the open till. The owner tells us that at that point everything seemed to happen at once. "Old man Walker says, 'Whatcha' doin'?' I lifted my head off the ground when he spoke, just in time to see that other fella [Paul Cass] yell and get between the gunman and Mr. Walker. Right after that, I heard the gunshot. It was awful. Then the two thugs just took off."

The article continued with details about the 911 call and the paramedics trying to save Paul's life, but those details just made me cry. *Focus on the good things*, I kept telling myself. *Paul died a hero. He was a hero.* That's what I would tell Noah when he was old enough to understand, whenever that was. I certainly didn't feel old enough to understand. *But Noah won't remember Paul like I do, so it won't be as difficult,* I realized with both relief and intense sadness.

I didn't read any more of the paper. Dad wanted me to, and he thought I was, because my head was buried in the paper for some time, but honestly, I just kept rereading about my husband the hero. It just seemed too fantastic, all so ethereal, as if I were in a dream, a bad dream, but a dream all the same. How could this possibly have happened? Why did Paul have to be in the corner grocery then? Why that store of all the multitudes of all-night groceries? Why couldn't he have stayed home sick that night? Why ... oh, a million things why?!

A HOME WITH A VIEW

The house on Shadow Brook Lane was the fourth house we looked at. I was coming up on the end of the semester and graduation, but having made it to the second trimester of my pregnancy, I was feeling like I had to do as much as possible while I felt relatively decent. A first trimester complete with morning sickness and a full load of classes had been rough, and I had heard the last trimester could be a bear as well. So, I had decided that now would be a great time to look for houses. I don't know what I was thinking. Despite my enthusiasm at the beginning of the day, my interest was waning. I was tired and hungry, and I knew I still needed to study for finals.

However, this house was different before we even entered it. Pulling up to the curb, Paul helped me out of the car while our realtor got out of her large sedan with the garish realtor magnet stuck to the side. I looked up at the large two-story colonial house standing on a small rise in front of us. It was inviting and imposing at the same time.

"Paul, are you sure we need something so large? It looks nice, but I just don't know." I knew my tiredness was coming out in my tone.

Paul put an arm around me, trying to help share the burden of what I carried, even if he really couldn't. "Brea, trust me. You, well we, talked about wanting a large family. We may as well have the space now and not need to move later."

"I'm rethinking that whole 'large family' thing just about now," I muttered under my breath, but purposely audible enough for him to hear.

Paul smiled apologetically. "Okay, sorry. Why don't we just look inside and then we'll call it quits for the day. Deal?"

"Deal, but I think when we're done here you owe me a lunch. I don't care what it is as long as it comes with a chocolate shake. I'm starving."

Paul chuckled. My craving for chocolate shakes was not something I even tried to resist, and it had become our little joke. We figured our son was going to be born addicted to chocolate. "All right, it's a deal." What happened next was the best part of the home tour. While our realtor was busy getting the key out of the lock box, an elderly lady appeared at our side. When she said, "Hi," we both jumped, not having seen her approach.

"Oh, I'm sorry to startle you. I just wanted to introduce myself. I'm Martha Fereday. I live in the home next door to this one."

"Nice to meet you," Paul responded, while he extended his hand to her.

"Yes, I'm glad to meet you too," I added, absent-mindedly rubbing my belly.

"If you don't think me too forward, after you look at the house, would you like to come over for lunch? If you don't have further homes to look at, that is. I'm just not fond of eating alone, and I'm guessing that little one of yours," pointing at my expanding belly, "doesn't like you to go too long without something to eat."

I looked up at Paul for confirmation. He nodded in a way that said, *Whatever you want is fine with me.*

"Martha, we'd love to join you. I'm Brea and this is my husband,

Paul. That's very thoughtful of you. Actually, I am rather hungry."

She smiled in return. "I may be an old lady, but I still remember a few things. I'll see you when you're done. Just come on over and walk in. The kitchen's at the back, and that's where you'll find me."

Then she surprised me by how spry she seemed as she scurried off to make us all some lunch. I couldn't begin to move as fast as she did. Paul walked patiently beside me as we made our way to the front door of a home that suddenly had a lot more appeal to it than it had a few minutes before.

The house itself was a pleasant surprise inside. We walked into a two-story foyer with a curved staircase leading to the second floor. It invited me to climb it, to see just where it led. But I resisted and turned instead to the left to see a formal dining room and then the other direction to see a small sitting room with early afternoon light streaming in unrestrained. I sought the source of the light and discovered a front window that afforded a view over the surrounding neighborhoods. I could see trees and houses and even a city park a few blocks away. It was a clear day, and the large expanse of blue sky seemed to stretch on forever, as if I were in the middle of someone's painting. I took a mental snapshot, to keep the moment with me forever. Already this place felt warm and comforting, exactly like home.

I reluctantly followed the realtor past the staircase to the great room at the back of the house. Attached to it was a large kitchen. I could picture our son crawling around this great room and into the kitchen where I would be making dinner or toddling to the front of the house to watch out the window for Daddy to come home, leaving little boy fingerprints all over the glass.

After that, looking at the house was a mere formality, at least for me. Paul eagerly showed me the first floor office just off the great room, opposite the kitchen. When we began this process of looking for a house, Paul had to convince me of the office arrangements. He wanted the larger space, an actual office as he called it, to be mine. As our baby grew, I wanted to create educational software for children, probably in the form of apps for any hand held device. I had created a prototype for my senior project. It was so much fun and such a natural fit for me that I could envision doing it from home when I had a stolen moment or two.

As we moved upstairs and looked at the bedrooms and bathrooms, I could already see in my mind's eye how I might decorate each room. The master bedroom was very large with a separate sitting area partially walled off. It struck me as the perfect place for Paul to have a working office. He agreed, and I could tell he was mentally moving in as well.

· · ·

We ate lunch with Martha before formally submitting our offer. We knocked on her front door as we entered, announcing our presence, and then made our way to the back of the house. She had made us grilled cheese sandwiches, and her timing was perfect. They were just coming out of the pan and onto waiting plates as we entered the kitchen.

She had filled the table with food. Besides the warm sandwiches, she had a tossed salad along with a bowl of cut up fresh fruit. Lemon slices and ice floated in a pitcher of lemonade. A bowl of chips and a smaller bowl of pickles rounded out the meal. I couldn't imagine a small woman, whom I assumed lived alone, having this much food on hand. "Wow, this looks delicious. Did you just run to the store for us?"

"No, darling, I just had a feeling I might need a little more this week," and without further explanation, she sat down and motioned us to do the same. She bowed her head, blessed our meal, and then invited us to, "Eat up."

My grilled cheese was crispy and gooey, just the way I liked it. "Martha, if you will make me grilled cheese like this, I'll offer the owners full price."

"Oh, thank you, but I wouldn't do that, my dear. Those folks have had that home up for sale for a long time, and they're starting to get impatient. I'm sure they'd accept just about any offer about now. Of course, I'm sure you'll make a fair offer. I even imagine they'd let you start painting or doing whatever you like right away, before you even close. That might help you get ready for the baby."

I exchanged a glance of wonder with Paul. This woman could be my adopted mother any day, and clearly, she was going to be like an extra grandma for our new baby. I didn't remember meeting someone who was so forthright right away, and yet she did it with such an ease that I had no cause for offense.

She looked at me and read my expression. "Don't be surprised, dear. When you're my age, you don't have time to wait for pleasantries to be over. I can see you want the house, you don't want to pay too much, and you are worried about being settled before your baby comes. It doesn't take much to figure that out. So the way I see things, if I can help you I will. Helping people is what makes me happy, and it keeps me from feeling too lonely or missing my husband too much. He's been dead for ten years now, and I miss him every day, but he knows I'm too busy helping people to join him just yet."

Nodding at my almost empty plate, she said, "When you're done with that, would you like some chocolate ice cream?"

I laughed out of pure joy. This woman would always have my back, and I had only known her for an hour.

ANOTHER HOME WITH A VIEW

The week following Paul's death was filled with one thing after another. The funeral took place the day after the newspaper article came out. Professor Haynesworth spoke and so did my father. I wanted someone to give a long eulogy, but I realized I didn't have enough details of his life. I knew a few childhood stories and where he grew up, but what was his first job? Did he have a favorite high school teacher? What was his first pet? Did he know his grandparents? I knew very little even about his parents since they died before we met. Did Paul look more like his father or his mother? I hadn't had enough time! I didn't know I needed to ask these questions already. We shared stories with each other, but we were just beginning. I thought we had a whole lifetime to share our histories. I guess we did; I just didn't understand the meaning of "lifetime."

Haynesworth spoke of his indomitable spirit. "Paul didn't

understand the meaning of 'can't.' He believed that if he could think of it, he could do it, and he had an uncanny ability to convince everyone around him that he could do it as well." He was right. That was Paul, always making plans, always achieving them. What would be his plan now? What would he suggest I do, if he could?

"Paul was a natural to work with people. He loved people and people loved him. It's a great tribute to him and his family that this chapel is so full today. May his memory be kept alive in all of us." Professor Haynesworth looked at me and at Noah sitting in my mother's lap and smiled.

My father gave the best eulogy that you can give with the knowledge that we had. I was surprised at how much he did know. I found myself falling in love all over again as he described Paul, his first trip to our house, his delighted yet scared reaction the first time he held Noah, his charming demeanor. I cried but I also smiled.

As the funeral ended, I was surprised to look at all the faces in the crowd. There were so many people! I knew or at least recognized most of them, but a few were strangers. I was astounded by the number of people who had made time to come to Paul's funeral. Virtually all the staff from the hotel where he worked had come. It made me wonder who was left to manage the front desk. I saw friends from church and our neighborhood, even people from early college years. Other faces I thought I could place, if given enough time. Many of them looked at me and smiled, but a couple at the back looked away and ducked out of the chapel quickly. I shrugged off their rudeness and turned to accept the embraces of those closest to me.

When we stepped outside of the chapel, the day hit me with its serenity. The sky was the color of Paul's eyes. Leaves were just starting to bud on the trees; red tinged their edges, like a whispered hint of auburn hair. An apple orchard was next to the church, but I was grateful that it was the wrong time of year for apples. I didn't want to see any apples right now.

After Paul and I were married, he still brought me apples. Every Friday morning or evening, depending on when he came home from work, he brought me an apple. He sometimes said nothing, just smiled, but usually he would lean down and kiss my forehead saying, "Apple of my eye, I love you." If Noah was in my arms, he would reach down and scoop him up, swinging him above his head. "And when you get a few more teeth, little man, you will be the applet of my eye," turning to wink at me as he did so.

The trees next to the church whispered these memories to me, sweetly, sadly, silently. I kept my gaze on them as I slid into the back of the mortuary's black limousine.

. . .

We buried Paul in the Summerhill City Cemetery, a few miles from our home. Paul had told me where his parents were buried in Ohio, but we had never found the time to visit their graves. I couldn't bear the thought of his grave being that far away, and if we hadn't visited his parents', how often would I be able to visit his graveside? Instead, I had found a double plot on the top of a small rise with a nice view of the distant horizon. It seemed fitting to look far off to see the setting sun; I had a long life ahead of me before I could join him.

Just a few people had gathered at the cemetery for the burial. A prayer was said over the gravesite, and just like that, it was over. Like a door shutting, it really was over for me. I looked around me at my family and close friends. They were here and warm and alive. As I scanned the faces and shapes around me, my gaze stopped on Noah, living, breathing, adorable Noah, six-month-old Noah.

I wasn't sure what was next, but my resolve was beginning to take shape. A little boy still needed me. I may now be a widow, but I was still a mother. Many wonderful people had mothered Noah in the last few days, but I was not one of them. I turned to my mother, who was holding Noah tightly.

"Mom, I'll take him now," was all I said. She handed him over, and I held Noah in my arms for probably the first time since Paul's death. I held him so tightly that he started to squirm. I loosened my grasp and said, "Noah, I love you. Mommy loves you so much!" Then I held him tightly again. He squirmed but he didn't complain. Soon he snuggled warmly in my arms, and then he began to silently cry.

I don't know why he cried. I don't know if he could possibly understand what was happening, or if he was reacting to everyone else's tears, but they weren't tears of hunger or pain. They were just simply quiet, cleansing tears. My resolve formed stronger, and I knew that we would survive, and somehow we were also going to thrive.

NOAH

Noah Paul Cass arrived in the middle of the night. He weighed eight pounds even. When they placed him in my arms he was alert and looked up at me and right through me. It was an overwhelming moment. He had a mass of dark hair, a cute little nose, and lips just like his daddy's. "Paul, he's so beautiful." I was overcome with emotion, but when I looked at Paul, he was as overcome as I was. "Do you want to hold him?"

"No. I mean, yes. I just, I just don't want to break him."

"Paul, sit down." He did so, and I handed over our new swaddled bundle to him. "Just cradle him gently, and if he fusses, softly bounce him in your arms." He did as he was told, looking both proud and petrified.

After staring down at him for some time, Paul finally spoke. "I never knew it would be like this. He's so tiny and vulnerable. I want to protect him, but I feel so completely inadequate. How do parents do this?" He looked up at me with the most plaintive look on his face; all I could do was laugh.

"Paul, it will be okay. We'll just do the best we can."

"Yes, but will it be enough?" I didn't laugh this time. I could tell he was completely serious.

"Paul, we'll just take it one day at a time. We can do that. Paul, we *can* do it."

"Okay, if you say so," was all he said, and then he grew quiet again, completely taken by our new son.

. . .

When we brought Noah home from the hospital, we had a welcoming committee made up of my parents, Professor Haynesworth, Amy, and Martha. Paul had earlier placed a large basket of apples on the kitchen table to greet the two of us. My parents were staying for a couple of weeks, but the others left soon after they had met new baby Cass, knowing we needed space and time to rest and get used to each other.

We did get used to each other, but we didn't get much rest, at least not at first. Noah wanted to play all night and then take short, little catnaps during the day – long enough to refresh him, but not anyone else.

One night stands out to me. Paul, more rested than I, sent me to bed after I nursed Noah. "You sleep, we'll be fine." When I looked skeptical, he added, "If I need help, I'll wake your mother." Adequately assured and pleased with his willingness to try, I went to bed.

As I climbed into bed, I realized the baby monitor was on. I could hear everything going on in Noah's nursery. I smiled as I heard Paul's soft voice, working to calm the little, fussy baby noises.

"It's okay, little boy. We need to be quiet so your mommy can rest. She's sooo tired, and no one wants a tired mommy. So take it easy on me; I'm doing the best I know how. If I get stuck, we'll get your grandma, okay? Is it a deal, little applet?"

There was a pause with only slight gurgling sounds, then Paul's voice came through, even softer, with a wistful quality, "I wish your other grandma were here. She would love you, too." It sounded like he was choking back tears, so uncharacteristic of him. I wondered if I should go to him, but I realized he hadn't meant for me to hear, and while I debated what to do, I fell asleep.

My parents left after two weeks and Paul went back to work, but Amy and Martha stepped in to help as much as they could. Martha brought us meals on a regular basis, and Amy dropped by after work, even staying over a couple of nights to spell us.

Eventually Noah gave us a break and decided to sleep when it was dark out, at least for three or four hours at a time. It was enough, and we started to recover from our sleep debt.

· · ·

By the time Noah was two months old, I was feeling like I had a handle on things, and Paul was turning out to be a natural father. We both basked in each new trick of Noah's. We especially loved Noah's little smiles, and Paul became an expert at eliciting them.

· · ·

One night, after Noah had just hit his four month mark, we got him settled in his crib, and then we both collapsed into bed, but Paul wanted to talk. We were usually too exhausted for much talk, but this particular night Paul seemed pensive.

"Brea, do you think we can really be good parents?"

"Of course, honey. We're already doing a good job."

But he was not to be placated. "No, I mean in the long term. Brea, I'm trying to be a decent person, to be worthy of being Noah's daddy, but I just don't know if I'll be good enough."

"Paul, what are you talking about? You are an amazing person. You are kind and loving. You're helpful and sensitive. I feel lucky every day to have you. What's bothering you?"

He hesitated and then said, "Brea, it's just that you're a better person than I am, and your parents are amazing too. Even Martha is

..."

"No, Paul, stop talking that way. It seems like someone had to have a talk with me about selling myself short. Don't you start doing that now. Paul, you have already learned so much about being Noah's daddy. Sure, you'll make mistakes along the way; we both will. But we just need to keep an open mind and fix the mistakes we make. If you have a bad day, just make sure the next day is better. Remember, we just take it one day at a time. You can do that, can't you?"

"Yeah, I suppose so. It's just not always that easy." I had never seen him look so dejected.

"Paul, I know that. But if we keep trying, it is possible."

He was quiet, his furrowed brow indicating he was considering my words. I remained silent, not wanting to interrupt his thoughts. Eventually his expression lightened. He wasn't exactly happy, but he at least seemed unburdened. He lifted his eyes to mine and placed his hands on either side of my face. Holding me softly like a china doll, he bent in to kiss me.

"Brea, you make me a better person. I don't know where I would be without you. If you will be patient with me, I hope to one day be worthy of you." Then he cradled me, and we slept wrapped in each other's arms until Noah woke us up at five in the morning.

OF ESCALATORS AND PLAYGROUNDS

After the funeral my parents went back home. My friends went back to work. Life was returning to normal for all around me. They were moving on, but I didn't know how to move on. I felt like I was stuck at the bottom of an escalator, not knowing how to get off. Stairs kept rushing past, and I had to keep moving to stay in the same place, only I never got anywhere. I could see the goal, the tiled floor in front of me, but no matter how hard I tried, I just couldn't make that leap, I couldn't even lift my toes enough to let the escalator push me forward.

I arose each morning, dressed and fed Noah, and sometimes I even dressed and fed myself. My determination to be a living, breathing mother to Noah kept me going. We played, we read stories, and we cuddled in the rocking chair, but I must admit he wasn't much for conversation. Although what I would say if he were, I'm not sure.

I found myself often staring blindly out an open window, all resolve and self-assurance leaking out of my fingertips and blowing away on the silent breezes passing through our yard. Paul and I had talked about this yard, about the children we would have who would play here, about the family backyard campouts, and summer picnics.

All that I was and all that I had become under his loving hand seemed lost. He had taught me to be strong and confident. I was neither now, not knowing who I was anymore. I felt so incomplete, worse than just feeling alone, I felt like half a person.

Noah would pull me back from these moments when he woke from a nap or as he played at my feet, slobbering on my bare toes with his incessant teething. He was supposed to be the first, but not also the last, of the little Cass "applets."

. . .

Martha came over almost daily. She brought a pie one day and a casserole the next. Sometimes it was a crossword puzzle book or a bouquet of flowers. I graciously accepted her proffered gifts, but declined the need for her company. She kept coming until I stopped answering the door. Looking back, I was ruder than I had been raised to be. She understood what I was feeling, and she would have provided the adult conversation that I needed, even a shoulder to cry on, but I preferred to wallow like a sulking teenager.

Amy stopped by a few times, but she took a different tack from Martha's. After the second time I brushed her off, she responded in classic Amy fashion with, "Hey, you know where to find me. I'll be there and I'll be waiting for when you're ready to enter life again."

The phone rang but I rarely picked it up. My parents left one message after another, sounding more desperate with each one. Eventually their messages had outright threats, "Brea, if you don't pick up this phone, we'll call the police and send them to your house."

I just erased the messages. I figured they were empty threats; my parents wouldn't want to traumatize me further. What would I say to my parents anyway? "Yes, Mom, I'm doing great! Noah's started crawling, and he's drooling on everything in sight. We're going on as if nothing has happened to shake our existence." If they really did call the police, what did I care anyway?

My real excuse for not answering the phone was the occasional reporter's phone call. Even when I didn't answer, they still left their intrusive messages. One reporter called when Mr. Walker was released from the hospital. "Did I want to meet him?" with the implied, "We'll be there with cameras to cover the blessed event."

No, I didn't want to meet Mr. Walker! I didn't want to see him and feel bad inside that he was alive, while my husband was dead. I never wanted to feel that way about another human being, but I couldn't guarantee the sight of him wouldn't prompt that. Although, maybe he would understand my emotions since his wife had recently passed away. Guilt overwhelmed me as I realized it was even possible that he wished it had been his life taken and not my Paul's, but it's not like I could have that conversation. "Hey, so Frank, let me be frank. Do you feel bad that you're alive while my young husband lies in a coffin, covered in dirt?" I guess I wasn't quite over the anger. And I wasn't angry at Mr. Walker. I didn't know who I was angry at – no one, everyone?

Another call came when the grocery store reopened. "Did I have a comment? Could they interview me outside the store?" Really? Did I want to get within ten miles of the place? I was assuming since it was reopened that the blood stains had been cleaned up, but I would look for them if I went there. I'm even certain I would see them, would feel them, and the smell of blood would fill my nostrils, and I would choke on the smell, on the memory, on my life.

That choking sensation woke me with a start. I had drifted off to sleep in an easy chair while Noah napped. I gulped a deep breath, fighting hard to keep back the memories of that first night, the first time I woke up gasping for breath. Would it never end? Would I always feel like I was holding death at bay?

"Time to leave the house, even if just for the afternoon," I said aloud. I quickly showered and dressed while Noah finished his nap. By the time he awoke, I had a diaper bag all packed and ready to go. I even threw my camera into my purse for good measure.

Scooping him out of his crib, I rubbed noses with him. "Noah, I love you so much, little one. Shall we go out?" He responded by grabbing my hair and holding on tight. "I'll take that as a 'yes.' Let's change your diaper and get outta here!"

A few minutes later, with Noah safely buckled into his car seat, I pressed the button to open the garage door. I put my key in the ignition and then stopped. Only at that moment did I realize I had no clue where to go. Amy was at work. Martha was only next door, hardly worthy of a car outing. Where should I go? I let go of the key. Where in the world was I going? Noah, all excited a minute ago, began to fuss in the back.

I could think of only the city park. It was summer now, but the day's weather was unseasonably "mild," as they called it. What did mild mean? Is it like mild cheese that doesn't have a bite to it? So mild weather doesn't pack a punch? I could use something that didn't pack a punch. The park it would be.

As I drove I noticed what summertime meant. Flowers were in bloom and bicycles lay on sidewalks. Somehow, inexplicably, time had continued to march on. I wasn't sure how. I hadn't noticed the passage of time or the change in the weather. Paul had been dead for two months now. He had left us in the spring, a time, I realized with cruel irony, of new birth.

As we pulled into the parking lot, I saw a few other cars already there with car seats in the back. I took a deep breath. Was I ready to pretend I was a happy, young mom just like them? Noah began to fuss again, and I realized we had been parked for ten minutes, and I had yet to unclench my hands from the steering wheel.

Noah, that's what I was living for, I reminded myself. I eased my hands off the steering wheel, stepped out of the car, and opened the back door to retrieve Noah. "How are you little one? Shall we go check out the swings?" Then with his genuine smile and my pasted-on version we went to face the real world.

There were three other mothers at the playground. Two were talking to each other while their children, two little girls, ran around them. The third was pushing her son in one of the baby swings. Gathering my courage, I walked to her side, and placing Noah in the other baby swing, I gently began to push.

"It's nice to get out after being cooped up all winter and with our rainy spring," she casually remarked.

I hadn't noticed the rainy spring. All had simply been dark and cloudy in my mind. "Isn't it," I responded, my eyes forward, never meeting hers. I didn't want her conversation. I couldn't handle it. Surely her life was just wonderful. I couldn't live with that. Or maybe her life was a disaster with a cheating ex-husband. No, with a quick glance I saw she was wearing a lovely wedding ring. But then again, so was I.

She glanced over at me with a strange look on her face. *She knows, doesn't she?* I thought. However, she shrugged and looked away. I then realized how vigorously I was pushing Noah. He wasn't complaining, but he was holding on to the sides of the swing tightly with a confused look on his face.

Slowing him down, I thought, *Who am I kidding? I can't do this. I can't even push a swing properly.* Tears began to run silently down my cheeks. *Husbands aren't supposed to die young!* I screamed to myself. *Husbands are not supposed to die at midnight in all-night grocery stores! It isn't right! Who dies like that, at midnight?*

Wait! I suddenly froze. It wasn't right. How did I miss it?! Paul should not have died at midnight in an all-night grocery store. Paul was working the night shift at the hotel. That was the middle of his shift. He was the front desk manager, but they had been installing a new computer system lately, so he'd been overseeing it on the graveyard shift. He should not have been at an all-night grocery store in the middle of the night!

PART 2 - WALKING IN THE DARK

LEAVE

We had only been at the park for a few minutes, but I scooped Noah up out of the swing and hurried to the car. I knew where to go now; we were heading to the hotel where Paul had worked.

I eased into traffic from the parking lot, my mind going a mile a minute. I didn't like what I was thinking, wondering, but at least I was thinking. I felt more alive than I had been since that horrible night. I also felt more dead than I thought possible.

There must be some logical explanation. I just couldn't think of what it would be. Did the hotel need something in the middle of the night? Unlikely, but what if they had? Why go to some little corner grocery? From the news reports, I knew where the store was located, but I hadn't thought about what that location meant before. I mentally did the math. It was six or seven blocks from his work, not too far, but weren't there convenience stores closer? I wasn't sure.

As I approached the hotel, I began to look for gas stations and corner groceries. The store where Paul lost his life was in the other direction away from the hotel, so he wasn't stopping off on his way home. But that didn't matter, he'd never come home that early anyway. What was going on?

. . .

I eased into a parking spot right up front. Taking Noah out of the car, we both headed to the front entrance. My heart was pounding, and my thoughts were swirling. I approached the front desk determined to keep my emotions together.

Jolie was working the front desk. When she saw us, her face lit up. She hadn't seen Noah for several months, except for at the funeral, of course, I reminded myself. Then her gaze shifted to me, and I read a smile of pity cross her face.

Is that what I was now? An object of pity? Of course I was. I pitied myself, for heaven's sake.

"Hi, Jolie. How are you doing?" It was a stupid question to ask, I realized too late. She can't appear too happy, that would be an affront to my suffering, but if she's not having a good day that would be bad as well, since she can't possibly be suffering as I am. Jolie looked appropriately conflicted about how to answer. I saved us both by continuing, "Is Anna in? Or George? I just have a couple of things I need to clear up."

"Sure," she responded, clearly eager to pass me off to someone else. She quickly disappeared into the back office to find the manager or assistant manager.

I used to know the schedule of the front desk staff and managers, knowing who worked when. It dawned on me I didn't even know what day of the week it was. When Jolie returned I asked, "Would you mind telling me what day of the week this is?" It sounded pathetic, but I knew I already appeared that way. What would it matter if I humiliated myself further?

"Tuesday," she replied, trying not to look directly at me.

George and Anna both appeared a few moments later. "Would you like to sit down?" George asked, directing me to the nearby lounge.

"Can I play with Noah?" Jolie chimed in, finding a way to rise above her embarrassment for me or at least mitigate it some.

I turned and handed Noah off to her before following George and Anna.

"We are so sorry that ... ," Anna started.

I raised my hand to cut her off. Platitudes, well intentioned though they were, were confusing right now. I wasn't sure how I felt and I was anxious for answers, answers I was hoping they could provide. "Do you know what happened on the night shift the evening Paul was shot?"

Both registered surprise at the question. George finally answered. "I'd have to look over the records, but I think it was a pretty uneventful night." He let out a small gasp at the insensitive comment he had inadvertently made. "I mean, nothing unusual went on here at the hotel."

"Why did Paul head out to the grocery store in the middle of his shift?" I asked, adding, "In the dead of night?" as if somehow I wasn't clear the first time, or maybe still trying to deal with the questions in my mind.

If I had thought they'd looked surprised before, I was mistaken. They looked at me, then at each other. As if by mutual agreement, Anna began, slowly, softly, "Brea, Paul wasn't working that night. He took a leave of absence about a month and a half before he was killed."

Knives couldn't have felt sharper to my heart. I wanted to stop the pain, to take the knives out and stanch the flow of blood that was beginning to drown me. Why didn't I know about his leave? Why didn't he tell me? If he hadn't told me about that, I had to wonder what else he was hiding. No, it bitterly dawned on me, I needed to make that past tense. What else had he hidden from me? He wasn't even here to answer for himself. How dare he chicken out that way!

I was boiling inside. What was he doing taking a leave of absence in the first place? And if he was on leave, where in the world had he been going all that time? The pain spread to my lungs as I took a sharp intake of breath. His "leave" coincided with his working the graveyard shift. What had he been doing?

I took a slow, deep, cleansing breath. No pain came this time. My hands were in tight fists, but I forced myself to speak calmly. "Did he say why?" I should have been embarrassed needing to ask the question, but my desire for answers overwhelmed any sense of shame.

"He said the three of you were going to be taking an extended family vacation, visiting your folks who were in ill health."

"Are you sure? My parents are perfectly healthy. They actually were in Europe until a week before Paul died. You didn't mix him up with someone else did you?" But, of course, I knew the answer to that.

They didn't insult me by trying to answer what was surely a rhetorical question. We all sat in stunned silence as possible answers swirled in our minds. I could see in their eyes the thoughts dancing past, none of them pleasant.

At my prompting, we all stood without a word. George reached out to me and embraced me. When he let go, Anna took his place. "Let us know if there is anything we can do for you." But we both knew the words were hollow, even if she meant them to be sincere, because it was readily apparent to all that the situation was beyond help.

I numbly walked to the front desk, took Noah back into my arms, and shuffled in stunned disbelief to my car. I had never dreamed that my husband had been lying to me, never entertained even an idea of such a thing. In many ways, this was worse than his dying. When he was shot, his physical body had died, but now the man I thought I knew was disappearing before my eyes. Did the man I knew even exist in the first place? What was real and what was fake? I felt overwhelming grief all over again. With his death I had lost a future with him, now it seemed our past was being taken as well. I was too shocked even to cry.

CALLING OUT FOR MOM

I don't remember driving home. The rest of the day was one long blur until I put Noah down to bed. When he settled down, I slumped to the floor in the hall outside his room. I was reluctant to be far from his side, afraid he would evaporate like the rest of my life.

With that fear came new frenetic thinking. I needed to understand what Paul was doing, had done. Even if it meant facing that fear, risking everything, I had to learn the truth. Before long I realized it was midnight, but I picked up the phone. "Mom?" I could hear an audible sigh of relief on the other end. "Mom, before you say anything, I need your help. Can you and Dad come out and help me with Noah? I have some things I need to take care of. I'll explain later. I don't think I could now, even if I wanted to."

With only a moment's hesitation, "Absolutely, dear, we'll check on flights and see how quickly we can make it. I'll call you back in a few minutes."

I had made a commitment to be Noah's mother above anything else. I hoped I wasn't backing out of that. No, I assured myself, this was a necessary step. If I was going to be any kind of a good mother to him, I needed to find out what his father was.

A minute later, the phone startled me. For the first time in days, I answered it. "Mom?"

"Yes, Brea, it's me. Dad and I will catch the first flight out in the morning. Should we rent a car?"

"No, Noah and I will come and pick you up. And while you're here, you can use Paul's car. He doesn't need it anymore." I was surprised at how matter-of-fact I was being. Having a task to accomplish was helping me be very practical. "But, Mom, I don't know how long I'll need you."

"That's okay. We are in the process of clearing our schedules. We'll stay as long as we're welcome."

"Thanks, Mom. I ... I know I've been shutting you out. I just ... "

"It's okay," she cut in. "We'll talk tomorrow when we see you. I'm just glad you finally let us back in. We've been worried, but there's something in your voice that tells me you'll make it. 'Til tomorrow. Love you."

"Love you, too, Mom," I whispered back. If she only knew where the determination in my voice was coming from, she might not be so sure of a positive outcome.

I stood up from my perch in the hallway and wearily made my way to my bathroom. I picked up my toothbrush and then paused at the reflection staring back at me. It had only been a short while since Paul left us, but I could see the grieving in my face, grieving that was now replaced with what? Anger, fear at what I would find, confusion? That was probably it - confusion. Was there another woman? I finally voiced the thought in my mind. It rattled around in there, like a fly trapped by a closed window. Surely, there was some other explanation, but that thought just could not escape.

I looked again at my reflection. Was I not enough for Paul? My blonde hair was longer than when we had met, but it had the same natural highlights and gentle wave. My face was still young and what most would consider attractive. Was something wrong with it? I

76

turned from side to side, critically staring at every imperfection. Was this happening even though my looks hadn't faded? What would have happened if Paul had lived and with time, they did fade? Or was it something else? Was it something wrong with me, who I was as a person? Where had I gone wrong?

I was jumping the gun, I knew. I didn't know if there even was another woman. *Get control of yourself*, I told myself. *Stick with what you do know.*

So what exactly did I know? I knew only one thing, that Paul told me he was working the night shift when in fact he wasn't. So what did that mean?

That I was too trusting is what it told me! Never did I question Paul's move to the night shift. Then again, I hadn't felt the need to question what he told me. I was a trusting person by nature.

With a little smile, this thought made me think of Professor Haynesworth. I was like him in this regard. When honesty is something that defines you, you expect it from others, even going so far as to assume others are honest. Some would say this made me naïve. I didn't know about that. Maybe it did, but I didn't think I wanted to live my life any other way.

I looked in the mirror again. I was more than what I saw reflected back. Paul knew that, didn't he?

Was he more than a handsome face? He was just so incredibly charming. Was that it? Paul's charm? He could have charmed the skin off a snake and had the snake slither away happy.

Sleep was far from me as I began to examine my life. Had Paul always charmed me into everything? Was his love for me real? Maybe I shouldn't have married him so quickly. But I pushed that thought aside, knowing that if I had it to do over again, I wouldn't have done things any differently. Questioning the decisions I had made wasn't going to help in the end. I trusted Paul. Trust wasn't such a bad thing, was it?

I honestly didn't know, but I did know that it was time to start thinking, time to start asking the questions I should have been asking all along. I determined to do all I could to figure out exactly what was real and what was a lie. Tonight I would make my own plans, and then when my parents came to help with Noah, I would find the answers I needed, answers so I could get on with my life, so that Noah and I could get on with our lives, one way or another.

My mother and father would be devastated by what I would tell them, but that could wait until after they arrived, maybe even until after I learned what was really going on. For now, let them have their peace, thinking the worst was over.

STARTING AT SQUARE ONE

Noah and I picked up Mom and Dad the next day at the airport. I watched them loading their bags into the back of the car. They were a good team. Mom was 5'8" and nestled perfectly under Dad's 6-foot frame. It was a protective embrace and never a domineering one.

My dad was going gray above the ears, and if I wasn't mistaken, it was more pronounced than when he had been here for Paul's funeral. I felt a twinge of guilt for my part in that gray. When Dad finished loading bags and turned to smile at me, I found myself bathed in his love. He would do anything for me, even trade his dark hair for gray, just as I would do anything for Noah.

Dad had been a consultant for years, working for himself. It had paid him well, eventually, after those money-building years. Now, with some wise investing, he could set his own hours and choose his own vacations. Mom had been his invaluable office manager through it all. I was grateful that they had been able to drop everything to come, knowing that most don't have that luxury.

Mom came up behind Dad. She was a beautiful woman with short, wavy, blonde hair sprinkled with gray. She had put on some weight over the years, just like Dad had, but she wore it well. It made her look more like a loving grandma that way.

She added her smile to his, but hers spoke chapters while his had been a single sentence of love. I could tell she had worried herself through many a sleepless night. The dark circles seconded this. More than anything, I could see the tentativeness in her smile. Could she let her guard down yet? Was I really on the upswing?

The words of reassurance I wanted to give her were stuck in my throat, cutting off my breath. It was with disheartening reality that I knew I would add to her worry before I would allay it. I didn't even trust my smile not to betray my concerns to her. Instead, I reached out to embrace them both before climbing into the car to drive them home.

Mom and Dad had barely brought their suitcases inside when I was itching to be on my way. The car ride had been quiet, except for Mom's playful words with Noah. I hadn't known where to begin. Now, unfortunately, it wasn't any better, but I didn't want to put it off any longer.

"Mom and Dad, would you mind coming and sitting down for a minute?"

"Sure," was the quick response. They both registered an eagerness to know what was going through my mind.

When we were settled in chairs in the great room, with Noah crawling around our feet, I finally met their gaze. Could I really do this? *Time to be strong*, I told myself. I would face whatever was coming head on.

"This is not the easiest thing to talk about, but something was up with Paul. I don't know what it was. I need to figure it out. It dawned on me yesterday that he had no good reason to be in that grocery store the night of the robbery. I did some checking and found out he wasn't even working at the hotel anymore. He had taken a leave of absence, supposedly so the three of us could go visit you two."

"Are you sure, honey? Was he planning a surprise trip?"

"Yes, I'm sure, Mom. There was no trip. He said it was because you were in ill health, and all of it was apparently taking place when you and Dad were in Europe. Paul was well aware of where you were. There's no mistake. He out and out lied to a lot of people. I don't know the reason for it yet, but my imagination is starting to get the best of me, and I'm not coming up with anything good."

I took a deep breath before continuing. "I'm not sure that I'll like the truth, but not knowing it is eating away at me." I looked at my parents, people who could trust each other, and just as important, a couple still very much in love. They had in their marriage what I thought had been present in mine, that was until yesterday. With a sigh of resignation, I continued. "I want to find out what was happening. It's for me and Noah, so we can move on together, but I need you here so that I know Noah is safe and happy. Then I can learn what I need to know."

Their faces registered the shock and hurt I expected. Thankfully, I also saw the fierce determination that had been my birthright, the determination that Paul had finally unleashed within me. I wondered if he would really want me to be self-confident right now.

Mom spoke first, but she spoke for both of them. "Brea, you do what you need to do. When you want to talk it out, we're here, but if you want to just think and mull it over, we'll understand. You go; we'll take care of Noah."

I hadn't realized I'd been holding my breath, until I released it. Admittedly, I hadn't expected any other response, but I was grateful to have it expressed. I looked at them both for a moment. I was ready.

I bent down and kissed Noah. "You have fun with Grammy and Grampy, okay little one? Mommy loves you." I almost added, "You're the apple of my eye," but I caught myself up short. It all felt like rotten apples about now.

Hugging Mom and Dad in turn, I said, "I have my phone with me. Call me if Noah needs anything. I'll be back when I can. Thanks again." Grabbing my purse and my newly created list, I went out to the garage.

This time opening the garage door and inserting the key into the ignition, I had no questions about where I was going. What I would find was another matter. I did, however, know where I was starting. I was going to visit the grocery store where Paul lost his life, hoping I could find what I was missing.

. . .

Harper's Mart didn't look like much from the outside. It looked as if it had been built in the middle of last century and hadn't been updated since. Even the sign out front was leaning to one side with faded blue letters spelling out "Harper's Mart." The small parking lot was empty except for one car in the back, I assumed the owner's, and a broken down truck with a big "For Sale" sign in the front window. "Boy, Paul sure knew how to pick 'em," I muttered to myself.

I stepped out of my car, making sure to lock the car doors behind me. Stepping gingerly over the cracking and weedy parking lot, I approached the front door. Not surprisingly, the paint was peeling around the doorframe. I pulled open the door and stepped inside. I didn't want to look down at the floor in front of the register, but I couldn't help but do so, even though no bloodstain remained. I stared at the empty spot, feeling acutely the hole in my heart.

"Can I help you?" came from somewhere behind the counter. I looked up to see an older man with thick bifocals. He still had a lot of hair, but most of it was growing out of his ears and in a ring like a fallen halo above his ears and around his head. It was hard to see where the halo-hair stopped and the ear-hair began. He stood up to greet me, but being vertical didn't increase his height much, being bent over with age. I felt sorry for this man who had been robbed of probably what little he had. My thoughts were straying from my purpose, and I was beginning to doubt this would help me any, but I was here, so I may as well ask my questions.

"Yes, I hope so. My name is Brea Cass. My husband was Paul Cass who ..." and I could tell from the look on his face I didn't need to finish my sentence.

"Oh, ma'am, I'm so sorry. I don't know what would've happened if your husband hadn't been here. But, I'm so sorry, so sorry." He looked as if he might cry, but I was feeling that way myself.

"Are you Mr. Harper?" I asked.

"Oh, no. Mr. Harper died years ago. I bought this place from him. Didn't see any need to change the name, though. I'm Walter, Walter Schultz."

"Nice to meet you, Walter," and I actually smiled at him. "I was just wondering if you could help me a little. I'm trying to figure out a few things about the night my husband died. Can you tell me anything you might remember about him that night? Anything he said or did."

He wrinkled up his brow in thought. "I can't think of anything out of the ordinary. He came in before my regular customer, Frank Walker, did. I think he was talking on a phone, but I can't be sure." He paused to drag the recesses of his memory for any remaining details. "I'm sorry, I don't remember much else other than him jumping in front of Frank and taking that bullet for him. He didn't even hesitate to do it. I'm so sorry," he said while shaking his head. "Such a waste, such a waste."

"Thank you. I appreciate your time." Then I turned to go.

"You know, Mrs. Cass, he was a nice man. I liked him."

I turned at that. "Why do you say that? Because he gave his life to save Mr. Walker?"

A little flustered he responded, "Well, no, although I mean that was a good thing. But no, he came in a few nights before the uh ... , the robbery. Real nice man. He bought some beef jerky and a six pack of soda."

This new piece of information piqued my curiosity. What was that about? "Was that the first time you'd seen him?" I asked.

"Yeah, that was the only other time. It was the middle of the night, too, just like, well, you know, just like that other night. He was real friendly like. He had such a nice smile, and he just visited with me for a little while. So many people are in a rush. It gets kinda lonely here in the wee hours. But he wasn't in any hurry. Just asked me if I liked having a store and if I got lonely and stuff. He even asked about my family. Told me about you and your son. A real proud papa."

"Thank you," was all I could think to say.

"He showed me pictures of your little boy, and he looked at pictures of my grandkids. Would you like to see?"

"Sure."

We spent the next little while looking at pictures of his grandchildren at various ages and stages of life. As I watched his eyes light up with each picture, I tried to imagine Paul's eyes doing the same thing when it had been his turn.

Eventually we said our good-byes and I returned to my car, after picking out a Dr. Pepper and a teething ring for Noah. Mr. Schulz wouldn't let me pay for them, even offered me anything I wanted in the store, but I declined.

Sitting in my car, sipping my drink, I took stock of what Mr. Schultz had told me about Paul. Other than Paul being "real" – real nice, real friendly, real proud – I wasn't sure what I had learned. Maybe there wasn't another woman, but when I catalogued the information in my mind, I had to accept I knew nothing for certain.

After thinking about it, I mentally added to my growing list of questions: Why was he in this neighborhood? As if the answer would magically come to me, I looked around. Why was he here? It wasn't the worst neighborhood, but it wasn't a charmer either. A pawnshop was on the opposite corner, but all the other buildings I could see were homes, mostly single-family homes. Down the street, I could make out a line of duplexes. Nothing jumped out at me. I was as lost as before.

"Okay, what's next," I mumbled, picking up my list. An internet search the previous evening had given me Frank Walker's phone number and address. Should I call and tell him I was coming? That probably would be the nicer thing to do.

Opening my phone and dialing, I put the phone to my ear. It was several rings before he answered with, "Yes?"

"Hi, is this Frank Walker?" I asked.

"Yeah, this is him. Who wants to know?"

"Oh, I'm sorry. I'm Brea Cass, Paul's wife." I let that sink in before continuing. "Would you mind if I came by to visit you?"

It was silent for some time, and then his voice, softer now, responded, "That would be fine. When would you like to come?"

"Is it all right if I came now?"

"That would be okay. Do you know where I live?"

"Yes, I have the address. Is five minutes too soon?"

"Oh, no, not at all. I'll see you in five minutes."

Mr. Walker lived only a few blocks from Harper's Mart. I could easily picture him restless and lonely at night, making his way there for some company.

He opened the door before I had a chance to knock. "Come in, come in."

Stepping inside was like stepping back in time. I saw furniture that he and his wife might have picked out together when they were young, a rose colored love seat with a curved back and wood trim and an overstuffed chair with a floral print to match it. A small TV sat on a rickety TV table a short distance away. From a back bedroom, I heard the meow of a cat.

Mr. Walker looked like he belonged back in the era of the furniture. He wore suspenders over a plaid shirt, with old dress pants. He wore no shoes, but his dark socks were worn with a toe or two poking out. His face was gaunt and reminded me of the cancer.

Frank cleared newspapers off the loveseat and beckoned me to sit. He sat down in the easy chair, looking as if he wanted to speak but being torn between expressing his gratitude and his regrets.

I had been fearful of this meeting, but I shouldn't have been. Someone's life had been spared, even if just for a short time. How could I not be grateful for that? I found that in my mind, I had separated the two events of Mr. Walker's life being saved and my husband's taken. I also had to admit the events of the last 48 hours had distanced me from the emotions surrounding Paul's death.

Breaking the silence, I asked, "Mr. Walker, I was wondering if you could tell me about my husband on the night he died, what he said, what he was doing, anything?"

That clearly wasn't what he had expected me to ask, so it took a moment for him to change gears in his mind. "I hadn't really thought about it. The police asked me all about the two men who came in but not much about your husband. Let me think for a minute."

"The store owner said he might have been talking on a cell phone," I prompted.

"Oh, yeah, he was. He was in the back of the store. It's pretty quiet that time of night, so I could hear him. I looked to see if someone was with him, and then I saw the phone in his hand. He was saying, 'The truth is I left the light on.' I remember it because it made me realize I always leave the lights on whenever I go someplace. Somehow the house doesn't look quite so empty that way when I come home." He paused to collect himself.

Something about what Paul had said sounded vaguely familiar, but I couldn't quite place why.

Mr. Walker continued. "I walked close by your husband. I think my presence kind of startled him, because he turned suddenly to look at me. But after he stared at me for a moment, he went back to his phone and said, 'No, turn the lights off.' Then I picked up my cat food and went to the register. I think he might have said something more after that like, 'Yes, that's right' or 'I know' or something like that, but I think that was it. After that, well, I suspect you know the rest, with your husband jumping in front of me and all."

My heart sank just a little bit deeper. I guess I had been hoping that he hadn't been talking on the phone after all, because I knew he wasn't talking to me. Who do you talk to on a cell phone at midnight? The only good answer for Paul would have been his wife, but that didn't apply in this case, did it? So who exactly was it? Where had he been that he had left the lights on? That sounded more to me like a house than a place of business, but I guess it could have been either. The bottom line was that I didn't know! I didn't know anything about where he had left those lights on or who he was trusting to turn them off. I couldn't decide whether to be angry or sad.

I could see that Mr. Walker was reading some kind of distress on my face. It clearly was disturbing him that he might have said something to upset me. I didn't want him to have time to change his story in an effort to somehow make me happier, so I quickly added, "Did he say anything else? The newspaper said he yelled or something."

"Yeah, he yelled all right. Mostly he was just making noise. He did say, 'No! Wait! It's not worth it!' I remember the words so clearly. Man, it's been a long time since I've seen such courage." Not wanting to meet my gaze, he glanced down as he whispered, "I sure do appreciate it."

Whatever my husband was guilty of, I couldn't ignore his heroism. The emotions that I had recently shut out began to sneak back in. All I could do was sit there while tears coursed quietly down Mr. Walker's cheeks and mine. We were united by a single act that forever altered both of our lives and both in opposite ways. Sometimes there just are no words.

The cat spared us. She sauntered into the room, oblivious to our grief, and demanded an explanation for the stranger sitting on her furniture. Frank flashed an apologetic smile. "I don't get much company. I guess Patches has gotten a little bossy," and with a real grin, he added, "You know, so unusual for a cat."

I smiled back. He really was a nice old gentleman. I tried to think of anything else to ask, but there wasn't too much to work with. Finally, searching for anything, I asked, "Do you remember what my husband was buying?"

Surprised, he thought back for a moment. "I don't think he had picked up anything yet."

Well, so much for trying to piece things together from that, I mused. I'd been hoping that what he was buying might tell me something. Was he talking to a woman or a co-worker or just an old buddy? Tampons or a beer would indicate entirely different things. I seemed to be getting nowhere fast.

I was reluctant to leave Mr. Walker's home so quickly, but I figured I had time for only one more stop before the end of normal business hours. So I made my excuses and let myself out, much to the cat's delight.

. . .

I got in my car but didn't turn on the ignition as I tried to understand what I was learning. All I could think about was Paul and how I had expected that he would grow old like Mr. Walker, that we would be together for a good long time, only mourning each other's loss when time had wizened and softened us.

Since Paul's death, I had thought about all his good qualities and what I missed most. We were, I had to admit, still learning to compromise, to be patient with each other, to always be kind, things I assumed Mr. Walker and his wife had developed over the years.

A memory came back in a trickle. It was our first fight as a married couple. I was struggling with a particularly difficult computer program for one of my classes. Paul came home from work to find me frustrated and no closer to a solution.

"Just do a search on the internet," Paul said.

"What would I be searching for? I know how to create the code once I figure out how to approach it."

"No, just put in this classroom assignment. I'm sure someone has posted their code from previous semesters."

I looked at him with disbelief. "Paul, that's cheating. It's plagiarism, maybe not with words but with code. I wouldn't do that."

"Why? Everybody does it. That's how all the rest of your class is going to figure it out. You'll still be using your brain to solve the problem, just in a different way." He wasn't even acting defensive. He seemed absolutely mystified by my reluctance.

"Paul! I DO NOT CHEAT!" I was losing my temper, something that didn't make me proud. I took a deep breath and quieted my tone. "I don't know how you were raised, but I was raised to do what was right in all situations. A 'D' for my own work will always be better than an 'A' for someone else's. I don't mind getting help from someone, like going to a TA for some direction, but straight up copying of another person's work is not right, and it never will be, regardless of how many people do it. Ask Haynesworth if you want another opinion on the matter."

He was fuming by now and had clearly caught my dig about asking a TA for help, seeing that he had been one. I regretted having thrown that in, but I wasn't ready to apologize for anything small like that when he clearly had no intention of apologizing for the larger issue.

However, I suppose it was the mention of Haynesworth that was the more cutting remark. I truly believed he would back me up on this, but since he was as close to being a father figure as Paul had, it was like a slap in the face to claim him for my side.

We both stared at each other, wondering how to end the stalemate. I caved first. "Paul, I'm sorry to have brought the Professor into things; that wasn't very nice of me. However, my position about the code stays the same. I will write it myself."

I expected Paul to apologize in return, but he just looked past me. Then without a word, he turned and went into the bedroom. I wasn't sure where we now stood.

I struggled a little longer with how to approach my assignment. I made a little headway, but not much. My thoughts were on Paul and our disagreement. I finally went into the bedroom to talk to him. He was busy working on his computer, but when he saw me his eyes lit up. He put his work aside, came to me, and took me in his arms. "I love you, Brea. You catch me off guard sometimes, but I love you with all my heart."

At the time, I took it as an apology, but now, as I contemplated Paul's apparent deception, I wondered. Where had he stood on what was right and what was wrong? Had he ever been the one to back down and apologize? I felt compelled to pursue those answers.

· · ·

I turned my key in the ignition. What was next on my list? My bank was on the opposite side of town, and banking hours being what they were, I figured it would have to wait until tomorrow. So I called the police station to see if one of the detectives assigned to my husband's case was in.

Detective Lentus was indeed in and happy to meet with me; so I drove directly to the station. Parking the car in the police station lot felt a lot safer than at Harper's Mart, and I climbed out without even a glance around.

I'm sure I had met Detective Lentus before, but I didn't remember him. He belonged to the hazy days that defined the last two months. He met me at the front door, so I didn't need to wait to be buzzed in. He didn't look like a detective to me. I suppose I was expecting someone good-looking, having seen one too many detective shows with the leading role played by some Hollywood hunk. I think I would have even settled for a studious or professorial look. What I got was none of those.

Lentus moved at his own pace, more like a sloth than the adrenalin-laden do-gooder I was expecting. Even his large belly didn't appear to want to expend the effort to stay above his belt, instead choosing to flop down, hiding the buckle from view. It dawned on me that I was being unusually harsh on a man I hadn't really met. Here was a man who was supposedly helping me and I was examining his wrinkled shirt and stained tie. I didn't even want to consider what stained it.

Focus on Paul. Focus on Paul. This is a nice man, I kept telling myself.

He led me back to his office and pulled out a chair for me. "What can I do for you, Mrs. Cass? I'm assuming you would like information on what's happening with our investigation?"

I paused. I knew it was unusual, but I hadn't given that investigation much thought. Paul was dead; finding out who did it wouldn't change that. My questions circled around what Paul was doing, the other criminals in the picture being simply a waste of my thoughts.

Knowing it was the right answer, and not wanting to expose my husband's personal betrayal, I responded, "Yes, that would be lovely." Lovely? I sounded like Audrey Hepburn responding to an offer of tea, but I figured correcting it would make matters worse, so I just looked expectantly at the detective as if that was how I always spoke.

He hadn't seemed to notice, and I barely listened as he told me they had no new leads. The camera in the store wasn't working, and the vague descriptions given by Mr. Walker and the storeowner hadn't produced any hits. Wearing ski masks had effectively hidden much of the intruders' identities. "The suspects didn't actually get away with much cash," he added in an apologetic fashion.

I wondered if much effort was being made to find them since they didn't "get away with much cash?" But I knew that was just the cynical side of me weighing in. I had to remind myself why I had come.

"Detective, I was just wondering if you could answer a few questions for me."

"Sure, the best I can."

"Do you know if my husband had picked out any groceries?"

His eyes opened wide in surprise. "No, he didn't have any. Is there a problem, or something I should know about?"

"No, I'm just trying to tie up some loose ends is all. Do you happen to have his cell phone?"

He was still a little taken aback by my first question and didn't respond to this second one. Instead, he asked, "You aren't trying to solve your husband's murder by yourself, are you? Because that is not a good idea. You never know who you're dealing with. That's a very dangerous situation to put yourself in." He paused to look at me to see if the words were sinking in. "Please, just let us do our jobs. We'll find whoever did this to your husband. It just takes time."

I realized in trying to cover my own embarrassment, I had unintentionally misled him. I wasn't sure how to repair the damage, but my husband's indiscretions weren't any of his business.

"No, no, I'm not interested in that at all," I responded before realizing that didn't sound believable either. Trying to salvage things, I added, "I'm just trying to piece together the last moments, the last memories of my husband. It's how I'm dealing with this whole situation."

He seemed at least partially placated. I plunged forward by asking, "Did you say whether you had his cell phone?"

"Um, yes, we do."

"Would you mind if I had it back? You don't need it for anything do you?"

"No, I don't suppose we do. Let me go check with my lieutenant."

I'm not sure how long he was gone, but he eventually came back with Paul's cell phone in hand. "Here you go, Mrs. Cass. Let us know if you need anything else," and with that he turned back to his desk, effectively dismissing me. But I was done with him for the time being anyway.

PHONE CALLS

It was a relief to return home, but it was with mixed emotions that I registered the smell of marinara sauce from the kitchen and the sound of charming little baby boy giggles coming from the great room. I wasn't even sure which of my parents was in which room, but it filled me with joy and sadness. I was glad they were here, but I was also sorry it was necessary and sorry that I wasn't the one doing either of the things that they were.

I quickly made for the great room. My stomach reminded me I hadn't eaten well for some time, but my aching heart trumped it. I yearned for little Noah.

As I entered the room, I called, "Noah," and he immediately turned at the sound of my voice, his eyes dancing. Flashing me his biggest smile, he got on all fours and crawled my way just as fast as he knew how. I scooped him up into my arms and held him fast. When he squirmed away from the tightness of my embrace, I set him down and sat down right beside him.

It was only then that I noticed my father. He was watching the two of us with a knowing smile. He had been waiting all day for this moment, just as much as I had. I grinned at him, a reassuring smile that I was going to get through this, and then turned my attention back to Noah. We played peek-a-boo and pat-a-cake until Mom called us for dinner.

I was hungrier than I thought possible and more exhausted than that. It was no surprise that I was emotionally and mentally drained. Much as I wanted to spend every possible second with Noah, I didn't resist when my mother sent me off to bed long before Noah.

I remember wishing, once again, that my bed wasn't quite so lonely, and then I drifted off into a dreamless sleep. But the sleep didn't last. I awoke at 2:20 am and my mind immediately started to attack the problems at hand. After a half hour I accepted that sleep would elude me, and quietly made my way downstairs.

Making a beeline for my purse, I retrieved Paul's cell phone. The battery was dead, but I knew his charger was in my den. The office space was filled with my things except for the odd item or two that Paul kept there for ready access, like car keys and phone chargers.

I paused at the doorway. Paul had encouraged me to embrace this office, to use it in any way I wanted. What would Paul think about how I was about to use it now? He had always trusted and encouraged me. Why hadn't I been able to trust him in return?

I sat down at my desk and placed his cell phone on the desktop in front of me. After plugging it in and turning it on, I pulled up his recent calls. The last call was an outgoing call at 12:34 am the morning of his death. Paul had identified the contact simply as "B P," whoever that was. I looked under his contacts and no other information had been entered. He was meticulous about recording as much detail as possible with all his contacts, probably a habit he picked up from needing to document computer programs so someone else could follow his thinking. It struck me as odd that B. P. had no other information attached, almost as if Paul was purposely hiding who B. P. was.

Without thinking about the hour, I called the number from his phone. As the time dawned on me, I was relieved, but disappointed, to learn the number was no longer in service.

I wasn't sure what to make of that. If it was another woman, did she know about me and change her number after Paul's death? That seemed somewhat calculating and devious, but calculating and devious were two words that seemed to apply to this situation.

A wave of grief hit me, mixed with hurt. The last person he spoke to before he died was not me. It felt like the wind had been knocked out of me. I slid off the chair with his phone still in my hands, landing on the floor in a heap. I curled up in a little ball and buried my head in my knees.

What was I to Paul? Did he care about me? I thought he did, but had baby tiredness clouded my sight?

I looked at his phone again as if it were the enemy. The more I learned the more I felt stabbed in the heart. I was tempted to fling the phone against the wall, to obliterate it.

As I stared at the screen, deciding what I would do next, it went dark, going into power save mode. When it did, I could see a muddled reflection of myself, dark like the screen. It brought me up short. Was I trapped in darkness? This wasn't about the past as much as it was about the future. I needed to learn what had been going on, so I could truly put it behind me and move on.

As I sat pondering the meaning of all that I had discovered and what might be ahead, I absent-mindedly fiddled with Paul's phone. I began to scroll through his contacts. I recognized most of the names but not all. Did these unknown names belong to passing acquaintances or people who played a role in his life, unbeknownst to me?

I looked to see if there was a listing with the initials B. P. under a different number, but there were no matches. Next, I returned to the recent calls to look for anything unusual. I wasn't sure what I was looking for exactly, simply hoping that I would recognize it when I saw it.

As I scrolled through his calls, I noticed that he had made two additional phone calls to B. P. One was forty minutes before the last phone call and the other was two and a half hours before that. But even though I scrolled back fifty calls, back to where the record ended, no other calls to B. P. could be found.

In the process of doing this, I noticed one other thing, that Paul had made repeated calls to Alex, no last name, just Alex. The last call had been two days before his death. I didn't know any Alex. Was Alex male or female? It didn't match with B. P., so what now?

Aware of the hour this time, I didn't dial Alex's number. Instead, I clicked on the info under that name on Paul's phone. It didn't surprise me to find that no other information had been entered for this contact as well.

I seemed to be going nowhere fast. I decided to scan through the other contacts to see if it was more common than I thought for him not to enter additional information. It was as I had originally expected. Every other contact had more information entered, such as an email or home address. At least there was still something I thought I knew about Paul that was correct.

It echoed as hollow comfort since this discovery just made it all the more obvious that something was different about Alex and B.P. I wished I knew what.

What else could I learn? I decided to check his text messages. There were no texts to B. P., and surprisingly, even though he had spoken with Alex frequently, there were no texts sent to or received from Alex either.

Allowing myself to smile, I saw a long list of texts back and forth with me. I pulled them up to reread them. Two nights before his death he had texted me from work. No, I had to admit to myself, he wasn't at work. He had texted me from wherever he was.

"Kiss the applet for me."

There were other texts, simple things.

"Be home soon. If still awake, wait up for me. <3"

"Need any milk? Bringing cookies." My response: "Yes!" His: "Skim ok?"

They were simple exchanges, but they reminded me of happier times when life seemed bright and clear. I loved him so much. I missed his smell, the touch of his hand on my face, or the feel of him coming up behind me and slipping his arms around my waist. My heart would race and I would turn to embrace him. These thoughts left me weak, overcome with the memory of Paul and being his wife, living my life with him.

Had that all been real? It was real on my end, that much I knew for sure.

I sat back in my chair and closed my eyes. I forced my thoughts away from Paul himself and focused on his phone and what I had found tonight. Questions were flooding through me with no sense of how to restrain them, let alone answer them. I wished I could at least connect them to each other, but that cohesion was elusive. Somehow, I needed to keep moving forward and pursue any answers I could find.

Not able to think of anything else productive to do in such wee hours of the morning, I reluctantly headed back upstairs. I peeked in on a sleeping Noah before returning to my bed for a few more hours of exhausted sleep.

DAY TWO

The next morning (it was Thursday, I was keeping track now) found me waiting in the parking lot when the bank opened for the day. I should have made this visit weeks ago, shortly after Paul's death, but I wasn't doing much of anything "shortly after Paul's death." Since his death I had checked our accounts and knew what we had in savings, but I hadn't checked on our investments. I had trusted Paul with the accounts before his death, otherwise I might have noticed that money was being transferred from savings rather than coming from a paycheck from the hotel. Now I was looking for anything unusual prior to his death that might explain Paul's late night activities.

. . .

An hour later, I returned to my car with no new information. Even though Paul had stopped working, financially I was in good shape. Buying the house outright with Paul's inheritance money had made it possible for us to set aside or invest the amount of a mortgage payment each month. Combine that money with some residual inheritance money and the small amount coming from Paul's life insurance policy and I would have plenty of time to figure out how to balance being Noah's mommy and making ends meet.

That news was good news, but it somehow disappointed me. I was so desperate for answers that I would have welcomed large sums of money disappearing from our bank account for some unknown purpose. Even strange deposits might indicate some new activity – legal or not. But there was nothing unusual. Paul didn't just disappear each night and do nothing. What in the world was going on?

Since he had quit his job, he must be doing something that would eventually bring in money. Money had always been important to him, much more so than to me. I heard him more than once refer to himself as a "self-made" man. Although I knew that we were doing well financially, it was his parents' inheritance that had given us a huge leg up. I never quibbled with his somewhat arrogant description of himself. It didn't seem important at the time, and I guess it wasn't important now either. It was just a reminder of the chinks in his armor that I had chosen to ignore.

· · ·

I moved on to the next thing on my list. While still sitting in my car I dialed Alex's number. After two rings a woman's voice came on the line with, "Hello."

My heart caught in my throat, but I steadied my voice and responded, "Yes, I was wondering if Alex was in?"

"No, not right now. Could I take a message?"

"Yes, Alex just won a free pizza from Pizza Pete's. I was wondering if I could get an address where I could mail the gift certificate?"

"Sure. It's 6540 Shadow Lane."

Jotting down the address I continued, "I assume that's in Summerhill?"

"Yep."

"Okay, thank you very much."

"No, thank *you*!"

As I hung up I made a mental note to send them a gift certificate. The deceit didn't sit well with me.

Apparently, Pizza Pete's, a popular hangout, had been a safe bet. However, I still didn't know who Alex was, be it a spouse or a roommate, and still could be male or female. If Alex wasn't home now, when would he or she be home? I figured I had called a home and not a business. The phone had been answered in a casual manner, and I seemed to remember that most of Shadow Lane was residential.

Not knowing what else to do, I decided to drive past the address. It dawned on me, too late, that I should have disguised my voice on the phone. Then I could have gone to the door and worked some other angle to glean more information. Oh well, I wasn't used to trying to manipulate my situation or the people around me. It wasn't in my nature.

I pulled up across the street from 6540 Shadow Lane. Now what? It was a cute little house, nondescript. That told me nothing.

While I sat contemplating my next move, a car pulled into the driveway. I slid down in my seat hoping I hadn't been seen. The car was an older model. When I heard the car door slam, I peeked out of my window to get a glance. I gasped. It was one of the "rude" mourners from the funeral! I had seen him only at the back of the church, but I was positive it was the same man. This must be Alex. I was at once relieved it wasn't a woman and at the same time confused. Why slink out of Paul's funeral if you were his friend?

I really couldn't go to the front door now. Surely he would know who I was, and if he hadn't wanted to meet me at the funeral and express his regrets, I couldn't see why he would want to meet me now.

Then again, maybe the direct approach *would* work. But what would I say? "I've been checking up on my late husband and you seem to figure in with whatever he was hiding. So, what's up?" Somehow, that seemed like a bad idea. I had to learn more before I talked with Alex. Somewhat disappointed, I drove away.

This day was turning out to be a waste. I was reasonably certain I now knew who Alex was, but I knew nothing else. Is that what detective work was like? A few answers with long periods of getting nowhere?

I hated the thought of wasting time. The desire and need to be Noah's mom tugged at me constantly, and I was spinning my wheels, getting nowhere. What should I do next? I was running out of ideas.

. . .

Pulling into my garage at home, I was just as lost as ever. I leaned my head onto the steering wheel, trying to devise a plan. My current approach wasn't working, so it was time to try a new one, but what would that be?

I got out of the car and dejectedly made my way inside. The house was quiet, an easy tell that Noah must be down for a nap. Making my way to the great room, I discovered my parents sitting on the couch, both reading, my mother a novel and my father the newspaper. They looked up when I came in.

Mom spoke first. "Hi, sweetie. Come in and sit down."

I sank into a chair beside them. "I'm not sure what I'm doing. I don't seem to be getting anywhere."

"Well, what are you trying to find?" Dad asked.

I had to stop and think about that. What was I trying to find? "I guess I'm trying to find out who Paul really was. I thought I knew, but every time I turn around lately, I find things I didn't know. I don't know what to think. I don't know what to believe. I'd just like to find the truth. Who was Paul?"

"Then focus on figuring out exactly that."

"What do you mean?"

"Well, it seems to me, you're trying to figure out what he was up to right before he died. Maybe you need to focus on who he was. Go back further into his past rather than looking at recent events. Who knew him before you met him?"

The answer was obvious. "Professor Haynesworth." I couldn't believe I hadn't thought of him before. "Thanks, Dad, you're brilliant!"

I jumped up and nearly skipped to my office to find his number. It would be delightful to visit with Professor Haynesworth, even if it yielded no new information whatsoever.

He picked up on the first ring. "Haynesworth, here. Can I help you?"

I loved a man who answered his own phone. "Professor, this is Brea. How are you doing?"

"Ah, Brea, such a lovely child. I am absolutely wonderful. But the real question is how are you?"

"Well, I've been better. Are you, perchance, free today or tomorrow? I was wondering if I could talk to you about Paul."

"Certainly! I have a class this afternoon, but I'd love to take you to dinner. Would that be all right?"

I hesitated. Once I determined a path for myself I was impatient to be on it, but I needed to talk openly with him. "I would like that, but I was wondering if we could speak more privately, if that's okay."

"Sure. I should have thought of that. How about I have Alaina whip us up a nice dinner at my place?"

Alaina was the Professor's longtime housekeeper. She was like a sister to him, a big sister that watched out for him. "That would be perfect. What time shall I come?"

"I think I can be done here in my office around six. Would you like to meet me here about then, and we can walk over together? I'd love a stroll with a beautiful woman on my arm."

I smiled at his words. He always knew how to put others at ease. "Sounds great. I'll see you at six then."

After I hung up the phone, I sat there in my den remembering with fondness that first class taught by Haynesworth, the introductory programming class. Computer science was Paul's minor. His major was people, or at least I always thought of it that way. In reality, he majored in hospitality management. He was a natural at dealing with people. I didn't understand at first why the computer science minor, but the way Paul explained it to me was that he liked working puzzles. People were easy to understand, no challenge really – for him, anyway. Programming, on the other hand, was like a puzzle. He liked being able to put the pieces together and seeing the finished result. Being a teaching assistant for that class combined his two loves – puzzles and people. He was good at both.

I sensed Professor Haynesworth recognized these traits in Paul and eagerly welcomed his assistance. Haynesworth was a no nonsense professor. He didn't like excuses, but he was happy to help if you were willing to put in the work. He was my perfect teacher. I spent that first semester so conflicted about Paul that I had to work harder than normal to pull an A. Often I found myself in Haynesworth's office working out the complexities of our various assignments. I wasn't about to go to Paul, and I think, in looking back, that Professor Haynesworth knew what was going on in my head as well as in Paul's. He always seemed to greet me with a twinkle in his eye and never questioned why I hadn't approached Paul with my questions.

I'm sure he was more observant than I had given him credit for at the time. That was precisely what I was counting on now.

DINNER FOR TWO

Six o'clock found me knocking on the office door of Professor Sherman Haynesworth. He pulled open the door almost before I finished knocking.

"Timely as always, my dear," he said with a smile.

"It's good to see you." I reached in to embrace him. It felt good to be wrapped in his teddy bear hug. I wanted to cry, but I had promised myself I would hold it together until we at least finished our walk across campus. We let go and briefly looked at each other, reading the knowledge in each other's eyes that this would be a raw evening.

"Let me grab my briefcase and we'll be on our way." With an agile motion that belied his age, he picked up the handle of his briefcase with his left hand while at the same time, always the gentleman, offering me his right arm. I gladly took it.

We were quiet as we made our way out of his building and into the warm evening. "Do you remember your first visit to this campus?" he finally asked.

Surprised by his direction, I turned to look at him. "Why, yes, I do."

"I remember it too."

"What?"

"Yes, you don't remember me, but I remember you. I never reminded you before. I suppose I didn't want to embarrass you, but you visited the computer science department in the spring of your senior year of high school, I believe."

I nodded assent.

"I happened to be in the department office when the receptionist needed a bathroom break. I willingly agreed to sit in her chair for a few minutes to monitor the phones. It was at that moment that you entered the office. You were with your mother and father, as I recall. Is that correct?"

"Yes," I responded, completely taken off guard.

"You impressed me from that very moment. Outwardly, you held back, but just under the surface I could tell you knew who you were and where you were going, and at such a young age. That's a rare thing, young lady. You had a plan of what classes you wanted to visit, and you had an extensive list of questions to be answered. But my high opinion of you only started there. What really struck me was how you treated me. You should have been surprised to find an elderly gentleman sitting at that front desk, but you acted as if it was the most natural thing in the world. I could tell by your questions that you assumed I was indeed the receptionist."

I started to object, but he held up his hand and continued. "What I remember about you was that even though you thought I was the receptionist, you treated me with respect and deference. I'll never forget that."

I stopped walking and stood with an open mouth. I remembered visiting the department office, but I honestly recalled no faces.

"See, just by the fact that you can't place me there in that office chair says that you didn't single me out and judge me for being an old man in an entry level position."

I was completely befuddled. This man was reaching into my soul. He seemed to know me more than I ever thought possible, and not only that, he thought I was a worthwhile person. I believed myself to be that, but the last few days had made me doubt everything I thought I knew. His kind words were making it hard to keep my promise to hold back the tears.

Professor Haynesworth continued, "When you were sitting in my class at the start of the semester, I was tickled and intrigued. Would my assessment of you bear out? I must admit I tested you a little to see if you remembered me, but you did not. Having already met you, I rightly 'guessed' that you were not from the Midwest, do you recall?"

"Yes, I do. I remember everything about that day. Well, everything except your actual lecture. Sorry about that."

"No, no need. You were smitten, I could tell," and he added in a conspiratorial whisper, "I don't blame you a bit. I must add though, that you were not who I had pegged you to be."

He watched as my face fell.

"You were much better," he said with a chuckle.

I elbowed him and laughed too. It felt good to laugh. Trust my dear professor to lighten my mood. We finished our walk reminiscing about campus life.

. . .

Professor Haynesworth lived in a house right next to campus. Looking like it had been plucked from an English village, the house was a Tudor style cottage, complete with ivy vines growing up the sides. I think it had been there longer than Haynesworth had been alive, but I don't know who would have built it other than the Professor. It fit him and few others. Even the rest of the homes in the neighborhood were entirely different. His house was completely out of place, like a koala at a state fair, but also like the koala, it was so charming that no one cared.

We entered the side door and were greeted by the sound of pots and pans in the kitchen accompanied by an enticing aroma. "Alaina, we're here. What smells so delightful?"

From the kitchen I heard the return, "That's what you always say. It's just food. Now don't track any dirt into my kitchen. This may be your house, but the kitchen is mine."

He dutifully checked his shoes for dirt, as did I. I didn't want to cross Alaina, much as I adored her. We looked at each other and giggled like school kids caught playing in the mud.

"I've got Brea with me. Did you remember?" he called out, as we settled our various bags on the bench by the door.

"Of course I remembered. What do ya' take me for? *I'm* not the absent-minded professor in the house."

Duly chastised, we both made our way to the kitchen. The wonderful smell was almost overwhelming. Alaina was in the middle of cooking up enough food to feed a family reunion, but knowing Alaina I would be taking a lot of it home with me at the end of the evening. She had her graying hair braided and twirled around her head as if she had once been a playful girl but was now a woman, tied up tight. I knew that was an illusion. She only appeared wound up and stern; inside she had a heart as big and warm as the sun.

It wasn't long before we sat down at his dining room table to enjoy Alaina's efforts. We invited her to sit down and eat with us, but she declined. A different time she might have joined us, but she had enough sense to know that we needed to talk, and talk without restraint.

Dinner lived up to its aroma, but it didn't stop us from talking. There was much to discuss, and we were both eager to begin.

All it took to get me started was a searching look from Professor Haynesworth. His look was honest, if a look can be that, and concerned. I knew I would tell him everything, and I did. I told him every detail I could think of, many more certainly than I had even shared with my parents. I felt unburdened sharing it with him, as if he were my confessor and the failings and faults all mine.

When I was done with all that I knew of Paul and his behavior of late, as much as I could detect of it, and all my efforts to learn more, he simply nodded. It was a nod of understanding and resignation. It wasn't hard to read the sadness that spread across his face.

"Brea, I can only express my extreme sorrow, but that's not why you're here. You have shoulders to cry on, if I'm not mistaken. What you need from me is different.

"You, child, are an open book to me. I can imagine if I had ever married and had a daughter, she would be much like you. You and I are spitting images of each other. I'm sorry if my looks make that an unfair comparison for you," he said with a grin. Serious once again, he continued, "But we think alike and act accordingly. It is not in our nature to lie. We might tell the 'kind' lie, the one meant to spare another's feelings, but out and out lie? No, we just couldn't do it, and this is good. However, it also means we can't conceive of someone choosing to act differently than that. We just can't understand that other people can lie and still live with themselves."

I let the reality of that sink in. I suppose that was part of what was bothering me about Paul. I couldn't understand the deceit. It made no sense to me, and I couldn't fathom that the husband I had known and loved had chosen to lie to me.

He continued, "Paul was always an enigma. I liked him right from the start. Everyone liked Paul; you couldn't help but like him. Nevertheless, he only let me see what he wanted me to see. I believe that's how he was with everyone. But even with that, I did learn a few things about him. When he fell in love with you, he let his guard down just a little and I learned a bit about him. I gather that's why you're here. To learn more about the man you married, am I right?"

"Right, as usual." I turned my chair to face him fully. "I guess I'm ready, or as ready as I'll ever be. What do you know that I don't?"

"Well, first off, it's not as bad as you're expecting. I would have warned you off if I had thought that. Thinking about it now, though, I think there were things in his character that might give you some insights. They didn't stand out at the time, but given what you just told me, they could be relevant.

"Even though Paul was my TA when you met him, that was the first time I worked with him. I had only known him before that semester as a student. He was very intelligent, but beyond that, I knew few facts of his life. Some of his character traits, however, could not be hidden. Paul, as you probably know, was always very determined. If he set his sights on something, he would go after it with everything he had and not back down. I believe that's why he was able to land a prize like you." He raised his eyebrows, asking for the verification that was actually rhetorical. "But I think there was more to it than that," he added.

Puzzled, I asked, "What do you mean?"

"It's actually the fact that you two got engaged that made me stop and think about my assessment of Paul. It didn't dawn on me right away, but I started to form an idea, and then I checked it with what I saw and knew about Paul. He was all about the challenge. He only showed that fierce determination when he was trying to conquer a challenge."

I paused to process that information. It certainly fit with what I knew, but it didn't make me feel any better. Paul had admitted that his interest in me started because he couldn't have me. I had always assumed that it continued because he got to know me. Was I simply the challenge at hand, the one to conquer? I hoped that wasn't the case, but I couldn't be sure, wasn't sure of much anymore. If it was true that I was merely a trophy to be won, was there any emotion involved? I loved Paul fiercely, but what had I been to him? I thought I had known, but these last two days made me wonder. I finally dared to ask myself the question I feared most of all. *Did Paul ever love me?*

Even though I trusted Professor Haynesworth, I couldn't bring myself to put voice to this fear. Somehow saying it would make it real, and I didn't want him to start giving me that "nice" lie about Paul to make me feel better. I needed truth.

Surely going after what appeared difficult applied to other aspects of Paul's life, and by extension, maybe not his love for me. "Do you have some other examples?"

Sensing my concern, he steered the conversation elsewhere. "For instance, Paul was always trying to win at something. The computer science department held a contest the year before you arrived. It was something about creating the best app, and the winner would get a chance to pitch it to several different companies – no guarantees about whether they would buy it, but at least they would give the winner a shot at it. Paul went after that with the fierce determination that I was talking about. For him, the challenge was not winning the contest; he just assumed he would win. The hard part, what he set his sights on, was selling his app to one of those companies. That's what mattered to Paul. Of course he won. His self-confidence alone may have scared away the competition, who knows. But darn it if he didn't sell that app. He presented to those companies, and he had a contract by the end of the day! As part of it, he finagled a second app sale that he promised to have within six months. Again he pulled it off."

"I didn't know that," I said quietly. "What else did he do?" This was an insightful conversation.

"I don't know any other specifics, but I got a sense that there were more of the same: contests, business ventures. It appeared that when he was after the chase, nothing would stop him. It's as if he didn't know how to quit, even if he wanted to. But once he achieved what he had set out to do, it was a different story. It seems he didn't stick with any one type of thing too long, apparently dropping something when it was no longer difficult to achieve."

Again, I wondered if I had become one of those things that was no longer a challenge. Was he off looking for the next best thing?

We both sat in silence. The gravity of our revelations to each other needed time to sink in. I could read the anguish in his eyes that I knew was reflected in my own. We both loved a man of such potential, and he had sold himself short, had fallen from the pedestal we had wished and fantasized that he was on. But worse than that, he was dead. He couldn't redeem himself, couldn't pick himself up and rise above any of these things. It was too late, everlastingly too late.

The tears I had held off finally came, silently but persistently, tracing lines down my face. I lifted my face to look into the eyes of this caring man, only to see the same tears falling from his eyes. It was raw and tender. I mourned for the professor and his loss as I had mourned for mine, as I continued to do so.

Only a few days before, although it seemed like years, I had been in deep mourning over the death of my young husband, thinking nothing could be worse. Did I regret learning what I had recently learned? Even though I didn't have any definitive answers, I was forming a picture in my mind of a man I had hardly known. Would I undo what I had discovered if I could? I honestly didn't know.

Haynesworth reached over to grab my hand and squeezed it gently, but then he tenderly turned my hand over to see my wedding ring. He let out a soft chuckle.

Surprised, I looked up. "What in the world are you laughing about?"

Seeing my stricken expression, he said, "Oh, Brea, I'm sorry. I'm not trying to make light of what's happening in the least. It's just that I know something about your wedding ring that you don't."

My confused look spurred him on. "Well, after you and Paul had your first date, Paul decided he was going to ask you to marry him."

"Are you sure?" I didn't know if he was kidding or not.

"I'm absolutely sure. You went home for Christmas the next day, and as soon as he had seen you off, he made a beeline for my house. We had lunch in this very room, although I don't think he ate much. He was a nervous wreck." The professor got a faraway look to his eye and his mouth turned up in a soft smile. "Paul wasn't sure what you thought of him, but he told me that for the first time in his life he could picture being married, settling down with one woman. I'm sure you know what a womanizer he was. He wasn't one to sleep around, but he was a constant flirt.

"Let me tell you, though, once he knew he had a chance with you, that side of him completely shut down. Feeling that way completely undid him. He even told me that he had always planned to stay single and never have a family. Families just weren't for him. However, over that lunch he talked about you non-stop and living his life with you.

"I thought he was jumping the gun, but he didn't hear a word I said. Well, I take that back. He did ask how fast he could go, and I told him he was going to have to sit back and let you dictate how fast things went. Otherwise, he might blow his chance before your budding romance had a chance to bloom.

"But even though he listened to that piece of advice, he was determined that he would be prepared should the moment arise. The next day, he insisted I go ring shopping with him!" He stopped to laugh heartily at the memory. "Brea, can you imagine that? Paul, the formerly self-determined bachelor, and me, the old bachelor, wandering around the jewelry store trying to find the perfect ring for you? And all this because of one date and just the hope of more! We were both a little flustered, but Paul's excitement was contagious. Everyone was congratulating the two of us. They all assumed I was his father and that he must be proposing at Christmas time. Neither of us had the heart to tell those well-wishers what a chance he was taking and that he had no idea when or if it might actually happen."

I smiled despite myself at the image of the two of them in the jewelry store. "I never knew that," I said softly. "That story is nice. I'm surprised I never heard it before."

"I can explain that one," the professor replied, looking chagrined. "I was so out of my element. I agreed to go with Paul, but only on the condition of anonymity. I made him promise to never tell a soul."

"He must have been carrying that ring around with him for months," I mused. "He gave it to me right after I told him I loved him for the first time. I think he said he'd been waiting for me to say that. Wow! I had no idea. That's kind of sweet."

"Yes it is," he agreed.

It was a relief to learn something new about Paul that wasn't disappointing.

"Hey, did I ever tell you about how I met Alaina?"

"No, but that's got to be a good story." As he started his tale of meeting Alaina when she was cooking on campus, young but with the sauciness she was known for, my thoughts drifted. It was nice for a change not to be talking about Paul.

. . .

I recall driving home in the dark after making our teary good byes and being loaded down with leftovers. When I eventually found my answers, or as many as I could find, we would talk again. There was no doubt in either of our minds that Professor Haynesworth would reprise his role as surrogate father to Paul, only this time it would be as surrogate grandfather to Noah. We were bound by the mutual loss of a friend.

My phone rang on the way home, and I fumbled to find it and answer it. When I finally did so, no one was there. How rude people could be sometimes! Normally it wouldn't bother me, but I had so little fuse left these days. In my mind, I immediately blamed Paul for that, but as I did so I was quickly annoyed with myself for being *that* person, the one who takes offense at the littlest thing and never takes personal responsibility, insisting on blaming others instead. While learning that Paul was not who I thought he was, was I also learning that I wasn't as nice of a person as I thought I was?

The car lights illuminated the road in front of me but nothing else. How I wished I could see even that much of where my life was heading. I felt completely surrounded by darkness, but was it darkness of my own creating or had someone else pulled all the shades and turned off the switch, plunging me into this frightening abyss? I didn't know the answer.

It was a relief when the porch light on my house came into view. At least a small piece of safe harbor still existed. Coming into the house so late at night I was surprised yet pleased to see my father waiting up for me. He looked up from his crossword puzzle and smiled. "Hi, sweetie. Mom went to bed when Noah did, but I thought I'd wait up. You know, for old time's sake." He waited for me to sit down beside him. "How did it go?"

I nestled up next to him, putting my head on his shoulder, feeling at least partially safe. "Dad, I really didn't know him. I still feel so much love for him, but at the same time, I feel hurt and betrayed. I don't even know if he ever loved me." That's as much as I could get out before collapsing in tears.

It took a few minutes to pull myself together. Wiping my tears with a tissue, I said, "Thanks for being here for me. Would you mind helping me up to bed? I think I need your shoulder to lean on a little longer."

Without a word, he wrapped an arm gently around my shoulder, and together we made our way upstairs. He even insisted on waiting for me to brush my teeth and get ready for bed so he could tuck me in before heading off to bed himself.

INTRUSION

I slept like a rock. At nine in the morning, my mother reluctantly woke me. "Brea, I'm sorry, honey, but you need to get up. The police will be here in a few minutes, and they're going to need your help."

I woke up with a start. "The police? What happened?"

"Someone broke into the house last night. We've already called the police, because we didn't want to wait any longer."

"What's missing? What did they take? Is everyone okay?" I realized that last question should have been my first, but my brain wasn't quite awake yet.

"Everyone's fine, dear. Noah's eating some cereal in his high chair and Dad's with him. We don't know if anything is missing. That's why we need you. Can you come take a look and see?"

"You mean there's nothing obvious that's been taken, like a TV or artwork?" I was trying to think of what we had of value in our home.

"There might be a computer missing. The only place we can see any disturbance is in your office. So we figured you would know."

I hastily threw on some clothes, not wanting to greet the police in my robe, and hurried down the stairs. Mom was right. Nothing was disturbed in the rest of the house, but my office was a shambles.

Stopping at the door, I stared with disbelief. The entire contents of my filing cabinet had been emptied onto the floor, not in one big, loud dump, but in a quiet, we're-looking-for-something-specific kind of way. I could tell this by the piles of files, not quite neat piles, more like sorting piles – you know, "I've gone through this stack, why don't you go through that one."

I looked at the top of my desk where my laptop should have been, only it was gone. The dust outlined an empty rectangle where it usually sat.

I tried to look around and call up a mental picture from my memory of what used to lay where. If I could compare what I was seeing with that image, I could piece together what was missing. They had taken the charger for my laptop, so these were thinking criminals, or at least that's what I thought, admitting at the same time that I could be completely mistaken.

As I looked at the empty socket that usually held that missing power cord, I realized Paul's phone charger was also missing, which meant ... yes, his phone was missing, too. Who would want his phone? Or more likely, whoever took it thought they were taking mine. It's rather doubtful that I would be charging a dead man's phone I realized with a laugh, even though none of this was actually funny.

I couldn't imagine that someone just stole the phone and the computer to sell them. Looking over my office seemed to indicate this wasn't a random robbery. The whole thing felt surreal. I should be outraged, but with all I had been through lately, I just felt numb.

At that moment, the doorbell rang. I let my father answer it while I continued to paint images of the room, both past and present, in my head.

A familiar voice said, "Have you figured out what's missing yet?" I turned slowly around to find myself face to face with Detective Lentus. It had only been a few days since I had seen him last.

"Mrs. Cass, I'm sorry we meet again under such circumstances. Since your husband's case is still open, my lieutenant thought it best to send my partner and me out to see what happened here."

"Of course. That makes sense. I, uh, I'm not sure what's missing yet. My laptop is gone and my husband's cell phone, beyond that I don't know."

"His cell phone?" I had just piqued his interest. "The phone we returned to you a few days ago?" His voice sounded testy.

I couldn't tell if he was mad at me for retrieving the phone or at himself for not knowing it could somehow be important. But then I sensed something else - fear, fear that his lieutenant might think he had messed up.

When he kept staring at me expectantly, it dawned on me that I had not answered his question. "Yes, that very phone," I confirmed.

"Was there anything on it?"

"Well, there was an Alex in his contacts that I didn't know. He, uh …" How could I explain tracking down his address and staking out his house? "He seems to have been a friend of my husband's that I hadn't met before. He even showed up at his funeral, but ducked out before I got a chance to meet him."

The obvious question now would be, how did I know he was at the funeral if I had never met him, but Detective Lentus never asked it. He just shrugged his shoulders and started looking around. I thought about how it must sound. Your husband has a friend, a male, who his wife has never met. Yeah, that didn't sound like much of a threat, probably a drinking buddy or a bowling partner. It sounded silly now that I thought of it. I guessed B. P. would sound even sillier, so I kept my mouth shut.

"Detective, whoever it was that broke in took my computer and ransacked my office. I'm guessing they thought the phone was mine."

"Oh," Lentus responded with obvious relief. "Do you have any idea what they might have been looking for?"

"No, I don't. I haven't had a chance to go through my papers to see what's missing. Although I don't know if that will help any. I can't think of anything of value or importance that I have in here."

Lentus made his way over to the window; it was ajar. With a sinking feeling, I knew that was the form of entry.

He looked at me and arched his eyebrows. "Was this window left open like this?"

Feeling like the fool, I responded, "It could have been. I often crack it a bit. Even when I close it, I often forget to latch it," I admitted, but defensively I added, "I've been a little preoccupied lately."

He ignored my excuse. "This looks like how they gained access," stating what was now obvious, but exerting his control at the same time. "Were any other rooms in the house disturbed?"

"Not that I know of. My parents didn't think so, but I haven't looked around yet to see if anything is out of place."

He seemed eager to leave now that it didn't seem important to his investigation. Impatiently he urged, "Why don't you go take a look around, and then we'll talk in here again."

Annoyed with his attitude, I turned to wander through my house. It was strange that nothing else was touched. There were valuable pieces of art, mostly gifts from Paul to me, but none of these had been disturbed. What had they been looking for in my den?

As I walked through the kitchen, I noticed my cell phone sitting on the counter where I must have placed it on my way upstairs last night. It registered one missed call. I picked up the phone to check it. No message had been left. The call came in at 2:23 am, and the number was blocked. That struck me as odd, both a call in the middle of the night and on a night when we had a break in. While pondering that, I noticed that the call before that one had also been from a blocked number. It was not a missed called, so clearly I had answered the call, but I couldn't place it. Looking at the time of the call for clues, it showed 11:04 pm the previous evening. That would have been shortly after I left Professor Haynesworth's, but I hadn't talked to anyone on the phone.

I stood where I was in the kitchen pondering the call that I could not remember, mentally retracing my steps of the night before. The time must have been when I was in the car. With realization dawning, I recalled getting a call and answering it only to find no one on the other end. That was it! I was proud of myself for remembering, but then I stopped to consider what it might mean.

If both calls were from the same person, was someone checking to see if I was asleep? Was that call from the person who broke into my house? It sounded far-fetched, but just as plausible as anything.

Happy that I had pulled my thoughts together, I returned to the office to show the detective my phone. "I wonder if whoever broke in was checking to see if I was awake, if I would answer my phone. See, here's a phone call from a blocked number at 2:23 this morning. I didn't answer it. And around eleven last night there was another call from a blocked number. I answered it, but no one was there." I then looked up at the detective and smiled. I don't know what reaction I expected, but a complete dismissal was not it.

"Yeah," he raised his eyebrows at me, "it seems they had a plan," and with that he turned away.

Okay, I had to admit, it wasn't an earth-shattering piece of information that directly tied itself to anything. So maybe it didn't really help, and it didn't help direct us anywhere. A blocked call is a blocked call, isn't it?

Then over his shoulder he threw me a bone. "If you'd be willing to give us access to your phone records, we can try to track it down."

"Yeah, sure," I eagerly responded. Why wouldn't I? Did this detective care about doing his job? Maybe I was just reading him wrong. It's possible I had just ticked him off questioning him at the station a couple of days ago. I didn't know for sure, but the sooner I looked over my office for what was missing, the sooner he would be gone.

"Um, I didn't find anything disturbed anywhere else. What would you like me to do here?"

He turned at my conciliatory tone. "Why don't you go through your papers and things to see if you can identify anything else that's missing. I've got my partner checking the outside of the house. I'll go direct her to this window, and then we'll head back to the station." I had been oblivious to the fact that another police office was somehow on the premises. Lentus had mentioned a partner when he first showed up, hadn't he? I shook my head to shake out the cobwebs.

"Call us if you discover what else, if anything, is missing," he added.

"Okay," I responded, knowing he wasn't expecting much. Regardless, it was time to do my part. I found a clean spot on the floor amid the piles and sat down cross-legged in the middle of it for the tedious task ahead.

MARTHA'S CAR

Two hours later I had learned two things. One, that my files were seriously out of date, and two, that I couldn't possibly tell if anything was missing. Other than the computer and the phone, I knew of nothing for certain that had been taken. I left a brief message to that effect for Detective Lentus and then went to find Noah. At least if I could play with my little boy, the day would not be a total loss.

I found my mom and dad in the great room on the floor with Noah. They were rolling a ball across the floor much to Noah's giggling delight. I sat down to join the game, and for the time being all my troubles were forgotten.

Before long, playtime and lunch were over. I read a story to Noah in our rocking chair and placed him down in his crib for a nap. He fussed only a little before drifting off to sleep.

I stood outside his door listening to the soothing sound of his breathing. I felt like I was playing at being a mom, as if this were all a dream. Waking up to the uncertainties swirling around me would be the nightmare.

With reluctance, I tiptoed away from his room and returned to my office to put things back in order. When I had gone through my papers earlier to determine if anything was missing, I had made a cursory attempt to sort my files. I had a pile of things I no longer needed that would go straight into the trash and an assortment of other papers that needed to be returned to my filing cabinet.

Working on the mindless task of shuffling papers allowed me to ponder recent events. I couldn't, for the life of me, understand why anyone would want my computer or any of my papers. I hadn't found anything missing, but what had they been looking for in the first place?

No matter which way I looked at the problem, I could think of nothing I knew or had that could be of value or interest. I felt like I was walking around with a target on my back with no idea what or who had placed it there. It was a vulnerable feeling, and the urgency to understand it just compounded all my frustrations with trying to figure out what Paul had been up to.

My thoughts drifted to the last couple of days. All I had to show for them was more questions and certainly no answers. I wasn't even sure what I was looking for. Was I stirring up something I would later regret?

Is that what was happening? Had I inadvertently triggered the break in? What had I learned that someone might think was important? Alex! That was the only loose end. He must have seen me outside his house. If he knew Paul, it would be logical that he would know where I lived. If he was behind this, what did he think I knew? What was there to know?

As my thoughts started to race to pull the pieces together, I felt a growing sense of alarm. What would happen when he discovered he had Paul's phone and not mine, would he come back? And surely when he looked at my computer he would find that there was nothing *to* find. He was looking for some knowledge that he thought I had;

what would he do when he didn't find it? I wondered what lengths he would go to to get what he wanted.

With fear creeping up my back, I thought of Noah and the danger I had just placed him in, not to mention my parents. There was no time to waste. I had to figure out what was going on and I needed to do it right now! Somehow, I had to learn what it was that Alex was after.

I quickly shoved the remaining files back into the drawers or the garbage can, only pausing briefly to hope I hadn't mixed up the piles. I had to learn more about Alex.

What should I do now? If he was worried about me watching him, maybe that's exactly what I needed to do more of – watch him. Only this time, I needed to guard against being seen.

I raced upstairs and rummaged through the closet. Finding a nondescript t-shirt, I quickly changed clothes then put my hair up under an old baseball cap of Paul's. A pair of sunglasses would complete the look. At least from a distance no one would recognize me.

After a brief explanation to my parents, where I gave them enough information to appease them but not enough to worry them, I went to the garage with a plan forming in my mind. I came up short. All the disguises in the world would be meaningless if I drove the same car I had driven the day before. I assumed since Alex knew Paul, that Paul's car would be an even worse choice. I sat down on the steps leading from the garage into the house. How could something so simple derail me? I determined that it wouldn't; I just had to come up with a solution.

With a sudden idea, I slipped out of the garage and made a beeline for Martha's house, pulling off the hat and letting my hair fall as I did so. As I reached up to knock on her door, I realized I had some explaining to do. I had shut her out, and at bare minimum, I owed her an apology.

What would I say to her now that I was standing on her front porch? Before I had a chance to formulate the words, the door swung open and Martha was throwing her arms around me.

"Brea, dear, come on in."

"Martha, aren't you mad at me?"

"Why would I be mad at you?"

"I've turned my back on you lately. I'm so sorry."

"Is that it? Well, my dear, everyone has to grieve. Some of us do it loudly and tell everyone about it. Others, like you, grieve in your own head, trying to spare the rest of us from your turmoil."

I thought she was being overly generous. I didn't think there was anything selfless in my grieving at all, but, knowing Martha, there would be no convincing her otherwise. Besides, I was grateful she wasn't mad at me. "Martha, you are a better friend than I deserve."

"No, Brea, but given enough years, I've learned a little patience. I knew you'd come around eventually. So, what's up? I saw you march over here with a very determined step. This is not simply an apology visit, is it?"

"Well, no it isn't. Could I borrow your car? You're welcome to use mine in the meantime." Catching her confused look, I had to acknowledge just how odd what I asked must have sounded. "Martha, it's complicated. I'll explain it all eventually. But for right now, I just need you to trust me on this."

"It's never a matter of trust; you should know that. I am curious, but I'm sure you have a good reason. Did I see your parents around, so there is someone to watch Noah?"

"Yes, you don't miss a thing, do you?"

"Not much, not much. I might have to stop by, though, to see that sweet little boy of yours. You won't mind, will you?"

"Of course not." I reached out to hug this gentle woman. I had forgotten how much I enjoyed her company and became aware of how much I needed her in light of all that had happened lately. We exchanged car keys and I sped off to learn what I could about Alex.

. . .

It was late afternoon when I pulled into Alex's neighborhood. At least I had the sense not to park right in front of his house this time. Instead, I found a side street off Shadow Lane, a short distance from Alex's house. A number of parked cars were scattered about. Slipping in between a couple of them, I felt inconspicuous. I didn't have a perfect view of his house, but I could at least see the comings and goings.

Being new at the stake out business, I learned I had not planned well in the least. I could have used a pair of binoculars, like the nice pair sitting in the top of my closet at home. Some food and water also wouldn't have been a bad idea.

Fortunately, I didn't have to wait long to see some activity. On the other hand, what I saw wasn't much. Alex came down the street in his car a few minutes later, turned into his driveway, then entered his house. Other than his stepping out of the house later for a smoke, nothing happened.

I wasn't sure how long I should wait around, not helped by the fact that I didn't know what I was watching for. My grumbling stomach won out, and I left for home around 9 pm.

Driving home, I made a mental list of what I would do differently tomorrow. Food was at the top of my list, but I knew that wouldn't help me with Alex. Now that I had wasted my evening, did I dare use Martha's car again? With a split second decision, I turned the car around to head to Amy's apartment. Maybe she could loan me her car tomorrow.

As I approached Amy's door, I realized that for the second time in the same day I was in a position of needing to apologize for how I had treated one of my best friends. Buoyed up by Martha's response I rang the bell.

It only took a moment for Amy to answer the door. She didn't say a word as she stood in the doorway but tilted her head to the side and gave me a questioning glance.

"I'm sorry, Amy. You've been trying to help me and I stubbornly wouldn't let you."

She still stood silently in front of me, placing her hands on either side of the doorframe, blocking any further entrance. I wasn't sure what to say now. "If it makes you feel any better, I'm here because I need your help." It came out sounding lame, and I knew it.

Amy's face relaxed into a grin, and she started laughing. I wasn't sure how to take that, so I stared back into her face.

"Brea, come on in." She dropped her arms and moved aside to let me in. "Do you have any idea how pathetic you look? You look like a puppy dog begging for his dinner."

"Are you mad at me? Because I wouldn't blame you."

"Of course I'm mad at you. But that doesn't mean I've stopped liking you. You're like my sister. We may disagree, even get mad, but we'll be the first to defend each other. So, what do you need?"

It was my turn to laugh. "You always could cut to the chase." I wasn't in the rush that I had been in when I was at Martha's, so I explained what was going on to the best of my knowledge up to my failed stake out.

Before I could even ask to borrow her car, she could see where I was headed and beat me to the punch. "Okay, so you need a different car tomorrow. You can borrow mine, but only if you take me with you. When do you want me to pick you up in the morning?" She smiled her self-satisfied smile, knowing I couldn't refuse her.

STAKEOUT REDO

Amy came by bright and early at six in the morning. After talking it over, Amy had suggested we show up before Alex might head out for the day. Then we could follow him if need be. He wouldn't know her, so if she followed him for a short distance we surmised it wouldn't arouse any suspicion.

We arrived at the same side street I had used the previous night but parked in a different spot and settled in. This time the car was well stocked with snacks, my pair of binoculars, and even a couple of pillows if we needed to take turns catching a short nap.

The house was dark and quiet; we were probably in for the long haul. "So, how's Noah these days?" Amy asked. There was an edge to her voice. It hadn't dawned on me that shutting her out also meant cutting her off from Noah, who was growing and changing every day.

"He's ...," I wasn't quite sure where to begin. "He's crawling all over the place now. His favorite game is peek-a-boo." My answer sounded inadequate. "Oh, Amy, I'm really sorry. Do you want to come over later and see him?"

"Yes. Of course I would. I'll come for dinner, and you can feed me while you're at it."

I smiled. That was sounding more and more like the old Amy I knew and loved. "So, what would you like for dinner?"

"Something homemade would be nice. I'm getting tired of TV dinners. Do you know how much sodium is in those things? You need to take better care of me; you know that, don't you?"

Our combined laughter was like a healing ointment and all was forgiven. "I can't believe what a jerk I've been lately."

"I know, but there's hope for you now. So, really, what is Noah doing these days?"

I started to rattle off his latest milestones and misadventures. It was like coming home.

We had soon settled into such a comfortable exchange that we almost missed Alex when he came out his front door. I caught movement out of the corner of my eye and sat up with a start. "There he is!" I exclaimed just as he opened the back door of his car and ducked in.

"Where?"

"Just watch. He's in the car. I can't tell if he's going to leave or not because he's messing around in the back seat. Quick, grab the binoculars."

Amy held them out to me just as Alex came back out of the car and stood up. She let out an audible gasp and then snatched them back from my ready grasp to put them to her eyes. "I don't believe it. When you told me the name Alex, it sounded familiar, but I never thought in a million years it would be that Alex."

"You know him?"

"Yeah, I do." She sounded just as surprised as I felt.

"Who is he? How do you know him?"

She let the binoculars fall and turned to me. "His name is Alex Roberts. Do you remember when I first met Paul I was working as an intern at the hotel?"

I nodded.

"Well, Alex worked there too. He was the maintenance man. I didn't know him all that well, but I would see him every once in a while at our staff lunches. Alex was single at the time, and he started coming on to me at the lunches. One time he asked for my phone number, and I gave it to him. But later when I thought about it, I wasn't so sure I wanted to date him. I can't say why, just something bothered me about him. So I made sure to run into him and then give him the cold shoulder to discourage him. He got the message and didn't call me ... at least not then."

"When did he call you?"

"Long after I had left that internship. He called me about seven or eight months ago. He had to remind me who he was, because I had forgotten him. After he refreshed my memory, I was worried he was going to ask me out after all that time, but that's not what he wanted at all. He was asking me about *you*."

"What?"

"Yeah, he said he was helping Paul put together a nice surprise for you with the new baby and all. It must have been either right before or right after Noah was born. He wanted to know where you liked to shop and your favorite places to hang out. I thought he was putting together some gift certificates or something. Oh, and he asked for your phone number. I guess in retrospect that doesn't make much sense. Paul could have told him your number."

"Sure, but why would he want it anyway?"

"I hadn't thought of that. That's a good question. I haven't a clue. I'm sorry if I told him anything I shouldn't have. It just seemed legit at the time."

"I know. I would have done the same thing in your shoes. But I wonder what the whole thing was about. Paul didn't give me gift certificates or anything that seems to fit with what you're describing."

I grew silent, thinking back seven and eight months ago when the world seemed to be full of color and light. "Paul was so sweet and helpful after Noah was born." I was so lost in thought I hadn't realized that I had audibly spoken until Amy responded.

"What did he do that you remember most?" Amy asked. Her voice was quiet to match my own, as if anything louder might shatter the moment or bring a flood of unwelcome tears.

I didn't answer at first. What did stand out the most? As I flipped through the memories in my mind, I noticed that Alex had retreated into his house. Knowing that more empty waiting time stretched before us, I felt the need to respond. I wasn't sure I trusted my voice, but I began anyway. "You know some of the things he did already – the apples and the roses, making me dinner, that kind of thing." I stopped to allow myself a wistful smile. "I think my favorite memories come from the simple moments. I remember Paul bathing Noah by himself for the first time. He was so nervous that he would do something wrong or somehow hurt our little boy. I had to talk him through each step. At one point I even offered to take over, but he said that no, he was going to do it. After that, Paul bathed Noah whenever he could.

"When they both had a few baths under their belts, Paul showed him the magic of bubbles. He would get a soap bubble on his hand and then blow it into the air and Noah would start those baby belly laughs. Or he would take a bubble and gently transfer it to Noah's hands and then clap Noah's hands together to help him pop it.

"I guess it's just a million little things like that that I remember, that I miss." I then added, "I hope they were all real."

"Brea, they were real. I don't know what was up with Paul, but it doesn't change those moments."

We both lapsed into silent contemplation. I took the binoculars back and fiddled with them, wondering what was next.

Amy's voice broke into my thoughts. "There he is again."

I lifted the binoculars to my eyes to get a better view. Alex was standing by the back of his car, watching expectantly for something. Thankfully, he wasn't looking in our direction. After a few minutes, another car pulled in behind his. As it did so, Alex went to the back seat of his car and retrieved an item that was slightly bigger than his hand. It appeared lightweight and fairly slim. The only thing I could think of was that it looked like a handheld game or a glucose monitor, but other than that, I could tell nothing about it.

By now the other driver had gotten out of his car. He came into my binocular's view as he met Alex to take the object from him. I could see the back of his head as he and Alex began to engage in some sort of intense discussion. I dropped the binoculars to focus on listening to their words, but I couldn't catch even a snippet of what they were saying. Amy was clearly trying hard to hear what they were saying as well.

After a few minutes, the second man turned around to leave. As he did so, his face stirred something in my memory. "Do you know who that is Amy? He looks familiar."

"No, I've never seen him before. Where do you think you know him from?"

I probably wouldn't have placed him except at that moment Alex moved in beside him. Seeing their faces together reminded me once again of the funeral. He was the other rude mourner at Paul's service. It caught me by surprise merely because I wasn't thinking along those lines, but as I considered it, it wasn't surprising at all. If they were associated now, it made sense they would have been associated then as well. It was one of the few things that actually fit together. Amy was looking at me expectantly. "He was at the funeral, Amy, with Alex. I guess it makes sense that Alex was there to pay his respects, given what you told me about him, but I don't have any idea who that other man is.

"Amy, did you notice that thing Alex handed to him?"

"Not really. What did it look like through the binoculars?"

"That's the thing, I don't know." We watched as the second man pulled out of the driveway and Alex returned to his house. "Could you tell what they were saying?"

"No. They were talking seriously about something. You could tell by the looks on their faces, but I haven't a clue what they said. We're just too far away. But trust me; I wouldn't want to be any closer."

I agreed.

. . .

After several hours with no more activity on the part of Alex, Amy and I decided we weren't cut out for long hours in the car. Besides needing

a bathroom break, we were tired, and truth be told, we wanted to spend time with Noah.

When we got home, Noah was tickled to see me. He looked hesitantly at Amy, as if he might know her, but he wasn't sure. It was lunchtime, and by the time we had finishing making and eating our sandwiches, Noah had warmed up completely to Amy.

Much as I wanted to play with Noah, I stepped back and let Amy take that role. They played peek-a-boo, pat-a-cake, and tickle games until both collapsed from laughter and exhaustion. While Amy climbed onto the couch for a nap, I took Noah upstairs for a nap of his own.

BACK UPS

During their naps, I took the opportunity to check my email. But when I went to the den, I remembered the loss from the day before - my computer was gone.

My alternative was to traipse back upstairs to my bedroom. In the sitting area, which we had converted into an office for Paul, sat his laptop, undisturbed since his death. I sat down in his office chair and looked around me. Other than dusting surfaces, I hadn't spent much time at Paul's desk since he died. Everything around me whispered of Paul. I thought for a moment that I could almost catch a whiff of his cologne.

I looked at the desk in front of me. Beside his computer sat pencils, pens, and an assortment of note pads. Some random post-it notes littered the top of his desk. It whispered of a life interrupted. I had not turned on the nearby lamp yet, and the light coming from my bedroom cast eerie shadows on the walls around me. I reached over quickly to switch on the lamp to chase away the ghosts.

A little unnerved, I started up his computer and brought up my email. My inbox was stuffed to overflowing, but none of it was important. Thinking that this might be my computer from now on, I started to customize the computer desktop to my liking. I felt torn, as if I were moving on and erasing all traces of Paul. I decided to put the settings back to what they had been.

I stood up, walked over to my nightstand, and pulled open the drawer. Inside was my backup flash drive. I always kept it there where I would have ready access to it in an emergency. Unfortunately, I couldn't remember the last time I had backed up my files, probably before Paul's death. On the other hand, I didn't think I had actually changed any files since then.

I mindlessly copied my files onto the laptop. I thought of it as "the" laptop, neither Paul's nor mine right now. I was going through the motions, but my heart wasn't in any of it, and after the necessary responses, I turned everything off.

Staying where I was, I put my head in my hands, wondering where to go from here. Fiddling with my thumb drive in my hands, I decided to put it in the top drawer of the desk in front of me. I opened the drawer and threw it in, then just as quickly shut it leaving my hand on the drawer handle. It felt like a betrayal to so casually use what used to be Paul's. I didn't like the look of his pencils and pens, daily accumulations that reminded me how much I missed him.

I wondered when it would start getting easier. Feigning courage, I opened the drawer back up, slowly this time. It made me smile to see his odd assortment of paper clips, erasers, pencils, pens, and rubber bands. I remembered buying the drawer dividers for him to keep things neat and clean, and he had been quite compliant in keeping things sorted.

My eyes narrowed as I stared at the little bin into which I had just thrown my flash drive. Paul's back up drive was usually kept in that exact spot, but now the only one occupying that space was mine. Where was his?

I started to rifle through the remaining drawers of his desk but came up empty handed. Turning around I scanned our bedroom for possible places to look. I went over to our bed, checked his nightstand, and then to the other side to check mine, but I again came up empty. What was going on?

My eyes swept our bedroom again, but nothing stood out to me. I moved to Paul's dresser, frantically pulling out his drawers one after the other, searching behind and beneath clothes. By the time I reached the last drawer, I was pulling clothes out and shaking them before dropping them into a pile in the middle of the floor.

Irrational and panicked by now, I wasn't even sure where to look next. The clothes on the floor made me think of our walk-in-closet, so I moved to try that next.

As I flipped on the switch in our closet, our small wall safe came into view. Paul had thought it was a good idea to install it when we bought the house, while I had thought it was a waste of money. But Paul convinced me with talk of the jewelry he would buy me over the years. He'd only had time to buy me a few pieces. They were securely tucked away in the safe for the parties we had yet to attend.

I pushed clothes aside, bringing the safe into full view. It had been so long since I had opened it that I had to stop and think about the combination. I needed to try a couple sets of numbers before I got it right. When the door slid open, I was disappointed to see only my jewelry cases inside. I slammed the door in frustration, but it only bounced back open as if to taunt me. I looked at the contents in front of me again, feeling defeated on every hand. Only then did I notice something I hadn't before. One of my jewelry cases was perched at an odd angle, as if it were sitting on top of something else.

I tentatively reached inside and picked up the case. Underneath it, in the far corner of the safe, was Paul's small USB flash drive.

Curious yet nervous, I pulled it out. Leaving the safe open, I returned to Paul's sitting room office, bringing the flash drive with me. I turned Paul's computer on and after booting it up, I inserted the drive. It contained only two files. I opened the first and immediately recognized it as a computer program. There were no comments to guide me through what it did; I would have to step my way through it line by line. I minimized that window for future perusal and opened the second.

It was a JPEG file. Opening it revealed schematic drawings, but very little was labeled. It was not at all apparent what the drawings were meant to be. They looked like technical specs. The only labels were numbers. I couldn't tell if they were part numbers or maybe measurements or coded id numbers. I sent the drawings to our printer so I could look at them more closely.

It was only as I went down to my office to retrieve the print outs that I realized the printer had been left behind by the intruders, as if I needed any further proof that they were looking for something specific.

There were four pages of specs. Looking at them in print didn't help me understand them any better. Clearly the item was of rectangular shape, almost brick like. Unfortunately, that didn't narrow down the possibilities much.

I tried to think of some way to search the internet for something to match this, but there just wasn't anything I could pick out that was unique enough to key in on for a search. Even after showing it to my parents and Amy, who was now awake, we were nowhere closer to an answer.

When Amy agreed that an internet search would be pointless, I remembered the other file. The drawing of the mysterious box had so intrigued me that I had forgotten about the program on the screen upstairs. I remembered it at the same moment we heard Noah stir. The program could wait; I wanted to hold my son.

PROGRAMMING MYSTERIES

It wasn't until after Noah went to bed that night that I had time to focus on the computer program. Once I told them about it, Amy and my parents had both offered to play with Noah while I concentrated on it, but I wanted to celebrate the return of Amy and enjoy our little gathering. It was a little peace amid the storm.

When at last Amy had gone and Noah was nestled in his bed, I crept downstairs, taking the laptop and thumb drive with me. I settled on the couch in the great room with a plate of cookies and a glass of milk by my side. I knew the treats seemed incongruous with the task at hand, but that was exactly the point. I wanted the comfort of milk and cookies to see me through whatever I might find.

As I started to study the code, I began to learn a few things. First, this was not a complete program. It was meant to be part of something else. This was simply a function that performed one task as part of a bigger application. Without the other information it was difficult to understand what role different variables played. None of the variables even had names that helped to identify what they were. I could tell that most of the variables were defined as numbers, but they didn't include any decimal digits, so it's unlikely the numbers were related to money. A couple of variables held dates, but that wasn't unusual so it didn't tell me much.

I analyzed the code from different perspectives, making certain assumptions and checking to see where those assumptions would lead. None of my ideas shed any light on the situation.

After several hours of analysis, I had an understanding of only a few things. The function appeared to be called or used when something went wrong, because it was designed to return an error message, with information about what was causing the error. Beyond that, the only thing I could determine is that the error had something to do with duplicate entries. This seemed straightforward. I couldn't understand why it was in our safe.

Puzzling over what this app was about and why Paul had written it reminded me of Professor Haynesworth's stories. Paul had sold a couple of apps before, so I wondered if this was something he was going to try to sell also.

Other than what I had learned already, I wasn't sure what to do with the program in front of me. I decided to return it to the safe from which it had come until I could gain more of an understanding of what it was all about.

As I gathered up Paul's computer, I caught a glimpse of the night outside my window. It was pitch dark outside. So many things had taken place in the middle of the night lately. I looked out the window and shivered. Darkness engulfed my heart. Why couldn't we see things in the dark? I wished I could just be a nocturnal animal for a moment so I could see into the night. Even if I could be assured of the dawn it would free my heart from the hold the night had upon it.

As these thoughts swirled in my head, I saw a light go on upstairs and heard the pad of my father's footsteps. I would welcome his company.

"Dad, what are you doing up?"

"Looking after you. Are you going to stay up much longer? I thought you might like a blanket or a cup of tea."

"Thanks, Dad. I'm going to call it a night. I've figured out all I can for now."

"Then I will be your shining knight and see you safely upstairs."

"Thank you, Sir Knight. I would appreciate that."

Once again he waited while I got ready for bed, which tonight included returning the thumb drive to the safe along with the print outs and moving shirts in front of the safe to hide it. I was relieved to put it all away, even if just for the evening.

"Good night, Dad, and thanks for everything."

"Good night, Brea. I love you," were the last words I heard before falling fast asleep.

WEEKEND PLANS

I awoke Sunday morning to the sound of a myriad of voices downstairs. I lay in bed listening, but I couldn't make out the words, only that the sounds were happy. I looked at my clock and was surprised to see it was almost noon. Hastily throwing on some clothes, I descended the stairs.

What greeted me was a happy Noah surrounded by both grandparents, Martha, and Amy. They all heard my approach and turned to look at me. Their expressions all bore the same message in one form or another, "This is life as it should be." I had to smile in agreement. I didn't know exactly who had convened this group or if it had happened all on its own, but it was definitely "as it should be."

I slipped into the kitchen to grab a banana while I watched my parents and friends dote on my son. Maybe I really couldn't do this on my own, but thankfully, it was becoming clear that I didn't have to, nor should I.

Eventually Dad joined me in the kitchen, scrounging for some lunch for the crowd in the adjacent room, or at least that was his excuse. "So what did you learn last night? You were at it for quite some time."

"I'm not sure. That seems to be the problem with all of this; it doesn't make sense. I looked over Paul's program last night, and while I understand the basics of what it does, I don't know the point of the whole thing. I wonder if it's part of an app he was getting ready to sell. It isn't a complete program by itself, but it looks like it will fit in with something else. Although I don't know what that other part is either."

"So, where do you go from here?"

"I was thinking about trying to track down more information about the apps Paul sold when he was in school. Maybe that will help explain what I found."

"Sounds good."

"I hope so. I thought I would start by calling Professor Haynesworth to see if he knows anything."

"Okay. Go ahead and do it. Noah is fine. If anything we're fighting over him, so no worries there, okay," he said with a smile.

"Thanks, Dad." Then without any words of protest, I retreated to my office to make a phone call.

. . .

Alaina answered the phone on the first ring. "Haynesworth House," she answered, as if it were a great English manor house.

"Hi, Alaina. This is Brea. Is the Professor home?"

"Yes, he is. I'll get him for you."

It was only a moment later when I heard the cheerful sound of Haynesworth's voice. "Brea, dear, what can I do for you?"

"I've found a program Paul wrote, and I'm wondering if it's part of an app he was getting ready to sell. Do you know any more about the apps he sold before, like who he sold them to?"

"I don't, but give me a couple of hours and I'll see what I can learn. If you haven't heard from me by dinner time, give me a call." He often made comments like that, as if he really were an absent-minded professor, but I had yet to have him disappoint me or see him lose his focus. I think he just liked the image of being an eccentric old man, so we all humored him.

"I will definitely do that. Thank you for your help."

"No trouble at all, especially not for you, child."

. . .

I sat at my desk after hanging up wondering what was next. I began to write out my thoughts on the pad of paper in front of me. I wrote the name, "Alex," in big bold letters across the top. What did he have to do with any of this, if anything? Was he more than simply a friend of Paul's? Was something odd going on in his life or were my anxieties playing tricks on me? Either way, I didn't feel like I had learned all I could about that angle yet. For all I knew, it wasn't relevant to what Paul was doing instead of going to work, but it was one of the few avenues I had open to explore.

I was surprised to notice that I had jotted further, "Paul – app?" My brain was having a hard time adjusting to the slow nature of investigating and learning. Just like me, it craved answers that appeared elusive.

While I was waiting to hear back from Professor Haynesworth, maybe I could learn something more about Alex. Since I knew where he worked, I picked up my phone again and called the hotel.

When the phone was answered, I asked for either Anna or George. Before long, Anna was on the other end. "Brea, it's good to hear from you again. What can I help you with?"

"Anna, I was wondering if you could tell me anything about Alex Roberts?"

"Um, sure," she hesitated. Clearly, she wasn't expecting that question. "What do you want to know?"

"I'm not sure. Is he a good employee? Was he friends with my husband? How does he strike you as a person?"

"Well, he was a fine employee. As an employer I'm not allowed by law to go into detail, but I'll just say I had no complaints."

"Was? He doesn't work there anymore?"

"No, he quit about six months ago or so. He had been gone a few months when Paul took his leave."

"Can you tell me why he quit?"

"Legally, I can't, but I couldn't anyway. He never gave a reason."

I wasn't sure what to make of that. The bottom line is it didn't mean anything, which just disappointed me.

Anna broke into my thoughts. "And to answer your other question, Paul and Alex got along fine. They often grabbed lunch together. I seem to remember that they could easily get lost in conversation. Other than that, I'm sorry, I can't tell you much."

"No, that's okay. What did he do at the hotel? I understood he was a maintenance man?"

"Yes, that's what he did. It meant he had his finger in everything. He had a basic working knowledge of most things in the hotel but not expertise particularly in any of it. You always have to know when to fix something yourself and when to call in an expert. He was pretty good at that."

"Thanks."

"Does that help?" Anna asked.

I wondered if there was a note in her voice of fishing for what I was looking for exactly. Even if I wanted to, I couldn't tell her. I was fishing for it myself. "I'm not sure if it does or not, to be honest, but I appreciate your help all the same."

I hung up the phone and realized with a sigh that I was back in the position of waiting to hear from the professor. Once this quest had begun, patience had not been my strong suit. I figured I was going to have to keep myself busy to stay sane. At least I had the perfect crew in the next room to help me do that.

. . .

A few hours later found the adults gathered around a movie while Noah napped upstairs. Before it was over, I had started snoring, sprawled out on the floor. I couldn't say how the movie ended, and I'm not sure if anyone else could either gauging by the glazed looks in their eyes when I finally awoke, but it had served its purpose.

My phone rang a few minutes later. It was Haynesworth.

"What did you learn?" I eagerly asked.

"Well, the contest was organized by Dr. Jon Howard. He arranged the business contacts who were willing to consider the winning app for possible purchase. Also, you're in luck, because he said that one of them, the one who eventually bought Paul's winning app and another app later, will be on campus tomorrow for a recruiting visit. Would you like to meet him?"

"Yes! That would be fantastic."

"I thought that's what you'd say, so I set up a time for you to meet him. Can you do three o'clock on Monday afternoon?"

"Sure. Just tell me where, and I'll be there." I got the details from him before hanging up and returning to my family and other friends.

Once I told them of my plans, Amy was the first to speak. "I'm taking tomorrow afternoon off work, and I'm going with you to the university."

I smiled, admitting to myself that I had known all along she would go with me. It was pointless to refuse, and additionally, I knew that I didn't want to.

The rest of the day passed quickly as everyone sensed my impatience and took turns keeping me occupied. Even Noah looked at me with imploring eyes, as if to say, "Everything will be okay."

NIGHTMARES COME TRUE

I awoke Monday morning with a sudden start. It felt like that fateful night when I couldn't breathe. Only now, my breathing was fast and irregular. Had I been dreaming or were there actual dangers lurking nearby? I sat up at once, still breathing erratically, but aware of every sound around me. I could hear nothing but the sound of my own breathing panting in my ears.

What had awakened me? I hadn't been roused from sleep when someone broke into my house, why now? Still no other sound was evident. I consciously worked to calm my breathing, if for no other reason than to be able to hear sounds beyond myself.

Noah's baby monitor sat near my bed. Sounds of his soft breathing were just audible, but that was a comforting sound, not disturbing in the least. I eased myself out of bed to explore my surroundings, listening for any noise that was out of place as I did so.

Fifteen minutes later, I had completed a very thorough walk-through of the house. Nothing was amiss. Was I going crazy? I collapsed onto the sofa in the great room. Exhaustion overtook me, and I slumped over and fell back asleep.

. . .

I awoke at dawn when my mother came down from upstairs. The sight of me caught her off guard. "Brea, I didn't know you were here. I'm sorry I woke you. Did you sleep here all night?"

"No, Mom. I woke up in the middle of the night and came down here. You didn't by chance hear anything in the night, did you?"

"No, I didn't. Why? Did you?"

"I don't know if I did, but something seemed to wake me." I wasn't sure how to describe exactly what woke me, because I wasn't sure myself. Maybe it really was just a bad dream. "Oh well, I'm fine now. Would you like some breakfast since we're both up? I'll cook."

Mom started to protest and then thought better of it. "Sure, that would be great. Who knows how soon Noah will be up? We might as well enjoy some time to ourselves while we can."

While I whipped up some scrambled eggs Mom made toast, and we chatted about average, everyday things. It had a feeling of normalcy to it and began to calm my worried mind. We were almost done eating when Dad came down the stairs with a little boy in his arms.

Noah was still rubbing the sleep out of his eyes, but when he saw me, he smiled and put his hands out, chattering, "Mm, mm, mm." I gladly took him into my arms.

"I'm not doing anything special at the moment. I'll get his breakfast for him, Dad."

"Thanks," Dad mumbled, still a little tired himself. He left us to go turn on the morning news.

Mom turned to go upstairs with, "I think I'll go grab a shower."

Noah was delighted to have me feed him his breakfast. It looked like returning to our old routines was important for him too. He was still a big fan of rice cereal, which I would mix together with fruit of some kind. This morning it was bananas. While more ended up like glue in his hair, it was a moment we were both enjoying.

Eventually, I handed Noah off to Dad. I wanted to go upstairs to search through Paul's computer for anything out of the ordinary. It would be tedious, but maybe there were files that might give me some hints as to what I was looking for. I could also look at his browser history, bookmarks, and emails. It was doubtful to me that I would find anything. Paul had shared with me all his passwords since the moment we were married. I didn't think that whatever he was hiding would be right there under my nose, but at least I had to look.

Even though I had talked myself into believing Paul would hide nothing in plain sight, I found as I searched that I was expecting to find some astounding revelation every time I opened a file. After several hours of tedium, I disappointedly admitted there was nothing to find. It was a huge let down, only mitigated by the prospect of speaking to the man who had previously bought Paul's apps.

Dejected, I started to get ready to meet Amy for our scheduled afternoon meeting. The ominous feeling from the middle of the night began to prey upon my mind, and I questioned its meaning while at the same time trying to dispel it.

I was ready early, but rather than wait around and stew, I decided to head over to Amy's apartment. I arrived a little bit early, but Amy was ready for me; so we took off for the university with the windows down and the radio blasting. I was learning to have fun again, even in the midst of my inner turmoil.

The plan was to meet Taylor Argent in Professor Haynesworth's office, so being early just meant we could visit with Haynesworth while we waited. He had us both smiling and laughing so much that before we knew it, Mr. Argent was knocking on his door.

He was a tall, well-dressed man who gave off an unmistakable scent of money. "Hi, I'm Taylor Argent," he said, while extending his hand to each of us in turn. When we introduced ourselves, he paused while looking at me. I wasn't sure what to make of it. He quickly grabbed an extra chair from the edge of Haynesworth's office and turned to face me. "What can I do for you, Mrs. Cass?"

I felt a bit uncomfortable, as if he were coming on to me, or more accurately, kissing up to me, only I wasn't sure why. I threw a questioning glance at Amy to see if she had picked up on it as well, but

I could read nothing on her face other than impatience for me to start asking questions. I turned back to Mr. Argent. "Yes, I was wondering if you remembered Paul Cass. He was a student a few years back and, as part of a contest, sold a couple of apps to you."

"Of course I remember Paul. I was sorry to hear of his passing." Then he got a rather beguiling smile on his face, "But any friend of Paul's is a friend of mine."

"Why?" I bluntly asked, tired of whatever game he was playing.

My question surprised Taylor Argent, but he composed himself quickly, responding with, "Because Paul sold us a couple of very profitable apps." He looked at me as if I were the clueless one, which actually seemed to fit at the moment.

"I'm sorry. That all happened before we were married. Could you tell me a little more about it?"

He smiled. "Absolutely. There was a bidding war over that first one, but we won out I'm happy to say. We paid him a half a million dollars for that app and the second one together, but it was well worth it. I've stayed in contact over the years, you know, just a phone call every six months or so. I practically begged him to come up with more apps for us." Then his face fell as dawning came. "You didn't want to meet with me to sell me one of his apps, did you?" It was more statement than question, but I now understood his eager behavior from before.

"No, I'm afraid not." His face was completely crestfallen now. "But," I said, and his eyes perked up expectantly, "he was working on something when he died. Had he talked to you about it?"

Almost breathlessly he replied, "No, but I had told him I would buy just about anything he could produce for me. So, if you are interested in selling it ..."

"I'm afraid we're jumping the gun here. I'm just looking for information right now. I'm not interested in selling anything at this point."

. . .

By the time we were done talking a little while later, it was clear that

Mr. Argent knew nothing more that could help me, but it was also apparent he would do practically anything to secure a deal for whatever Paul had produced. I never let on that it was only a partial app or anything about what it did. I was interested in receiving information, but I wasn't ready to give any yet, even if that came off as self-serving. I viewed it more as being cautious.

During the course of our conversation, my sense of concern and worry had begun to escalate. I was now confident that the break-in at our house had had nothing to do with me after all. The fact that Paul had sold apps before for a large sum of money, coupled with the fact that he had felt the need to place his flash drive in our safe, made it clear that the burglars were after Paul's computer, not mine.

I wasn't sure yet what to do with that knowledge, but the whole idea of it made me extremely nervous. And what in the world had he done with the five hundred thousand dollars he had earned from his app sales? I suppose he could have spent it before he met me, but that didn't seem likely. He wasn't driving around in a fast car or living in a fancy place. It was one more mystery, one more point of confusion.

. . .

The drive home was quieter and more subdued than the outgoing trip had been. We talked little as Amy sensed my need to process what I had learned. After returning Amy to her apartment, I headed for home.

As I pulled the car into the garage, my phone buzzed in my purse. I turned off the ignition and fumbled to pull my phone out. The caller ID said it was Summerhill Police Department. My stomach dropped. I hoped I wasn't in trouble for asking around.

"Yes, this is Brea."

The voice of Detective Lentus sounded in my ear. "Mrs. Cass, we just wanted to let you know that the phone calls made to you the night of the break-in traced back to a burner phone."

"A burner phone?"

"Yeah, you know, those disposable phones you can buy anywhere. They aren't registered to a name or address, so they're basically untraceable. They're popular with drug dealers and criminals in general. Sorry, but it's a dead end."

I may have been mistaken, but his voice sounded a little excited, as if a burner phone added intrigue to the whole situation, as if my troubles were entertainment to him. But, I had to remind myself, he had called to inform me when he didn't have to. He was extending me a courtesy.

"Thanks for getting back to me. I appreciate it."

"You're welcome. I'll let you know if we have any other leads."

While we talked, I had made my way out of the car and into the house. By the time he hung up, I was sitting at my desk. I pulled over a pad of paper and absent-mindedly doodled "burner phone, BURNER PHONE, Burner phone," like I used to doodle my future married name when I was newly engaged. *Is this what I've been reduced to?* I wondered to myself.

I retraced my writing, emphasizing the B and P as if they would suddenly help answer my questions. I let out a squeal. Mom, not far away, came running.

"Mom! B P stands for Burner phone. Paul was calling a burner phone the night he died." With a gasp, my excitement at this discovery sharply died. Why would he call a burner phone, let alone enter it as such in his cell? I could think of no good reason.

What did I know about his calls to B P, the burner phone? About all I knew was what Mr. Walker had overheard. Under my earlier writing I wrote, "The truth is I left the light on." As I stared at those words, I wondered again why they sounded familiar to me.

I gasped as two words stood out to me – "truth" and "light." It was the phrase that Paul commonly used before he met me! He would tell people they could call him Apollo, the god of truth and light. And Apollo's last word was "ON." Paul was involved in the robbery!

With clarity like a clear yet jagged piece of glass, I knew without a doubt that Paul was being his old self, the arrogant, self-assured Apollo. He had visited the store earlier to case the joint. Then the night of the robbery, his phone call was the final go-ahead signal to his accomplices. He was saying, "This is Apollo, and it's on."

I tried to look at it another way, tried to excuse away the hidden meaning I could not deny, but to no avail. His words were like a puzzle, one of Paul's favorite things. I soon had to accept that my efforts to undo my conclusions were pointless.

I didn't know why they killed him. Maybe it was an accident. But Paul brought this on himself. Paul did this to us.

I sank to the floor unable to speak further. My breath started to come in rapid gasps as it had in my nighttime dreams. This was what the night warned me of, told me was coming. Yet despite the warning, I could do little to stop the torrent of truth that was drowning me, engulfing me in darkness and filling my lungs with the dirty floodwaters of my life.

I believe at some point Mom got an inkling of what my pale face indicated. But insightfully she simply backed away, shutting the door and leaving me to conquer the demons she no doubt knew I wanted and needed to face alone.

DECISION

Dad brought me dinner at 7:00, when it was clear I wouldn't be coming out. He said nothing, just opened the door and set down a plate of food on my desk where my computer was supposed to be. Before I even looked up, he had slipped out the door, shutting it behind him.

The food grew cold, but my heart felt colder. *Why, oh why?* I kept asking. Paul had a good career. We had plenty of money. He didn't need to turn to criminal activity. I realized "need" wasn't really the right word; it was always a choice. But Paul wasn't in some desperate financial situation, where he might feel driven to illegal activity. He had a job, at least before he walked away from it.

In all the scenarios I had thought of for what Paul was up to, I had never considered that he was involved in the crime that ultimately took his life. Everything made even less sense now, now that I understood more about what was going on.

I thought about what I knew of Paul. He was so charismatic. He could get anyone to do anything. People would follow him wherever he led. With an ever-sickening feeling, I understood. Paul was not only involved; he was the ringleader. That was the only thing that would be consistent with what little of him I still felt I knew. This had all been his idea.

Then why did he focus his energies on a grocery store robbery? That seemed beneath him. I was beginning to wonder if I even wanted to know any more. So far, knowledge had only brought me more heartache. I wasn't sure how much more I could take.

Paul had always been a good husband and father. He played with Noah. He helped around the house. He encouraged me to pursue my interests and use my intelligence. Why was this the way he had chosen to use his intelligence? That came off as sounding oxymoronic, that he was so intelligent that he planned something that in the end killed him. I think I would have taken a little less brainpower and a little more life. It appeared it was a bit too late for that.

It felt like Paul kept dying over and over again, and each time was worse than the last. What kind of daddy would he have been if he had lived? Would he have gone from being a father who played with his son to one that taught him to follow in his footsteps? I was becoming more and more cynical the later the hour, and with that cynicism came an increasing sense of separation. I imagined that I was watching my life on a big screen, as if it wasn't me, as if the recent events were just part of some fictional play merely dancing before me for my perverse amusement. Paul was becoming more of an enigma to me, as if I had never known him at all.

I started to think over the events of the last few days. Maybe I could capitalize on that out-of-body feeling and sort through things without emotion. What loose ends did I still have?

Trying to figure that out, I thought of places I had been in the last week. I had been to the hotel where Paul used to work, Harper's Mart, Mr. Walker's house, the police station, the bank, outside Alex's house on multiple occasions, Professor Haynesworth's office twice, and home. I didn't think I was missing anywhere.

I began with the place I thought was easiest to dispense with, the bank. However, the bank, in a strange way, with the absence of any change to our accounts, was a loose end. If Paul was involved in criminal activity, why hadn't our bank accounts increased? The answer to that may simply have been that he was just getting started. That would explain the reason no money had come in. Although such little money was stolen from Harper's Mart, nothing probably would have changed anyway. For that matter, did criminals deposit their money in a bank? I didn't know. It's not something I had sat around thinking about before. I snickered to myself; if someone robbed a bank, would he then deposit his take in another bank? It was getting late, and I was clearly getting slaphappy. Putting myself back on track, I realized the bank was a dead end.

What else could I glean? What about Alex? I was willing to bet about now that Alex had been Paul's accomplice, probably along with the other man I had seen him with at the funeral.

It was small comfort to put to rest any idea of another woman. That scenario didn't fit with any of this, but that realization didn't help me any. I still had to grapple with how to move forward with my life, a life that I had willingly joined to someone as seemingly dishonest as I was honest. There were simply no answers for that right now. Ignoring what I could not solve, I turned my thoughts to the problems at hand.

In trying to put things together piece by piece, I thought back to Paul's phone again. The calls that went back and forth between Paul and Alex were the reason I investigated Alex in the first place. They had occurred regularly, I recalled, up until a few days before Paul's death. I gasped. The calls to B P started after that. They had probably just switched to the burner phone. It was starting to click into place. My heart started to beat faster with each new piece of understanding. I took a deep breath and focused again.

If it was the case that Alex had been Paul's accomplice, I had been half-right about the break-in all along. It must have been triggered when Alex saw me outside his house. I'll bet he was wondering what I knew about their activities. The only thing I wasn't sure about was what Paul's app had to do with any of this, or if it was even related. Although answers were starting to come together in my mind, some things still had yet to make sense.

What were they looking for in particular when they broke in? Probably anything that would connect them to Paul, that's why they took the phone. They were just trying to cover their tracks. I imagine the computer would be an obvious choice whether they were looking for the app or not, and then for good measure they went through all the papers. I was attempting to think this through, but I wasn't sure if any of my assumptions about the break in were actually correct.

I paused from my musings and gazed out my office window. It was dead night outside. A chill passed through me. I seemed to be up in the night a lot lately. Somehow, it was appropriate. Paul's illicit activities took place at night, but even more than that everything just felt dark and was getting darker by the minute, if that was possible. I was still searching for the light, for the hope that all was not lost.

It was a sobering moment. All my determination to look at things in a clinical and detached manner disappeared into the blackness around me. The vacuum of emptiness seemed to pull the life out of me and draw moisture out of my eyes. Before I knew what was happening, tears were flowing freely down my face. All attempts at control disappeared in the ebony of the night.

I cried silently as I watched the night outside my window. I reached over and opened the window, willingly allowing, even welcoming, the dark inside, letting it flood my soul. Unlike the night when Paul died and all the times since, I didn't fight it, no gasping or struggling for breath. Instead, collapsing to the ground, I gave in and let myself drown in the cold black waters of hell.

. . .

I lay passed out on the floor when images, dreams I imagine, came into my mind. Paul stood before me with tears that he must have stolen from me, for my face was dry, hot and dry. He looked at me with sadness. It wasn't the pity I had garnered from others. I don't know how I knew, but I knew it was sadness for what he had done and what he was putting me through. He said nothing, just shook his head and looked down. It was the most sincere apology I had ever experienced, especially since Paul didn't normally back down, didn't apologize.

But somehow, it wasn't enough. "Why?" I cried out, "Why? Wasn't our family enough for you? Why did you go looking for something else? Didn't you know I loved you?! Still love you!"

He looked up at me again, his face etched with the devastation of my accusation. "Do you love me, Paul? Did you ever love me? And what about Noah?" But when I looked for the answer in his eyes, he was gone.

. . .

I roused with a start. Looking around me, I could see that the dawn was coming, beginning to penetrate the dark night. Thoughts of Noah came to my mind. How would his father's actions affect him in the future? I wondered if this would follow him for years to come, if not publicly, at least internally. Why couldn't he go through life with a father who simply died a hero? His death, alone, was certainly bad enough. Why make it a burden that he would always carry?

I realized with acute clarity that what I knew could remain my knowledge alone. Paul was dead. I think few would argue that he hadn't already paid for his crimes. Let Noah at least have a good image of who his father was. That might be the best present I could give him.

Resolved, I stood to greet the early day. I opened my office door, and as I did so, my father and mother came from the great room to meet me. I hadn't realized they had stayed up all night with me, but there they were, still dressed in yesterday's clothes, as was I.

I looked in their eyes, eyes of love and concern. Yes, I would indeed give Noah a gift this day, but it would be the gift of a mother who tried to live as honestly as she could. If I stopped being that person, I would rob Noah of both his parents. I whispered, "I need to call the police."

They both simply nodded.

MORE

We all retired to our beds to grab a little shuteye before Noah demanded our attention. I needed to compose myself before calling Lentus with my latest theory of events. I knew inside that I was right, even though every ounce of me wanted to be wrong. Still, I was uncertain what the detective would think. A little more sleep wouldn't hurt about now.

We all got a few hours of sleep before Noah, unaware of our long night, decided he was ready to play. I got to him first, but Mom and Dad weren't far behind. Their eyes told me what I'm sure mine reflected, that what sleep we had gotten had been restless at best.

Mom went to take a shower while Dad and I descended the stairs. I took Noah into the kitchen to feed him while my dad retrieved the morning's paper from the front steps and then retreated with it into the great room.

As I was finishing washing the last of Noah's fingers at the end of

155

his meal, Dad entered the kitchen with a grave expression on his face. He was holding the newspaper. "Brea, there's been another grocery store robbery. It sounds eerily similar to the one where Paul was killed. This time, thank goodness, no one was injured."

His tone of voice told me I should take this seriously. "Okay, so tell me about the robbery, as much as you have learned so far."

Dad pulled a chair out from the table to sit down while I finished separating my little boy from the cereal layer on his face. He waited until he had my full attention. "The robbery occurred at about 12:30 this morning. It took place at an all-night corner grocery store in an older neighborhood of town. It was described in much the way you described the neighborhood around, what was it, Harper's Market?"

"Harper's Mart. But, go on."

"Well, two men wearing masks entered the store. One of them was carrying a gun. The owner's brother, who was the only other person in the store, was behind the cash register." Dad paused to consult the newspaper article in his hands. He had a pained expression, as if he was reliving Paul's death.

I picked Noah up out of the high chair as Dad started again. "One of the men spoke and told the owner's brother to open the till and then lie down on the ground. He did as he was told. One of the two men reached across the counter, it appeared, and grabbed some cash out of the open register. Then apparently they left.

"But here's the strange thing, in my opinion, anyway. They didn't actually get away with very much money. The store just doesn't keep much loose cash around at night. They have one of those time safes, where you can put money in the slot but can't retrieve it until morning. So here you have two guys who have gone to the trouble to swipe some money. They don't get much, and they don't react in any particular way."

"What do you mean, Dad?"

"Well, wouldn't you think they would be upset or disappointed? Maybe they would shoot the cashier or shoot up the store, maybe grab a six-pack or some other kind of merchandise? I didn't say anything to you before, but I always thought it was a terrible shame that Paul was killed over a small sum of money. Although, given what we have learned lately, I'm not sure what to make of the whole situation anymore.

"That aside, I know stores have taken safeguards against having lots of money hanging around at night, but still, I would expect some kind of reaction when they don't get much cash, anything. You know, like at Harper's Mart demanding the old man's wallet or taking something else. I'm not a criminal, but if it were me, I think I'd do something like that, don't you?"

I hadn't been asked the question before of what I would do if I were one of the thieves. I didn't think I could put myself in their shoes. I suppose I could understand Dad's point, though. Why would you walk away calmly from a penny-ante take?

Could the two robberies actually be connected? There were similarities, but not everything was the same. I wondered if those things were enough to connect them. How many different ways would you set up a robbery anyway?

Mom came downstairs, combing her wet hair. She saw the looks on our faces and immediately asked, "What's up?"

Dad filled her in while I changed Noah's diaper, all the while thinking about what was ahead of me. Did I want to learn any more about what had been going on with Paul? I wasn't sure if I was ready to deal with the information I might found. I didn't want to go further into the darkness, but could I find the light if I didn't? Too many questions plagued my mind. The whole thing had an uneasy aura about it, as if it were important, only I didn't know why.

Breaking out of my trance, I announced, "I need to go to that grocery store. If Paul was involved in the one at Harper's Mart, and this is related, I need to know. I've been thinking, too, that I need to solidify my theory of Paul's involvement before I call Detective Lentus. Dad, did they mention the name of the store or enough of the location that I could find it?"

"I don't recall, but I'll go check the internet and find it for you," and he got up and left the room.

Mom suddenly spoke. "I'm going with you, Brea."

I turned to look at her in surprise. She was the one who pledged that they would stand back and let me do things on my own, but I saw in her a determination, and I knew not to refuse her. I resorted instead to asking, "Why, Mom?"

"I'm going stir crazy in this house. Time to get out," was all she said.

I raised my eyebrows but simply replied, "Okay, I'm sure Dad can handle Noah. I'll go shower and we'll head out." I called into the other room, "Dad, any luck with an address?"

"I'm on it. Got the name, and I'm just writing down the address for you."

"Thanks, Dad. Can you keep Noah? Mom wants to go with me."

Without missing a beat, he called, "Sure." He was so quick to respond I wondered if Mom and Dad had been plotting this intrusion. I turned to give Mom a questioning look, but she had already retreated upstairs to finish getting ready.

. . .

An hour later Noah was bathed and dressed, and so was I. Dad shooed us out the door as if we were heading out for a shopping trip instead of what we were really doing, investigating a murder. I chuckled to myself wondering what Detective Lentus would think of me now.

Mom turned, "What's funny?"

"Nothing really, Mom. This is just so absurd, isn't it?"

"Well, that's one name for it," she said as she grinned at me.

I found that this felt more like a fun excursion with Mom along. She was putting me at ease. Maybe that was exactly what I needed and the whole reason she wanted to join me.

"Mom, which car would you like to take on our adventure?"

"Why not take Paul's SUV? I've already reset the radio stations."

"Are you serious? You mean we're going to listen to your oldies this whole trip?"

"Yes, do you have a problem with that?"

We were smiling as we got into Paul's car. I was glad that my parents had been using it. They had only made runs to the store and probably the toy store, but it was enough to affect a change - it no longer smelled like Paul. This thought, I quickly acknowledged, was both sobering and relieving. I was losing memories of him already, and he had only been gone two months. I wanted to get over his death, but I wasn't sure I was ready to let go of things like his smell. All the questions I had about Paul made this even more confusing.

Mom broke into my thoughts, "Brea, it's okay to move on. It's what Paul would want you to do."

I gave her a puzzled glance. "How did you know what I was thinking?"

"Brea, it's not too hard to guess. You're getting into Paul's car for the first time since he died. That can't happen without a flood of memories and emotions.

"I want you to figure out what's been going on just as much as you do. Only I have a different focus. I know you need to find answers, and you are searching hard to find them. Personally, I don't really care what they turn out to be, but they are a means to an end. I'm hoping you find those answers so you can move past them, and I know ultimately that's what you're really searching for anyway."

We held each other's gaze for a silent moment. I *did* want to move past this, to feel like I *could* move past this, but it had become so all-consuming that I had forgotten to think about what would happen afterwards. I didn't like to admit she was right, but she was. "Okay, then. Let's go figure this thing out."

GROCERIES AND OTHER THINGS

The robbery took place at the uniquely titled All-Nite Grocery. I noticed right away that the neighborhood was similar to the one surrounding Harper's Mart. Dad would be pleased to know that his instincts were already panning out. All-Nite was a little store in a mostly residential area, but low income residential. The parking lot was also just about as beat up as the one surrounding Harper's Mart.

I hesitantly got out, but Mom leaped out as if we were heading to Macy's. *Trust Mom*, I thought. She was going to make this an adventure. There were a few other cars in the lot, and we wove through them to get to the front door.

All-Nite Grocery was built to last, but in a run-down looking way. It was a red brick building, but the mortar looked like it was a home done job – uneven and often on the bricks themselves. A large wooden doorjamb surrounded the more modern glass door. The jamb looked like it had been made out of posts as big as old railroad ties, solid looking but dirty. On closer inspection it wasn't so much dirt as community message board, written in various colors of ink – "Jay - see you at Sues", "Gone fishing", "Schools closed for lack of interest", "I know where you been", "Sally now gives haircuts" followed by a phone number, etc.

I hesitated at the door, but Mom yanked it open and strode on in. I had no choice but to follow. Once inside, I wondered what we were supposed to do now. I started to take in the store. It was similar in layout to Harper's Mart. There were a few aisles of convenience foods, a cooler at the back, mostly packed with beer, and the checkout counter by the front door. A logical layout, so the resemblance was not a surprise. It looked like the cash registers and other equipment were the same vintage as well.

I was disappointed, but I wasn't sure what I was expecting. Did I think there would be writing on the wall giving me a message?

Now that I was here, I wandered around the store a bit and picked up some goldfish crackers for Noah. Mom grabbed us something to drink.

I had brought a photo of Paul with me, so as we checked out I showed it to the cashier. He didn't remotely recognize the face. If Paul had done a cursory check of Harper's Mart a few nights before the robbery, I wondered if he had checked out this store at the same time. I knew it had been a long shot since this was a couple of months later, but I was grasping at straws.

A few dollars and fewer minutes later we walked out the door. I was tempted to add to the community doorjamb, but nothing witty came to mind. Dejected, I made my way back to the car, a few steps behind Mom.

As we were fastening our seat belts, my cell phone rang. It was Dad.

"Brea, I've been doing some checking on the internet. There were two other corner grocery robberies in the last two months. They fit the same pattern. They're in quiet residential areas, and each time it's two masked men with a gun, and they tell the clerk to lie down. The type of mask varies, but that's about it. One doesn't say how much they got away with, but the other one says it was under $200."

"Thanks, Dad. I hadn't thought about that. What about earlier? Do you think there might be some others before Harper's Mart?"

"Already checked it out. Nothing."

I laughed. "Trust you to be two steps ahead of me. Okay. Do you have any addresses?"

Dad had both addresses, so we wrote them down and headed to the closest. It was called Stan's Emporium.

Apparently Stan had a sense of humor or a high opinion of his establishment since it was a corner grocery, just like the other two. Determined not to walk away empty handed, I brazenly asked for Stan or the current owner once I entered the store. Mom turned to wander the few aisles.

A man who looked to be 80, but might be 100, slowly stood up from his stool behind the counter. "I'm Stan the Man. How can I help you?"

I went with the assumption that the police wouldn't spend much time on this robbery from a month ago. So hopefully my questions wouldn't get back to Detective Lentus. "Stan, glad to meet you. I'm Brea. I was wondering if you could help me. There's no easy way to say this, but my husband was killed in a store robbery much like yours. I'm trying to make sense of it all."

"No sense to be made outta killin', young thing. No sense at all," he responded, shaking his head.

"You're right. There isn't. I guess I'm searching for whatever answers I can find."

"Fair 'nuf," he responded. "How can I help?"

"Can you tell me anything about your robbery? Anything unusual or different?"

"Well, let me see. You know, I told the police those two men seemed to take their own sweet time getting money out of the till. I thought they would be in a hurry, but not so. The police thought I was nuts for even mentioning it. Now, I don't know if it meant anything or not, but it was just somethin' I noticed."

I liked this man. He was thinking. "Thanks. Maybe that will help. I assume they didn't get much cash?"

"No. It was only 'bout $100. I've been robbed before, but this time was different. They didn't even ask if I could open the safe. It may sound strange, but I don't think they were after the money."

This was something I hadn't even considered before, but it started me thinking. If they weren't after the money, what did they want?

I was so wrapped up in the conversation that I almost forgot about Paul's picture. I pulled it out to show Stan. "Have you ever seen this man before?"

He opened his eyes wide to take a good look. "Yes! I have." He sounded surprised himself. "I didn't realize that was your husband."

"How did you know it was my husband?" It was my turn to be surprised.

"Well, you just told me your husband was killed in a robbery. I didn't make the connection right away, but I remember the robbery that took his life. You know, anytime a fellow owner suffers, you suffer with him. So, I followed it in the paper. I remember the picture of your husband, 'cause he had been in my store the night before that robbery. At the time I was thinkin', 'Boy, if he had just stuck with my store, he wouldn't have been in that other place and gotten shot.' Like I said before, no sense to it."

I was appreciating this man more and more by the minute. "Do you remember anything about him from the night he was in your store?"

"I'm sorry, but there wasn't much to remember. He just bought a few things. You know, in the middle of the night people are either talkative or silent, as if they're half-asleep. He was the chatty type. He asked me about the store, pretty standard stuff, nothin' special."

That was more "special" than he could know. It was showing a pattern. Much as I didn't want to admit my husband was a thief, I was getting excited by the thought that I might finally be on the right track.

There didn't seem to be much more to remember. Mom had stayed back, letting me have my space to talk to Stan, but when she could tell I was done she was at my elbow. This time she had sandwiches for the two of us and a couple small bags of snacks. Stan rang up the purchase, but when he saw she was with me, he refused to take our money. He reminded me of Walter from Harper's Mart, which made me smile.

After thanking Stan, we took our food out to the car. We sat in the front seat eating the premade sandwiches with potato chips and cheese puffs, washing them down with the drinks from All-Nite Grocery. I relayed to Mom what Stan had told me, and we sat quietly wondering what one could possibly want from a place like this.

We finally visited the last store on our list, Corner Mart. It was a quick visit. The only employees in the store were a couple of teenagers who were chatting behind the counter. When asked, I learned they weren't around when the robbery took place, were not actually interested in answering any of my questions, and no, they didn't recognize Paul. Of course, they barely looked at the picture, but even if they had, I doubt they would have been observant enough to recognize him, even if he had been there an hour earlier.

Tired after our partial night's sleep, we headed home. We didn't talk much on the way, either too thoughtful to speak or too tired to try.

After I pulled into the garage, I dragged myself inside as far as the great room couch where I collapsed, knowing I still needed to call Detective Lentus. My last thought before drifting off to sleep was that I would call him when my thoughts were coherent.

A POLICE VISIT

When I arose from my nap, and with a weight in the pit of my stomach, I dialed the number Detective Lentus had given me. It was 5:30 pm, and I didn't expect him to be in, but at least I could leave him a message. I didn't want to put this off any longer and risk losing my nerve.

A female voice answered the phone with, "Summerhill Police. May I help you?"

"Yes, I was looking for Detective Lentus. Is he in?"

"No. But would you like to leave a message?"

"Yes. This is Brea Cass; he's been investigating my husband's death. I just came across some relevant information that I wanted to share with him."

"Okay, I'll pass the message along," and she hung up.

I held the phone in my hand, looking at it, knowing I had just committed myself to a course of action. It was the right course, but that didn't mean it would be an easy one.

I don't know how long I stood there staring at my phone, but while I held it, it buzzed in my hand. It was a number I didn't recognize.

"Yes, this is Brea."

"Mrs. Cass, this is Detective Lentus. I understand you were trying to reach me."

I was shocked that he would call back so quickly. I had misjudged him, to be sure.

"Mrs. Cass? Are you there?"

"Um, yes, I have some information about my husband," was all I could get out. How should I start the conversation I needed to have with him? Excuse me, but my husband's accomplices are the men you're looking for?

For the second time in as many minutes, Lentus surprised me, this time by his kind response. Sensing my hesitation, he simply responded with, "Would you like us to swing by your house to discuss it?"

That sounded so much better than going down to the station, to being exposed in the open squad room. I breathed a sigh of relief and answered, "Yes, that would be helpful," even though I wasn't sure I would breathe again until after he had come and gone.

"When would you like us to come?"

"Anytime is fine. When are you on duty?"

"Well, we're off for the day, but we can still come now if you like."

I realized the phone number I hadn't recognized was his personal number, a home or cell number. My walls broke down, and I honestly replied, "As soon as possible. I just want to get this over with."

"No problem. I'll call my partner, and we'll be there in half an hour. Is that okay?"

"Yes, that's fine. And, Detective, thank you."

I had briefly met Lentus' partner, a Detective Higgins, when our home was broken into. I only vaguely remembered her, but I recalled she came across as a no-nonsense cop. I hoped she was also gentle.

. . .

I was holding Noah in my arms when I heard them knock right on time a half hour later. Dad went to answer the door, and Mom reached out to take Noah. I took a deep breath and went to join the group at the front door.

I barely glanced at the two of them. I could see that Higgins was as thin and neat as Lentus was paunchy and sloppy. Maybe they balanced each other out. Then again, maybe they fought with each other all the time. As I thought it, I realized I didn't care.

Without a word, since I didn't trust my voice yet, I turned and ushered them into my office and shut the door behind them. They looked at me expectantly but waited for me to begin. This was, as they say, my party.

With no reason now to beat around the bush, I formed the words I had been dreading. "Detectives, I believe that my husband was involved in the robbery that led to his death."

I imagine these two were used to keeping a straight face, but both of them registered a look of shock mixed with disbelief. I'm not sure if it came because of what I was saying Paul had done, or the fact that I was the one saying it.

It was clear they were eager for me to continue, to explain why I had made this grand statement. "It all started with his phone, Paul's phone, that you gave back to me." I looked at Detective Higgins, not wanting to look Lentus in the eye, knowing I had weaseled that phone out of him.

"He made a phone call from the store that night, but it wasn't to me. In fact, I thought he was working at the hotel, when instead I found out that he had taken a leave of absence several weeks earlier. I've just been trying to piece together why my husband hadn't told me about the leave and where he went each night. I didn't think the phone call had anything to do with your investigation."

Lentus nodded in concession to me, so I continued. "When I checked his calls, he had made a call to someone he identified simply as B P. He called that same number two other times earlier that night, but I could find no other calls made to that number at any other time.

I called the number, but it was no longer in service. The only thing that makes sense is that B P stands for Burner Phone."

Even I had to admit that what I was saying sounded far-fetched. I knew the next thing I told them would take a leap of faith on their part. They didn't know Paul, had never known Paul. I found myself in the awkward position of needing to teach them about Paul and then impugn him. I was dreading this part most of all. It was strange that I wanted them to believe my husband was a criminal. I began to talk more rapidly, eager for them to hear and understand all the contributing factors. I didn't want to lose their attention before I had laid it all out.

I started by telling them about Paul calling himself Apollo, god of truth and light. When I added in what Mr. Walker related to me, I could read two things in their eyes. First, it was clear they had not interviewed Mr. Walker about what Paul had said on the phone, not finding it relevant; and second, a look of dawning, as if what I was saying might actually be plausible.

While they were still with me, I added, "I believe Paul was in the store early to do a final case of it before they went forward with the robbery."

"What do you mean, 'a *final* case'?"

"Well, Mr. Schultz from Harper's Mart recognized Paul from a few nights before the robbery. He had come in about the same time of night to buy a few items."

My story was holding their attention. They were leaning in to catch everything I was saying.

Next, I explained to them about Alex and all that I had learned about him, his relationship with Paul, the phone calls back and forth between the two of them, even his visit to the funeral. When I told them that the break-in occurred the night after I parked in front of Alex's house, their interest heated up. Unfortunately, I didn't have much more than that.

Lentus noticed my pause and offered, "You know, that break-in never made sense. They never searched the rest of the house for anything valuable. The focus was clearly on this room and this room alone. It makes sense only in a context such as looking for something specific like evidence that would lead back to them. The irony is that it appears in the very act of covering up, they may have given themselves away. It's at least a plausible theory. Is there anything else, Mrs. Cass?"

"Not really, only little things that don't quite add up." I proceeded to tell them about the bank accounts, even though they showed nothing, and about my supposition that Harper's Mart had been the first.

"Do you think there would have been others?" Higgins asked.

I hesitated, a little sheepish. I didn't want to admit how much investigating I had been doing on my own, but I was in it now, so I plowed ahead. "Yes, I think the other two went on without him. There have been three similar robberies since then."

It was now Lentus who spoke, "Yes, we knew about those, but I wasn't aware that *you* were." He threw me a questioning glance, which I chose to ignore. He continued, "I seem to recall telling a young mother not to go about investigating this on her own," but when I looked up, I saw he was smiling.

"I know. But before you say anything else, I also showed Paul's picture around at the other grocery stores. Stan, at Stan's Emporium, recognized Paul from the night before his death." That drew a thoughtful gaze and a nod from Lentus.

Even though I was talking about things I didn't like to acknowledge, I began to understand why Detective Lentus got excited by this. Adrenalin was starting to course through my veins. I felt a strange mixture of excitement and repulsion.

Eager to help, I turned to my desk drawers and files to find a picture of Paul, bank statements, anything I could think of. I thought of telling them about the flash drive and its contents upstairs in the safe, but I didn't yet know what it was or if it had any relevance to the grocery store heists in the least.

The detectives, thankfully, didn't draw it out any longer than necessary. I think they realized this was painful for me but that I was trying to do the right thing. When I finished talking and collecting items for them, they got up to leave.

"Thank you for your help. I ..." Lentus, the talkative one of the two, seemed at a loss for words.

His partner came through for him with, "You are doing an amazing job of taking a difficult situation and trying to make the best of it. You can be proud of that. We have a great deal of respect for you."

Lentus added his agreement to that statement with a gentle nod.

"Thank you," I quietly responded, my voice not capable of anything stronger.

. . .

When I closed the door behind them, I took a long awaited, cleansing breath. It wasn't over, but it had at least begun.

"FAMILY" DINNER

With my "confession" complete, I felt a clearing of my mind. I had come clean, but I also had passed along the burden. I felt no need to pursue answers on my own; the two detectives, I felt sure, would find the answers we both needed.

I discovered both of my parents in the kitchen with a goopy-faced Noah. "So what's the flavor tonight?"

"Spaghetti and crackers," Mom responded while Dad made helicopter noises with a spoon, going in for a landing in Noah's open mouth. I couldn't help but mimic everyone's smiles.

"You know what? We need a party. Let's have a big old party tomorrow."

My mother looked at me to see if I was serious or seriously nuts.

She settled on the first and consented readily. "Sounds good, Brea! Let's make some quick plans and we can run to the store for what we need."

"Why don't you go shopping for real?" Dad suggested. We both looked at him in surprise. "You both need it. We boys will stick together here. Take my credit card and go have some fun!"

"Really?" I squealed. I sounded like a teenager again. I knew it, but I couldn't contain my excitement. I started to laugh to cover my embarrassing squeal, and before long, everyone joined in.

"Okay, so back to our party plans. Who do you want to invite or do you just want it to be us?" my mother asked.

The question had such an obvious answer that all I had to do was smile, and my mother responded with, "I know, Professor Haynesworth, Martha, and Amy."

Straightening my shoulders, I said, "You know, I think it would be a good idea to tell everyone what I've learned. It's not going to get any easier, and I'd rather they hear it from me than see it on the news or read about it in the paper. I owe them that." I thought about that statement for a moment. "No, it's not that I owe them, it's that I want this. I want to be the one to tell them the truth."

My parents just gave me that now familiar nod. I was on the right track. I was going to make it out of this with my head held high.

. . .

I let Mom and Dad make up a menu while I retreated to my study to call Amy. When she answered, I asked, "Amy, can you come over tomorrow for dinner?"

"Of course!" I could hear the unspoken, "Duh!" in her voice.

"Great! I thought I would invite Martha and Professor Haynesworth as well. I've learned a lot more about Paul and I want to share it with all of you." With a brighter tone, I added, "And then we are going to party. We are going to celebrate all that is good! How does that sound?"

"That sounds great! What time should I come, and what can I bring?"

We worked out the details, and I hung up the phone with a smile. After that, I called Professor Haynesworth. He eagerly agreed to come, promising to bring whatever Alaina felt like putting together, which meant he would bring enough food all on his own to ensure no one went hungry. This would be a grand party indeed.

Next, I went to visit Martha. When I knocked, I could hear Martha's sweet, yet powerful, voice coming from the back of the house, "I'll be there in just a minute." For such a small woman, who seemed to be shrinking more each year, her voice appeared to compensate, growing more robust with the passage of time.

She swung open the front door and looked up into my face with a smile of pure joy. "Brea, darling! Come in, come in! Tell me how you're doing." I had yet to fill her in on why I had borrowed her car, but she seemed unbothered by the situation. "Are you finding the closure you've been seeking?"

"You know a lot more than I ever give you credit for, don't you?"

"Of course I do. So how is it going?"

"I'm getting closer. That's partly why I came over. I wanted to invite you to a party tomorrow at my place. The situation got a lot more complicated, and I thought I would explain it all to you, Amy, and Professor Haynesworth at the same time. Then I just want to enjoy spending time with my improvised 'family.'"

"I like the sound of that, but are you up to it? You look exhausted."

"Well, I can't say that I've been getting a lot of sleep lately," I confessed. "One day I hope to make up for all this sleep debt, but I can't see it happening any time soon."

"Take advantage of your parents being here. Sleep, sleep, and do it without guilt. Think of it as your duty, so that you can be a better mom once they go home."

Always trust Martha to give me the wisdom I needed but wouldn't listen to from anyone else. "Martha, what would I do without you?"

"I don't know. I just know you'd be miserable," she said over her shoulder as she led me to her kitchen. When we arrived, she pulled out a chair for me and placed a ham sandwich and a warm muffin on a plate in front of my seat, as if she had been expecting me.

"Did you know I was coming? And for that matter that I haven't eaten dinner yet?"

She smiled with an all-knowing smile. "No, dear, but I've been reading the stress on your face in the last few days, and I know what that means. If you've been missing out on sleep, I naturally assumed eating wasn't far behind. However, tonight you look like a weight has been lifted. Am I correct?"

I nodded agreement, and in between bites of sandwich and moist apple-banana-pecan muffin, I promised her full disclosure the next day. An hour later, armed with a plate of extra muffins for the rest of the household, I made my way home filled with the food of love and friendship.

. . .

In the end, I didn't go shopping with Mom, not even to the grocery store. Instead, I took Martha's advice and slept. I went to bed early that night and slept until midday.

When I woke up in the morning, I felt vibrant and full of life. I even felt beautiful again. The day was sunny and held warm promise.

. . .

That afternoon, just as I settled Noah down for his nap, Professor Haynesworth arrived with a car full of food. As we carried in fried chicken, potato salad, deviled eggs, pasta salad, fruit kabobs, and homemade chocolate cake, I mentally rearranged things in my refrigerator to accommodate the leftovers he would refuse to take home. Even accounting for what I would share with Martha and Amy, it would be a tight squeeze.

We had just arranged all of Alaina's offerings on the kitchen counter when the doorbell announced another arrival. It turned out to be a two-for-one. Amy and Martha both stood on the porch, beaming and heavy laden with all the food they had been wanting and waiting to share with me for the last two months. Tears came to my eyes as I understood the depth of love and concern these two had for me.

I would have hugged them both right then and there on the front porch had their overladen arms not made it impossible. Instead, I swept the door open wide and welcomed them inside.

While Mom and Dad arranged the berry pies, biscuits, chicken salad, and spinach salad from Martha and the chips, soda pop, cookies, vegie tray, and deli tray Amy had purchased, I ushered my friends into the great room.

While I contemplated how to deal with all the inevitable leftovers, avoiding thinking about the upcoming conversation, my friends arranged themselves on couches and chairs expectantly. Once again, in not so many days, I found myself needing to deliver difficult news.

I was nervous but shouldn't have been. Once I started, it was easy to relay everything to my friends. They gasped, they cried, they shook their heads, and they offered their love and support. It was as I knew it would be.

However, I was also anxious to move on. So I corralled everyone with, "Okay, enough of that. I'm starving. Let's go party!"

As we entered the kitchen, I heard Noah crying from upstairs. "I'll go get Noah. Please, go ahead and start without me." I could read the hesitation in their eyes. "If you don't, I'll think you're just trying to pity me!" With that challenge laid down, I bounded upstairs to collect my son.

When I returned with Noah a short time later, I was happy to see everyone eating and chatting merrily. Mom and Dad had made meatballs and quiche along with a broccoli salad and my favorite snickerdoodle cookies. We could have fed a football team and had leftovers.

I did notice, gratefully, that despite the abundance, everyone, including Alaina, had avoided serving any form of apples.

. . .

The party lasted well into the evening. It was a perfect summer night, and we threw open the windows, letting a gentle breeze dance around the happy gathering. When we were done passing food around, we took turns with Noah. Everyone played with him in his or her own way. Amy got down on the floor and crawled beside him. Martha held him and read him stories. Professor Haynesworth impressed him with a zooful of animal noises. Dad played tickle games while Mom played peek-a-boo. I just held him, amazed at my good fortune. I had a beautiful son, and I was surrounded with people who loved and cared about us. How could I want anything more?

It was drawing near to Noah's bedtime. Before he got too sleepy, I insisted we all gather to take pictures. At first, I couldn't find my camera. It wasn't in my office like usual. Had it been stolen? Then I remembered a week earlier putting it in my purse to take to the park with Noah. That seemed like a lifetime ago. My plans to take pictures that day hadn't really panned out, had they?

Now I just needed to find my purse. Everyone started looking. Mom started to walk me through the last time I had it. We finally deduced that I had last used it when we had checked out the grocery stores that had been robbed.

"It must still be in Paul's car! We were so tired when we got home that I bet I left it and just walked into the house without it."

Sure enough, I got to Paul's car and upon opening the door, found my purse on the floor. I had apparently knocked it over with my feet.

Bending down, I started to gather up the contents of my purse. I reached under the seat to check for any runaway items. My hands touched something solid. I grabbed hold of it and pulled it out. I wasn't sure what it was. It was a handheld device of some kind with a key pad and a small screen.

I hadn't heard Amy approaching, but she had followed me out to the car. "That's a collection device, you know like a utility reader. It's called an Automatic Meter Reader."

I turned to her with a look of confusion. "A what?"

"Okay, so you know how the utility companies have meters around your home? Well, they have remote devices like that to read those meters. No more traipsing from home to home. Some of the devices can be used by driving by the house, but the latest ones allow them to be miles away and just collect your information by plugging in your location. Some of the meters even send out information continuously, so the reader automatically collects it as it's sent."

"How do you know all of this?"

"My dad works for a utility company. He showed me something like that once."

I looked at it again, processing what she was saying. As I stared, something tickled the back of my mind. I turned it over and over in my hands, trying to jog my memory loose. "Wait!" I exclaimed, as a matching image came to mind. "I think this is what I saw Alex handing off to his friend." I looked at Amy again, "What do you think this one's for?"

She shrugged her shoulders and said, "I haven't a clue." Neither did I.

I placed the reader in my purse along with all the other items I could find. For good measure, I reached under the seat again. I was surprised once again when I touched something hard. It was heftier than the last item. I pulled it out for a better look but paused to check that this was the last of my surprises. When I deemed that the space under the seat was at last empty, I stared at the heavy, rectangular item. It also looked familiar, but I couldn't place it, as if it was somehow out of context. I turned to read Amy's expression, but it was clear from her knit brow that she couldn't place it either.

I gathered everything in my arms and headed back inside, still pondering the last item I had found. Setting everything but the camera down in my office, I went to find the others and snap some pictures.

It wasn't long before Noah was in bed asleep. Automatically everyone lowered their voices and began to wind down. As Mom and Dad cleaned up, I divvied up the leftovers with my friends and saw them one by one to the door.

Martha paused and looked directly at me. "What's up? You're distracted."

"You read me too well. I just came across another puzzle. I think it's going to be one of those long nights again where I can think."

"Okay, you do what you need to do. And this time, let me know when I can help."

"I will," I conceded. Then we hugged, and I was left with my thoughts.

ONE MORE NIGHT

Now that everyone had left, I sent Mom and Dad up to bed. Then I retrieved from my office the two items I had found in Paul's car. Sitting down on the carpet in the great room, I placed the two items in front of me. What were they, and why did Paul have them?

I started with the Automatic Meter Reader, as Amy had called it. I picked it up and turned it over in my hands. What was this for, and what did it read? There were no identifying marks on it, no serial number or manufacturer. I didn't know if Paul had bought it, had it made, or made it himself. While I sat pondering, I realized I needed to add to the list - or had he stolen it? I wasn't used to thinking of Paul that way, and the thought made me squirm.

As I did so, the night began to close in around me, but I was not the same person from two nights ago. In a strange way, Paul had taught me to be different. He may not be able to speak from the dead and tell me he loved me. He may not be able to right all these wrongs, but he taught me that I could still choose my way. I could be strong. I would be strong. I would push back the night. Erasing it was not in my power, but choosing not to let it in was.

I shut the night out of my sights and concentrated my energy on the two things in front of me. I could make no sense of the reader, so I turned to the heavy, rectangular item. It had a slit down one side, kind of like a knife sharpener, but that was where the comparison ended.

As I stared into the slit imagining what it might be for, the obvious hit me with full force. How could I have not seen it immediately?

I had seen this object a million times and one that was big and boxy like this one very recently. Going through my mind like a camera, I examined the mental pictures I had taken when at Harper's Mart. This looked like his credit card scanner!

In turn, I thought of Stan's Emporium, All-Nite Grocery, and Corner Mart. Each picture in my head could be cropped to highlight the same bulky credit card machine. I felt my veins fill with energy, with life. With a little more thought and effort, I knew I could understand this and put all the pieces together. I was close, so close. So absorbed was I in thought, that I failed to notice how the night was deepening around me.

Staring at the credit card scanner, I began to trace its outline in my mind. An audible, "Oh!" escaped my lips as I saw its image dance before me in another form - the embodiment of the schematic upstairs in the safe. The safe! I had neglected any thoughts of the flash drive with the program and the drawing. Maybe I should have handed them over to the police for them to sort out after all, but that thought was a little late. Maybe it was meant to be this way, since I was putting the pieces together like Lego bricks, one at a time. They were fitting together perfectly. How then did the computer program fit in?

I was so immersed in my thinking that I didn't notice the literal darkness creeping closer, nor how the crickets outside had stopped chirping. I didn't notice, until cold, hard hands came from behind me, stifling my screams, closing in around my mouth.

Terror froze me to the spot as I was unable to comprehend what was happening to me or what to do. The hands did not move, and certain I would suffocate, I began to breathe rapidly out of my nose, my breathing growing more erratic and panicked by the moment.

A guttural voice rasped earthy and black in my ear, frightening me, making me feel like a small, helpless child. "Now, little lady, tell me what you know." He shifted his hands from off my mouth so I could speak, only to reposition them around my neck, not squeezing, but touching, threatening to tighten at his whim. The touch of his fingers on my bare skin sent chills up and down my spine.

As he shifted behind me, the contents of the floor in front of me became visible to him. "Hmm," was his surprised yet sinister sounding response. "I wish you hadn't seen those."

At those words I shivered, adding to my fears that I was now certainly dispensable. *Talk to him, get him talking*, was the only thought I had.

"What are they?" I naively asked. It was the wrong move on my part. I had forgotten how to play the stupid card, and I couldn't pull it off believably anymore.

"Don't play funny with me, lady. I can crush this skinny, little neck of yours, or if you prefer, I've got a gun and I'm not afraid to use it. Already done it once, won't make no difference if I use it again," he said with cruel abandon.

Shocked, I whirled on him to look him in the eye. How dare he talk so casually about killing my husband! Unfortunately for him, he had just replaced my fear with resolve. I stared deep into his eyes, the only thing I could see. He had a ski mask on, and his eyes were like black holes – all dark, with no light in them at all. My gaze seemed to penetrate and unnerve him, and he growled at me, "Turn around, lady." I complied.

Only when he hastily moved to put his hands back around my neck did I realize I had momentarily freed myself with my quick movement. I grumbled to myself at blowing the opportunity, because regrettably, now he would be expecting it. I didn't think I would get so lucky again, but he surprised me when a moment later he dropped his hands. That sensation was immediately replaced with what must surely be a gun in my ribs. I had never felt the muzzle of a gun before, but I had seen it played out on TV. It felt just how I imagined it would.

"Now," the man's voice began, "let's talk about what you know, shall we?"

I nodded readily, wondering in the back of my mind if either of my parents would come down to check on me. Much as I wanted to be rescued, I could think of no good outcomes if they became involved. They would be completely expendable in this man's eyes. I must keep quiet enough so as not to rouse them. At all costs, they must be safe. If I did not make it through this, Noah would have them, must have them.

The gunman was talking, but I hadn't heard him, and I suddenly feared that I would do something wrong and potentially trigger a bad reaction. "I'm sorry," I whispered. "What did you say?" I knew by speaking I was taking a risk, but I hoped it showed compliance.

Impatiently he stated, "I want to know what your old man told you. Start talking."

"I, uh," I wasn't sure what to say that he would believe. I tried the truth. "He didn't tell me anything."

"How stupid do you think I am? He comes to us with this great idea last summer, already had most of it planned out even. And then when we're getting ready to pull it off, he tries to back out! I figure the only way a smart man does an about face like that is if his old ball and chain put him up to it. That's the way I see it."

I forgot my danger for a moment in my relief at what he had just said. "He tried to back out? Really?"

"You deaf, lady? Yeah, he tried to talk us out of doing it."

I was elated and incredulous. "But he never backed down from anything."

"Are you trying to argue with me?"

"No, no," was my quick reply. My mind was spinning. Was this true? I hardly dared believe it.

"Yeah, he tried to quit on the whole thing, but we weren't stupid. So then he says, 'Well, you go ahead then, but I want out.' Like that was going to work. Fortunately, we had our ways of convincing him he should stick to the plan."

"What ways?" He was so into his story that he failed to notice he was the one sharing information, not me.

"We knew about you and your kid and where you lived. My

colleague," he said it as if they were legitimate businessmen, "found out even more about where you liked to go and what you liked to do. It was enough, shall we say."

"Oh!" I thought of Amy's comments about Alex asking all about me and my interests. I just hadn't known why before this moment. That must have been when Paul was trying to back out. But before I thought through it further, I knew I needed to keep my assailant talking.

"So, were the signals Paul's idea? He told you everything was a go, by saying he left the lights on, didn't he?"

"Hey, I thought you didn't know anything."

"Paul didn't tell me about it, but I guess I figured a few things out." I wasn't sure why I continued to talk. If anything, I was sealing my fate even more the more knowledge I had, but I couldn't hold back. I was so close to understanding what had been happening, and somehow I was either going to get out of this despite what I knew, or I would die in the process. One way or the other, I hoped to exit knowing what had happened.

A question had come to mind with this man's disclosure. "If Paul was willing to go through with it and cooperating, why did you shoot him?"

"He was an idiot! Right after the go signal, he gave us the stand down signal. He was still trying to weasel out of it."

"What signal?" There was more to this than I had thought.

"Paul said, 'No, turn the lights off.' He wanted us to stand down, telling us the gig was off."

I had forgotten there was more to the conversation that Mr. Walker overheard. I pulled it up from the recesses of my mind. He *did* tell me Paul said those words, and then he said something that, in light of what I had just learned, must have been strong assurance that they should indeed stand down. It was something like, "Yes, I mean it," although the exact words escaped me. I hadn't realized until now that such simple words were actually an argument with his accomplices, with this man right here!

I was desperate to learn as much as I could. Thinking quickly, I wondered if by appealing to this man's ego I could keep him talking. I feigned sympathy for his plight. "Why would he do that? You were so close."

"Yeah! But Paul was a softie, thinking we shouldn't risk it if anyone other than the clerk was in the store. What a big baby. Who cared if someone was there?"

"Is that why you had to shoot him?" I almost choked on the words, but this vile man was becoming more relaxed as he talked, especially as I seemed to side with him.

"I didn't really plan on shooting Paul, but he was threatening to mess up everything. Then the gun just went off." He almost sounded apologetic, strange given he was here threatening me. And why do they always say "the gun just went off"?

I was shocked by this whole turn of events. My husband was involved in this up to his eyeballs, but he was also trying to be the hero, to do the right thing while doing the wrong thing. It gave me courage to try to find the right thing to do in this wrong situation, to be brave against my attacker.

The more my assailant talked, the more comfortable he had become, letting his guard down. While he was still holding the gun, it wasn't pointed at my back anymore. Instead, it was held loosely in his hand, pointing off to the right of me. If he reacted suddenly and pulled the trigger, he would miss me.

In a split second, I reached down and grabbed what I now knew to be a credit card scanner with my right hand, then swung my arm in a swift but long arc, gaining momentum as I spun my body around. It hit him squarely in the head, knocking him into the sofa behind him. Taking aim at his gun hand, I swung down on it and the gun came loose and fell to the floor. He was still slumped against the sofa, but he started to moan and then stir. I quickly hit his head again, and he fell back, silent, apparently knocked out. Hesitantly, I picked up the gun with my free hand and moved away from him, all the while still staring at him, looking for any further movement on his part.

Setting the credit card scanner down next to the phone, I picked up the receiver and called 911. It took me two tries, my hands were shaking so badly.

The commotion had done what our conversation hadn't, and as the dispatcher answered the phone, both of my parents entered the room. It was hard to hear the 911 operator over my parent's gasps, but I thought I made out, "Summerhill Police Department. What is your emergency?"

The words came fast and disjointed. "This is Brea Cass. I've just had a man attack me in my home. He's still here. I hit him in the head, so he's passed out at the moment, but I'm afraid he'll wake back up any minute."

She verified my location and immediately dispatched officers to my home. Then she instructed me to stay on the line until they arrived.

As I held the phone, my mother relieved me of the gun, while still training it on the masked man. My father went into the garage and returned with a sledgehammer. They were going to protect their little girl just as I was trying to protect them and Noah.

I think it took the police only a couple of minutes to arrive, but it felt like an hour, every second that passed another moment of fear that he would come to and fight like a caged animal, only without the benefits of the cage. In the meantime, the dispatcher was doing her best to calm me down.

When I heard the knock at the door, I relayed that information to the dispatcher and hung up. Two officers had arrived, and I quickly brought them back to the great room to see the aftermath of my encounter, including my handiwork of knocking the intruder out cold. They started by pulling off his mask. I immediately recognized him as the second man from the funeral, the friend from Alex's house, but then I had expected as much. They handcuffed him and in the process purposefully roused him. It was like watching my father catch a garter snake in the yard. I wanted to watch and make sure the animal was captured, but I was also afraid it would escape and come after me in the process. I hid behind my mother, even after she had handed the gun over to the police.

Soon an additional set of officers arrived. They hauled my would-be attacker away, so the first two could sit down and take my statement. I hadn't realized I had been holding my breath until I let it out as my assailant was finally driven away. With relief, I turned to give my full attention to the officers still in my home.

By the time they left, the morning sun was coming up over the horizon. I had not slept a wink, but I wasn't tired since adrenalin was still pumping through my veins. I joined my mother at the kitchen table as if we were starting our normal breakfast routine.

My father walked into the kitchen carrying the items from the great room. "Are these yours?"

In all the chaos I had forgotten all about them. "Yes, I suppose they are." I put my hands out to take the two objects from my dad. As he handed them to me, I noticed that a crack had opened at the seam of the credit card scanner. It must have happened when I hit the intruder with it. Grabbing a screwdriver from the kitchen catchall drawer, I pried the whole thing open. Wires and computer boards met my eye, and then a loose chip fell out onto the table. It was the last missing piece of my puzzle.

I stared at it. With sudden clarity, everything now tied together. I looked up at my parents. "I think I know what this is all about! I need to do a little research on the internet to back up my theory, but I think I finally have the answer."

I don't honestly know what their reaction was, being completely wrapped up in the apparent knowledge before me. I gathered up the Automatic Meter Reader and the pieces of the credit card machine. Without looking at my parents I said, "I'm going upstairs to do a little research. Will you call Detective Lentus for me to see when he's free? I doubt he's in yet, but I'm sure he'll get any message you leave for him."

"Okay," was all Mom said. Dad probably added his now familiar nod, but I was halfway up the stairs intent on finding the closure I was certain was at my fingertips. I'm sure my parents had questions, but they said nothing else.

Upstairs I hastily put on some clean clothes not even bothering to shower. As I was gathering the relevant items from the safe, the phone rang.

Not surprisingly, now that I knew him a little better, it was Lentus. "Mrs. Cass, I'm still at home, but I can be in the office in ten minutes if you'd like to meet then."

"Well, I need a couple of hours to check something out, and then I can meet you. Would ten o'clock be okay?" I asked.

"Sure." But unexpectedly he continued, "I was planning on calling you this morning anyway. We have Alex in custody. We picked him up yesterday. He's not talking, and we haven't been able to figure out who his partner is yet, but we're checking his known associates. I'm sure we'll catch him soon."

I quickly responded with, "Actually, you already have him in custody. Some of your fellow officers hauled him away from my house this morning. I don't know his name, but he's the other man from the funeral. We also had an interesting discussion while he was here."

"What?" was all he could get out.

"I'll give you all the details when I come in. I doubt the other officers have even had time to write up a report yet. When you picked up Alex, it must have spooked his partner. He came looking for what I knew. And, Detective, I know a lot more than I used to."

I could practically hear Detective Lentus salivating on the other end of the phone. With a smile, I simply added, "I'll see you at ten," although I was sure it would drive him crazy to wait that long. Regardless, I had to know what I was talking about before I showed up.

Settling in front of the computer, I began the research that hopefully would confirm my theories. Ironically, I thought, a year ago Paul would have been doing this exact research. It would have been interesting to see his browser history from that time. I'm sure it would have been illuminating.

In short order I found all that I needed. Satisfied, yet exhausted both physically and emotionally, I shut off the computer and climbed onto my bed. Tired as I was, sleep was elusive. I lay still, letting my mind wander and absorb recent events. Despite the summer season, I began to shiver. The sheer magnitude of all that had happened, and was still happening, overwhelmed my frame. I grabbed the comforter on my bed and wrapped my body inside its warmth, but my shaking would not subside.

My thoughts turned to the gathering the previous evening. As I thought of each of my friends and family members, my body gradually warmed and calmed itself. Before long, I closed my eyes, bringing their faces to mind one after the other. As Professor Haynesworth's face came to mind, I thought of what he had told me about Paul.

I sat up with a start, all thoughts of sleep chased from my mind. I now understood something that had been troubling me. Why had Paul done it? I had asked myself that question not having a clue of the answer, but the professor had given me the key. Paul was all about the challenge! This elaborate scheme, I could easily see, would have been something that intrigued Paul. He would have wondered if it was possible. Once he determined it was, I imagine he would have been too caught up in what he could do, the challenge he had conquered. Not until it was too late would he have stopped to think if he should actually be going through with it. I smiled a sad smile thinking about what could have been.

Paul had definitely made mistakes, but understanding why and how he made those mistakes gave me a sense of control back, even if it was tinged with sadness. But it also gave me courage. I was ready to tell Lentus the rest.

TRUE CONFESSIONS

I arrived at the police station in a timely manner, and as I suspected, Detective Lentus was standing by the door waiting for me. I wasn't surprised to see his partner, Detective Higgins, standing beside him.

They quickly ushered me into a room where we could talk. I could see the anticipation in their eyes. I didn't bother to ask if they had checked on my assailant, feeling certain they already would have.

Out of respect, they waited for me to begin, but I was as eager as they were to get this out in the open. "I have learned a lot more since I last sat down and talked with you. It started with this thumb drive," I said, pulling Paul's flash drive out of my bag. "Sometime after the break-in I noticed that Paul's back-up flash drive was missing. I ended up finding it in a safe we have upstairs. It contains only two files, this program and this schematic," showing them copies I had printed for them before coming. "I felt just as puzzled as you look right now. I couldn't figure out how or if these connected to the robberies, so I neglected to tell you about them earlier. They were simply loose ends I couldn't account for." I reached into my bag again and pulled out the two items from Paul's car. "Then yesterday, I found these two things under the front seat of Paul's car."

I started with the rectangular object. "This is a credit card scanner. I looked up this model online this morning. Apparently, it's a bit of an old style, but still commonly used in convenience stores. It attaches to the side of the cash register so the credit card can be swiped for payment. I recognized this model from somewhere. It's the same as the one at Harper's Mart, All-Nite Grocery, and..."

"Stan's Emporium and Corner Grocery," Lentus completed for me.

"Yes, exactly. The schematic here is of this very model."

"May I see that?" Lentus asked, pulling the schematic and credit card machine closer. He and Higgins looked from item to paper and back, noting the identical nature of each characteristic. "You're right. It's the same thing. But why did Paul have this?"

"I'm getting to that. I was at the same point in my thinking as you are now when Alex's accomplice surprised me. He broke into my house wanting to know how much I knew about the robberies. I didn't know nearly as much as he thought I did, but he was rather talkative, and I learned a little more." The two detectives were hanging on every word.

"The relevant information at this point is what I learned about this credit card scanner. Eventually, I ended up hitting my intruder over the head with it." They both raised their eyebrows at that. Apparently, they hadn't been fully briefed about the incident at my home. Mixed with their surprise, I detected a hint of admiration in their eyes. I continued, "After I hit him, I noticed it was cracked open at the seam. Prying it open all the way I discovered this chip," holding up the offending item. "That's what made it all come together."

"Is this program you printed out from Paul's thumb drive on that chip?" Detective Higgins asked.

I was impressed. "I don't have any way to check it, but yes, I believe it is. Earlier I was able to figure out the purpose of the programming code, at least what it did, but not why it was doing it. However, when I put it in the context of this chip, things start beginning to make sense."

They were still confused, but I understood that look. "Let me explain how this works. Have you ever been to a store and swiped your credit card only it didn't seem to work, and you had to swipe it a second time?" They both nodded. "Have you ever worried that you might get charged twice for the same purchase because of that? But it hasn't happened, has it?" Again, they were nodding their agreement.

"Safeguards are built into the system to prevent that, so it doesn't happen. Paul's app played on that. Let me briefly explain what I just learned from my internet searches today about how all of this works. Harper's Mart works through a bank to handle all its credit card transactions. So every time a credit card is swiped, an electronic transmission is sent to that bank, the merchant's bank. That bank acts as a middleman and in turn sends a message to the cardholder's bank to check for availability of funds. Based on the response they get back, they return a message to the store saying the charge is either authorized or denied."

They were nodding their heads, so I went on. "What Paul created was a fake swipe. His app, on this chip, when embedded in the credit card scanner, sent an electronic transmission to the merchant's bank. It didn't include any data; it wasn't meant to. Instead it was acting like a swipe that didn't quite work right, a fake 'double swipe,' if you will. It was sent with the sole purpose of producing a bogus error message indicating that a double swipe had occurred."

I could see they were still with me, understanding the steps so far. "But Paul's app went further than that. You know how when you get an error message on your computer it attempts to identify what the problem is and what you might try as a potential solution?"

"Yes," it was Higgins again. "Did this error message do that somehow?"

"It did. It asked the question, 'If a double swipe just occurred, which card was double swiped?' It then tapped into the information at the merchant's bank to answer that question. It did this by going back one transaction, to the last successful credit card swipe processed at the bank, saying, in essence, 'Aha! That was the correct swipe, this swipe is a mistake.' Then, and here's the key, it sent back the message to this chip, 'You just made a double swipe of credit card # 1234-4567-7890 with this name, billing address and security code.'"

"Wow! That's brilliant!" Lentus was wide eyed. "It's high tech credit card theft."

"That's exactly what it is." I was mortified at what my husband had done, but, like Lentus, I was a bit impressed at the same time. "The chip can send as many fake error message pulses as it wants. And every time a pulse is sent, a new credit card number with all its information is returned."

I could see the two detectives' minds working. Higgins spoke first. "How is that information retrieved? How did these crooks get the credit card info back out of the chip?"

"Exactly!" I picked up the reader. "This is the type of device used to read utility meters. It can read information from some range, for instance ten miles, away from the meter or, in this case, the credit card machine. As information is collected at the store, it is automatically sent to this device and wiped from the memory of the chip embedded in the credit card scanner. The beauty of this device is that you could take it anywhere within that defined radius and vary that location as often as you wanted. It's not traceable to any specific address or location."

Higgins was processing it quickly. "If you're right, the real credit card, the one whose information was stolen, could have been swiped virtually anywhere, at any store who used the same bank as Harper's Mart. It would be incredibly hard to track down the source of the breach."

I nodded my head. "You're catching on fast. As credit card information is stolen, the only common link would be the merchant bank, who is the middleman. The credit cards themselves may have been used at a huge variety of stores. Those various locations would be completely irrelevant, and any connection between them would only be coincidental. Even if the problem were narrowed down to one merchant bank, the leak is not technically at the bank, so it would be difficult to find its source."

Before I could continue, Higgins, with greater understanding dawning, broke in with, "If they used the same scheme at the other grocery stores that would really complicate matters, adding multiple merchant banks to the mix. Finding a common connection would then be even harder, making it difficult, at best, to trace where the stolen credit card information was coming from."

"Wow," was the only thing Lentus could add as the magnitude of the credit card theft that could occur began to register.

"Paul and his accomplices only staged robberies. They swiped what little cash was available, but having only a small take didn't bother them, because it was never the point." I said.

Both detectives were following every word, and I could see the wheels churning. "Were they using the robberies to install the chip in the credit card scanners?" Lentus asked.

"Close. I think they had identical machines to those in the convenience stores. That explains why this credit card reader was in Paul's car. I imagine it's also the biggest reason for Paul to case them. He was checking for compatible machines. They could preload the scanners with the chip and then swap the old machine for their new and improved version."

"I see," Higgins exclaimed. "That's why in each robbery the clerk was told to lie face down on the ground. They didn't want the clerk to see what they were up to. They were busy swapping out credit card scanners. Is that why Paul stepped in front of Mr. Walker, to block his view of what they were doing?"

For once, I was the silent one.

"I'm sorry. I didn't mean to sound callous. I just got caught up in ...," he quickly added.

"No, it's okay. It's possible that's what happened, but from everything I've learned, I believe Paul was done with this scheme. He really was trying to save Mr. Walker's life." I grew quiet, hesitating before continuing. "When that man broke into my house last night, he told me that Paul had tried to stop this before it got started. He tried to back out, but his two 'friends' wouldn't hear it. They threatened to hurt Noah and me if he wouldn't go through with it. I believe him. I don't think he had any reason to lie to me about that.

"It also fits with what I now know about Paul's character. He was very intelligent and liked to see where that intelligence could take him, without considering if it was a place he should go. I did not know him to back down from anything, but I believe becoming a father changed him. At least, I hope that's the case."

The shared excitement of discovery was dampened now. I soberly pushed forward, the honesty of the moment painful. "The plan was all Paul's. He wrote the app. He figured out the credit card machine and meter reader angle. It was all him. He must have let Alex in on his scheme who then recruited the other man you have in custody for accosting me during the night. Only at the end did Paul realize what he was doing, he just realized it too late.

"The man that broke into my house last night was looking to see what I knew, to try to protect himself. He claims to have not wanted to shoot Paul, but he seemed quite upset with Paul for wanting to pull the plug. I don't know," I said, shaking my head. "He did come to Paul's funeral. How strange is that?"

We were all silent for a few minutes. I finally stood up to leave. "All of this is yours now. Do with it what you will. And if you have any questions, you know where to find me." I then walked out of the police station for what I hoped was the last time.

AFTERMATH

The next few weeks passed in a rush. Details were forthcoming from the detectives as they became available.

However, the best detail they decided to deliver in person. After calling ahead to make sure I was home, they showed up on my doorstep with big smiles on their faces.

"What is it?" I couldn't help smiling in return.

Lentus walked right past me, as if he owned the place, but in such a jovial mood I just shrugged my shoulders and followed him into the great room with Higgins on my heels.

"Brea, we just got the results back about the embedded chips. You had it mostly right."

"Mostly?"

"Let me explain," he said with a twinkle in his eye. "Our analysts examined the credit card scanner you brought in. We also confiscated the credit card scanners from the convenience stores, and they evaluated those as well. What they found was interesting."

Higgins took over. "The program on the flash drive was indeed embedded in the chip of the credit card scanner you gave us. It did exactly what you thought it did and could have had devastating effects with a great deal of difficulty tracking down the source of the problem.

"The credit card scanners from the stores also had been modified. They performed exactly as the one you found, with only one small variation." Then she turned to her partner. "Would you like to tell her?"

Lentus smiled. "With the machines that had been placed in the stores there was a significant difference. When the credit card information was transmitted to the Automatic Meter Reader two numbers were transposed, making the information useless."

It took a moment for what he said to sink in.

"Mrs. Cass, it appears that Paul really did back down, and he found a way to do it despite the pressure he was under to see it through. With that one simple change he protected hundreds, probably thousands of people from having their credit card information stolen."

I was so pleasantly surprised by what he said that I was momentarily speechless. Then one more thing clicked. "That also explains something," I said.

It was the detectives' turn to be surprised. "What?" asked Lentus.

"Well, when Amy and I were watching Alex's house, he and his friend were having a heated discussion while holding an Automatic Meter Reader. I didn't know what the device was at the time, and we couldn't hear their discussion. But if they were trying to get credit card information and it wasn't working, then, well, I can understand their frustration."

I looked at the other two and they were nodding agreement. "Hooray for that frustration!" I cheered. Then our rich voices rang out with laughter and joy.

When the laughter subsided, I found myself still smiling from ear to ear. There were parts of my husband's life I could still be proud of, and with those parts, the pieces of my own shattered life began to come back together. Paul had done something right, risking everything, ultimately his life, so that others would not be hurt.

"Thanks for coming over to tell me. I know you didn't have to do that, but telling me all of this … well, it means a lot to me." I then surprised all of us by reaching over and hugging Detective Lentus and then Detective Higgins.

. . .

The visit by the two detectives brought me as much closure as I could hope to have. I learned that the two suspects weren't talking yet, but I didn't care. The investigation was ongoing; however, I found my interest in it waning. The two people responsible for my husband's death were in custody. They had been charged with various crimes including my husband's death, and the evidence was mounting against them.

I was tired. I just didn't have the emotional or physical energy to devote to the crimes that had been committed anymore. Noah was almost nine months old now. He was the whole reason that I could carry on, and yet despite my best intentions, I hadn't actually been fully present for him for the last three months, not since Paul's death. I had certainly made an effort, but my heart had been distracted. The answers about Paul meant a great deal to me, but as my mother had predicted, the answers weren't the end, they were a means to allow me to begin again, to reconnect with my life and with Noah. Gradually that's just what I started to do.

I took over more and more of the parenting duties, while my parents faded gracefully into the background. I set up regular get-togethers with Amy to keep me sane and to ensure that I not cut her out of my life again.

Martha, sweet Martha, joined us for lunch virtually every day. Often it was just the three of us: Martha, Noah and me. Mom and Dad would make excuses about errands they needed to run, but I knew they were just trying to help me get back on my own feet.

Noah and I learned to enjoy the world around us once again. It was full summer by now, and we found that playing in the backyard made the hours float by pleasantly like feathers on the wind. More than once

Noah fell asleep for his nap on our picnic blanket. I would position an umbrella to shade him from the sun's rays, and then I would lie down beside him, tracing the edges of his hair and his chin, examining his bare toes, kissing the top of his blonde-haired head. Soon I would fall into a light sleep at his side, while my parents watched over us from indoors.

I think they knew before I did that I was ready to fly solo. In the back of my mind it seemed possible, but I was afraid to try, afraid I might fall flat, and then not know how to get back up again. As they disappeared not so subtly each day for longer and longer periods of time, I found I could make it. At first, I watched the driveway for their return, but before long Noah and I were so involved with each other that I didn't even notice their return until they actually announced their presence.

Finally, one day Mom and Dad announced their plans to return home. We decided to throw one last party. We would jointly celebrate Noah's nine-month mark and have a grand send off for my parents.

Plans were made, and the usual group gathered one Saturday evening. Haynesworth, Amy, and Martha joined Mom, Dad, Noah, and me for a barbeque in our backyard. Mom and Dad took turns at the grill, cooking up hamburgers, chicken, and some corn on the cob. I had convinced all my guests to be modest with what they brought to share, or I thought I had convinced them up until the moment they arrived, each one once again laden with a variety of dishes. Martha brought cake and two kinds of pies. The professor showed up with several varieties of salads and some homemade rolls. Amy, as always, could be depended upon to bring all the best that our local store had to offer, including chips, dips, and drinks. Since Noah was eating more and more table food, each one brought something just for him from bananas to cookies to juice.

It was a carefree gathering. I had not chased away all my ghosts, but I wasn't afraid of them anymore. It allowed me to enjoy my company and talk freely with them. No topics were forbidden. There had been a number of newspaper articles about Paul and all the intrigue surrounding his death. They were not overly kind, but they also weren't overly cruel. I suppose they were fair. We talked openly about them. It was a relief to do so, a relief to have no secrets, no lies anymore.

The phone rang several times while we partied outside, but I chose to ignore it. I was getting used to the attention, although I didn't relish it. Even the national news had picked up the story of the sordid credit card scheme with its twists and turns.

Instead of dwelling on what had happened, I was moving forward, making a life for Noah and myself. I hadn't quite figured out what to tell Noah about his father when he was old enough to understand, but I had time to figure that out. At least we were now travelling on solid ground.

Too soon it was time for everyone to call it a night. Mom and Dad were leaving tomorrow and still needed to finish packing. Before I had a chance to protest, Amy and Martha started to clean up the dishes, shooing my parents upstairs to pack. Professor Haynesworth worked on straightening up the grill, lawn chairs, and returning any number of baby toys to the house.

That left me with Noah. He was head to toe dirt and head to toe happy. I took him upstairs and plopped him in a tub of water and bubbles, completely comfortable leaving my "guests" on their own. They were truly family now, all my walls knocked down.

Noah had started saying "Mama" recently, but he often added "Umum" for Amy and even "Gaga" which worked for Grandma, Grandpa, and also Martha and Professor Haynesworth. It was an all-purpose title they were happy to share. As I lowered him into his bath, he reached out to pop a bubble and added, "Bubba" to his growing vocabulary.

Playing with bubbles kept us both entertained well into the raisin skin stage. I forgot that anyone else was even in the house. I, at last, pulled the plug on his bath when he stopped talking and started to nod off in the tub. Within ten minutes he was dried, diapered, and dressed for bed. He was sound asleep in his crib before I could even cover him with a light blanket.

Tiptoeing out of his room and down the stairs, I was pleasantly surprised to find all my family, either through birth or by choice, gathered in the great room, chatting quietly. The kitchen and yard were neat and clean, and my parents were all packed ready to go. It seemed no one wanted the evening to end, despite their earlier claims of needing to leave. I sat down to join the group.

It was an easy, light-hearted conversation. My parents shared some of their travel adventures, and Haynesworth told college stories. We were an odd little family, but family all the same. When the phone rang again, I decided to let the machine answer it and continue to be regaled by the amusing life of an absent-minded professor.

I could hear a woman's voice leaving a message. Something in her voice sounded anxious or nervous. Clearly this wasn't one more reporter, well-practiced in the verbal arts. With a curious ear, I listened in half-heartedly. Whoever it was mentioned something about it being a long time, Paul, and then the newspaper articles about him. She left her name and number then said words that left me cold, "I'm Paul's mother."

PART 3 – GATHERING LIGHT

AVALON

The others in the room saw my reaction before they registered its cause. Soon we were all listening as the message continued. "... I wasn't sure at first because he called himself Paul Cass, not Caste, which is his real name, but I just saw the picture that went with the story, and there's no mistake. That's my son. So please call me."

We all sat in stunned silence, hearing only the click as the call was disconnected. No one moved. Amy was the first to break the silence. "Isn't his mother dead? I thought there was a car accident." It came out as merely a whisper, as if anything louder might summon ghosts from the dead.

No one needed to answer her question. We were all thinking the same thing. Either this woman was lying, or Paul had been lying for some time. One more lie. Lies do not help.

Finally, Haynesworth spoke up with a solution to our unspoken concerns. "Brea, if you like, I can make a few inquiries to learn if this woman is who she says she is. You can then do whatever you like with that knowledge, but at least you will know the truth."

Barely audible, not trusting my own voice, I responded, "Yes, please." Then I added, "Paul told me his parents' names were Len and Ava, and that they were from Ohio. I don't remember ever having seen their pictures." Why hadn't I thought that was strange? It was a little late to be thinking of that now.

Reaching over to put a hand on my arm, he said, "I'll see what I can find out."

I stood up and announced with a louder voice, "If you don't mind, I think I'd like to be alone," and I started up the stairs. As I did so, I could feel their worried eyes upon me. I stopped midstride and turned to them. "No worries, okay. I've dealt with a lot of things lately, and I'm not going back to that dark place where I was. I just need a few moments to process this. Stay and visit with each other, or don't stay, whatever you like. I *will* talk to all of you soon. Don't worry."

I hoped they believed my words, because I didn't know if I did. Quite frankly, I wondered if I was starting the downward spiral all over again. I had gained so much strength lately, but my foundation was slipping out from under me, as if it were a quicksand made of lies, more lies than I had ever imagined possible.

I had no doubt what Professor Haynesworth would find, realizing with sadness that I trusted the words of a woman whom I had never met more than I trusted my own husband. My very name, Brea Cass, wasn't real. Even if Paul had legally changed his name, it didn't feel right. For that matter, Noah, Noah Cass, a completely innocent child, carried a name that was a lie.

Feelings and worries swirled as I made my way upstairs. Staring me in the face was the reality that I had not resolved anything regarding the way I felt about Paul. I had pushed all those concerns aside, buried them under tidbits of hope that he had admirable qualities. Despite my best efforts, two questions remained about Paul. Was he really a good person who had just made some mistakes? It truly seemed like everything I had learned of late taught me that he was decent inside, but I just wasn't sure. The real burning question, however, was did he actually love me?

Even though he was dead, I desperately wanted to know what he would have been like five years down the road. He had clearly made mistakes. I believed I could forgive those mistakes, if I knew he had turned a corner. But was his change of heart real? Would it have stuck? I had hidden these thoughts from others, barely even acknowledging them to myself until this new revelation. They seemed silly really. Paul was dead, dead and buried, but I had to know if I had made a mistake with him. I had to know what kind of man Noah's daddy would have been. I didn't even know how to approach the thought of whether he loved me.

Lying on my bed, staring up at the ceiling I wondered why this was important to me. Why, when it was too late to change anything?

Sometime in that long sleepless night I found a little piece of what I was seeking. I didn't have any of the answers yet, but at least I understood why the questions were important to me. I knew that Paul was dead, that was a reality, but I also believed he still existed somewhere, or hoped he did. If he *was* somewhere, could he see us? Would he watch over us? Even more, if he loved me, somehow I thought he would be waiting for me when I died. I could imagine him taking me in his arms. Or if he had never loved me, would he abandon me even then? With those thoughts, I fell into a fitful sleep just as the sun was rising in the sky.

Noah awoke a couple of hours later. I heard him on the baby monitor. I knew my parents didn't need to leave for a few hours, and they could get Noah. However, I also knew I needed to do this on my own, and I needed them to believe I could do it on my own. In my mind I could see what would happen if I stayed in bed and let them get Noah. They would cancel their plane reservations and stay.

Maybe it was my foolish pride, but sometime I had to take over full responsibility. I had made too much progress to backslide now. So tired and groggy though I was, I hurried into Noah's room to pick him up.

I got there just before Mom. She seemed surprised to see me, but I just picked up my son and put on the happiest face I knew how before turning to greet her. She was a little taken aback I could tell, but I could also see her mind processing the scene, trying to decide what the situation truly was and what her reaction to it should be.

I deliberately cut into her thoughts with, "Good morning, Mom. What would you like for breakfast?"

She had no response, still eyeing my cheerfulness with suspicion. So I ignored the question as well and started chatting with Noah while I changed him and got him dressed. At some point, and without a word, she slipped from the room.

In the end, my parents didn't want to leave. They could see through me, but they also knew all too well my stubborn streak. It would be pointless to try to stay. I do think they sneaked off to enlist Martha as spy and accomplice, to watch over me in their absence. For all I knew they even called Amy, but that was okay. Much as I wanted to pretend, I too knew that I was far from solid ground.

All too soon it was time for them to go. We carried suitcases to my car for the trip to the airport. I glanced over at Paul's car in the garage. My eyes lingered on it as I wondered if I should sell it.

My mother saw my gaze and read my mind. "Brea, it was so nice having Paul's car to drive around while we were here. I hope you won't sell it any time soon. We plan on coming back to see our grandson on a regular basis," and then she added, "If that's okay with you."

"Sure, Mom, you can come anytime," and I meant it, but I also worried that if they came back too soon I would never learn to be the single mom that I now was. So I added, "Why don't you plan on coming back for Noah's first birthday? We'll have an over-the-top celebration, and we'll spoil him stinkin' rotten!"

She couldn't say anything but, "Okay."

I looked at Dad and his eyes mimicked Mom's, but he too couldn't think of any other response. I had clearly laid down the law. I was going to go it alone for three months. Dad gave himself away by subconsciously glancing towards Martha's house. I smiled as my supposition about their visiting Martha was confirmed. My parents were as easy to read as I was.

I almost made a remark to let on that I knew of their precautionary measures, but I stopped myself, knowing it would come out sounding snide. That was not the way I wanted to end this rescue mission of theirs. Instead, I thought with gratitude of all that they had done for me. Setting down suitcases, I reached to grab my parents in turn. Mom was holding Noah, so our embrace encompassed Noah as well, and he giggled in delight.

"We really are going to be all right. You are welcome to call anytime, and I promise to answer, okay?" They nodded at my concession, and we piled into the car.

. . .

Too quickly they were deposited and gone. With a mix of loneliness and determination, Noah and I made our way home.

When we arrived, a message was waiting for us from Professor Haynesworth. His familiar voice said, "Brea, it was actually quite easy to check out Paul's parents. They are from Ohio like he always claimed. Len and Avalon, known as Ava, Caste were married there a little over thirty years ago. I could find no record of their deaths, but the phone number left in your phone message is registered to a Len Caste. I was able to find the address if you want it. Len and Ava had a son named Paul twenty-seven years ago. His birthdate matches your husband's."

I thought that was the end of the message, but he went on. "Brea, I also checked into what kind of people they are. I found newspaper accounts of their charitable works that tout their character and virtues. I even made some phone calls to people who know them. They are good, hard-working folks, from everything I could gather. I don't think you have anything to fear from them. Brea, I'm in class later this afternoon, but you're welcome to call me tonight."

I stood there stunned. It's what I had expected, but suddenly it was real. What should I do now? I hadn't a clue.

In a swift moment of decision, or as a way to avoid the decisions I really needed to make, I scooped up Noah and made a beeline for Martha's house. I wasn't going to stay cooped up with my own thoughts again.

I had barely finished knocking when Martha swung the door open wide. "Come in, come in, you two. I was hoping to see you." Just like

Martha, she got right to the point. "Did you hear back from the professor?"

"Yes. She's real," came spilling out of me. "She's alive. She's living in Ohio, and I have no idea what I'm supposed to do with that knowledge."

"Oh, dearie, come in, sit down, and we'll make a plan." Trust Martha to help me figure things out. Why had I ever shut this woman out?

A little later, and a half dozen fresh rolls and cookies later, we moved to her sitting room where there were comfortable chairs and a basket of toys for Noah to play with. Martha sat down deliberately in front of me, demanding my full attention simply by her posture.

"Brea, you are going to call that woman on the phone. You need to give her the benefit of the doubt. You, Brea, are a kind and inclusive woman. Don't let your fears change who you are. That wouldn't be right, and you know it."

I had always known her to be direct but not quite this direct. I had to smile, though, at her idea of "we'll make a plan." It seems the professor's phone call was not a surprise to her either. It was apparent that she had already thought this through.

Martha's continued words broke into my thoughts. "Now, what's the worst that could happen? If you call her and you don't like her, then tell her she has no place in your life."

I laughed. "Martha, you say that as if it's the easiest thing in the world to say. I couldn't tell someone that."

"Exactly!"

"What?"

"That's just what I wanted you to realize. You can't shut this woman out. She is the grandmother of your child. You can wait if you want, but Brea, you know deep in your heart that you need to talk to her. That is the kind of person you are."

I just stared at her. She was right, of course. "How do you do that?"

"Do what?" she responded, feigning innocence.

"Peg me so exactly. You're right. I wouldn't be able to ignore her forever. But what if she's horrible? Up until now, I haven't had a mother-in-law. Now I have one, but no husband to act as buffer, not to mention the fact Paul hid that they were even alive! What if he hid them from me for a reason, like they're monsters or something?

"Martha, I don't know how to deal with this. I don't know what to do!" I was sounding like a whiney child, but I didn't care. I was letting my emotions out, not bottling them up this time around. I'm not sure either approach was right, but I hadn't discovered the middle ground yet.

She patted my hand. "Brea, you'll figure that out one piece at a time. You're trying to eat the whole elephant in one bite. That doesn't work. Just do it one bite at a time. So start by picking up the phone and dialing. You can have some questions ready ahead of time if you want, or just go with whatever comes out naturally. I'll even offer to be with you when you call, if you think you need it. But you have to try. You need to see where this leads."

She was right again, but I didn't want to concede yet. I sat still, thinking through all the possible scenarios, but I soon realized they were merely speculation. Martha was right. I wouldn't rest until I called. I just hoped the professor was right that these were good people.

MOMENT OF TRUTH

The problem with meeting someone over the phone is that too much is left to the imagination, and with an imagination that had already been running wild for some time, this wasn't the best scenario. I did call Ava Caste. The first time, the phone rang several times before I heard a voice say, "This is the Caste residence. We're not home ..."

I didn't leave a message. I wasn't sure what to say, but more than that, I didn't want to put the ball in their court. I liked keeping what control I had, and I didn't want to be surprised by a phone call from them and not be prepared with what to say.

It had taken me two days to get up the courage to make that initial phone call, and I knew I would have to make another attempt soon. I kept busy to keep my mind off the inevitability of it all.

I read the newspaper cover to cover. Somewhere in the middle, I found an article about Paul's two accomplices. I saved reading it until I had finished the rest of the paper. Then I turned back to slowly digest its contents.

It appeared that there was no honor among thieves. Alex Roberts had accepted a plea deal in exchange for his testimony against his cohort, whose name was Chuck Mendosa. It appeared that Alex was pretty broken up about Paul's death. He insisted that he and Chuck attend the funeral, but Chuck prevailed upon him to continue with the robberies that had already been planned.

The details of the crimes were laid out and replayed for the newspaper audience. Included was Paul's involvement, but with the help of Alex's confession, Paul's change of heart was also highlighted.

Just as I thought, Alex and Paul had been friends for some time, having met at the hotel. They got talking, one thing led to another, and the crime was planned. Alex knew Chuck and brought him in on the "project" early on.

I didn't know if Alex was truly free from any guilt in Paul's death. He was, after all, speaking up to save his own skin, and I imagine I had grown cynical in that regard of late. But I found I couldn't summon enough energy to care. People talk about needing closure after something happens like what I had experienced, and often that closure comes from the conviction of the person responsible. But it dawned on me that I already had my closure. Paul was the one who was ultimately responsible for his own death. He had been the one to put all the elements into place.

Too many thoughts and issues were converging in my mind all at once. Could I be cynical about Alex but leave that cynicism behind when thinking of Paul? What if I never found any of the answers I was searching for; what then?

I didn't like considering it, but the first questions I needed to answer were about *me*. Regardless of who Paul was, how would I choose to live my life? Could I forgive Paul and move on, or would I live a life of anger and bitterness? I honestly didn't know, and not knowing made me shudder. Strange as it seemed, I found the questions about Paul had been easier to stomach.

Noah was asleep upstairs, so I called to ask Martha to come over. She knocked on my door almost before I hung up the phone.

Swinging the door open, I pulled her into an embrace.

As I let go, she leaned back to take me in. "What's up? You seem troubled."

"I suppose that's a good word for it. Come on in."

When we were settled in the great room I continued, "I was reading about Paul's cohorts again in the paper, and I gained closure, I suppose, about Paul's death."

"But that shouldn't leave you ill at ease."

"I know. It just made me realize how little closure I have about his life. That leads me to wonder if I ever will." I turned to look into her caring eyes. "Martha ..." I didn't know how to find the words. Taking a deep breath, I plunged ahead. "What happens to me if I can't get past this, if I don't find any answers, or I don't like the answers I do find?"

"That's a good question."

I expected her to continue, but that's all she said. Where was her usual wisdom? I was puzzled and finally prompted, "That's it? No advice for me?" It came out sounding desperate, but I imagine that was accurate.

"No, Brea. I can give you all the platitudes in the world, but what you're asking about is a deep, internal state. You *are* asking the right questions, though." Then she just smiled at me.

I felt even more frustrated and suddenly very alone. I wanted to glare at Martha, but I could more easily cut off my own ear than scowl at this woman who kept smiling, lovingly, in my direction.

She finally relented with one little piece of advice. "Why don't you let me stay here with Noah. You go visit your husband's grave. Stay as long as you like. If you have made peace with his death, maybe that's the place to find peace with your life."

A calm washed over me, as if her words were a warm blanket settling around my shoulders. I didn't know how what she suggested would help, but it felt like it would somehow. I looked into her eyes, and then without a word I stood up and gathered my keys.

"Brea, take all the time you need. I know where everything is in this house, so Noah and I will fill our bellies for supper." Then with a serious look she added, "Go fill your soul."

. . .

I spread a blanket out on the grass next to Paul's gravestone. His etched name was visible in my peripheral vision, but my focus was the distant horizon.

Martha had insisted I bring snacks along, but they remained untouched in my purse as I contemplated my future. Who was I really? How would I choose to live from now on?

I remained rooted to my spot. Everything around me stopped in seeming commiseration. The wind was still; no birds sang; nothing and no one moved. Only the sun continued, almost imperceptibly, to slide down to the awaiting horizon. With its march I saw my life ebbing away before my eyes. I would grow older, but unless I moved, nothing else would change. The hurt, humiliation, and heartache would always haunt me.

Just as the sun was ready to dip forever behind the earth, I shifted my legs that had fallen asleep. That tiny little shift brought another headstone into view a short distance away. Flowers were growing around it, and their delicate blooms were drinking in the last light of day.

I stared at them until the last dot of sun slipped away. Dark did not descend immediately, but dusk began to deepen. I watched the little blooms until I could see them no more. But I knew they were there, even if I could not verify it with my sight, and in the dark they were still beautiful.

With a gradual lightening that finally burst into full radiance, I realized I could do this! Paul had taught me to shine, and I would! I loved him. Even more, I knew that despite the fact that I still had questions about Paul, I could forgive him. Answers to those remaining questions would be welcome, but my forgiving him was not dependent on having them or even what they were. Forgiving him would be the gift I gave to myself and to Noah. I was beginning to allow myself to believe that he was the person I hoped he was, one who was setting his life straight. However, my forgiving him had nothing to do with what choices he was or wasn't making. It was a separate matter altogether; it was about my choice. I had it in me to forgive him, and I would choose to do so. With that understanding, a heavy burden was lifted off my shoulders. I was standing straight and upright again. I could do this.

. . .

I returned home to find Noah down for the night and Martha cleaning my house. My smile answered her question. We sat together and quietly talked well into the night. My smile never wavered. We both knew I still wanted answers about Paul, but there was now hope that the answers wouldn't devastate me.

. . .

The next morning, I realized I wasn't afraid of Paul's mother or father anymore or what they might introduce into my life. Even though their existence was a shock, it needn't shake me. I could take it in stride.

With renewed courage, I picked up the phone and called Ava Caste. This time she answered with a simple, "Hello."

What should I call her? I hadn't thought of that. "Mrs. Caste?"

"Yes?" It was a question, patiently awaiting my response.

"I'm Brea Cass, Paul's wife."

There was silence on the other end. I hadn't thought about this being just as difficult for her as it was for me. Finally she spoke. In her voice I could hear her tears. "I was hoping you would call. I so loved Paul. It was such a shock to hear of his death ... and everything surrounding it." She was tiptoeing around the crime, whether for her sake or mine I didn't know, but I understood.

She continued, "I didn't know he had married and had a child. It's like getting a little piece of him back. I got ready to call you a million times, but I didn't know if you would welcome it." She paused briefly, but not long enough for me to respond. The words were flowing out, having been held back too long and probably rehearsed in her head. "I didn't know what Paul had said about us. Would you even want us in your life? I'm sorry if I'm saying too much or reading too much into the fact that you called me back."

"No, no, it's okay," I assured her. "It was more of a shock than anything. Paul hadn't really told me much about you."

"Oh. I'm not sure if that's good or bad. When he left home so full of himself I didn't know when I would see him again. I never dreamed that I wouldn't. I'm sorry to pry, but did he say anything at all?"

I hesitated to answer, but lying now wasn't going to help. It never did, as I kept telling myself. "There's no easy way to say this, Mrs. Caste, but Paul told me that the two of you had died in a car crash a few years before we met."

I heard a sharp intake of breath on the other end followed by a sigh. "I wasn't expecting that, but maybe I should have since I know he changed his last name. I often underestimated him."

That was a leading comment, but this was not a conversation I wanted to delve into over the phone. I needed to see her eyes, and in return, see if she would look me in the eye when she talked to me of Paul. I wanted to feel with every fiber of my being that she was telling me the truth.

I purposely shifted focus. "Mrs. Caste, would you like to meet your grandson sometime?"

The voice on the other end immediately perked up. She almost squealed with delight. "I would love that so much, you have no idea!"

I hadn't planned on offering to meet. I hadn't planned out any of this. Once I had found the courage to call again, I didn't stop to think about what I would say or where I wanted the conversation to go. However, once I mentioned meeting, I felt good and warm. Surely this was the right course to take.

We talked over some logistics on the phone, and I said I would get back to her with our specific arrangements. When we were done she ended with, "Thank you for calling me. It means the world to me."

"You're welcome. I'm glad you called me in the first place," and I was surprised to realize I really meant it.

MARTHA AND MARMALADE

I allowed myself a month before I would be flying to Ohio to meet Paul's parents. I didn't know if that would be nearly enough time to prepare myself, yet I didn't want to put it off too long.

To help the time pass, and hopefully prepare myself, I spent more and more time at Martha's house. Her advice was always helpful, but her comforting presence became even more valuable.

"Martha," I asked her one day over toast with Martha's homemade orange marmalade, "do you think Paul loved me?"

"Of course I do, Brea. He may not have been a perfect man, but he wasn't fool enough to not know what he had."

Looking at her profile while she sat on the floor playing pat-a-cake with Noah, I wondered if it was really that simple. I just couldn't be sure.

Reading my silence correctly, she turned to me. "But, Brea, if you don't believe that, my saying it isn't going to make it so. Talk it out with me, I can listen as well as talk, you know."

Smiling, I nodded my head. "It's just been so much to process. I feel like I'm fighting a battle in my head all the time. I remember the sweet things he did for me. Did you remember how on Sunday mornings he would let me sleep in and make a special breakfast for everyone? Often it was homemade pancakes or waffles. Occasionally he would take Noah out and buy fresh pastries so that they would be waiting for me when I woke up." As soon as I said it, I knew that of course she remembered. Many a Sunday she was our guest at Paul's special brunches.

I had grown somewhat nostalgic as I thought of other times. "When I was going to school, some of my classes required me to do my homework in the computer lab at school or meet my group there. I remember one particular night when I had been there for hours. Paul showed up with a late dinner for me, just because he figured I would be hungry. I was, too. He didn't say much while I ate other than to ask how things were going. Then he left.

"I finished my project two hours later. When I walked out the door of the computer lab, I was shocked to see Paul sitting on the floor in the hallway. He hadn't wanted to disturb me, but he had been sitting there for those two hours waiting patiently for me to finish. He just wanted to make sure I got home safely so late at night." A small trickle of a tear ran down my face at the memory.

"That's so sweet," Martha responded.

"Yes," I responded, gaining my composure, "but then, as soon as I remember those kind deeds, I think about the lies. I think of how he kept a whole childhood from me, how he was keeping his mother from her grandchild. I can forgive him, but I'm still grappling with understanding it. What goes on in someone's head that allows him to be both kind and cruel at the same time?"

Martha took me in with her eyes. She turned away for a moment, busying herself with something at her sink. When she turned back, in her hand was a shiny, fresh apple that she extended to me. I hesitated before accepting it, turning it over in my hands, yet not taking a bite.

"Brea, don't confuse this with a justification for his poor choices,

215

but who exactly did you expect him to be? Did you expect him to be perfect?"

Her words caught me off guard, and I was suddenly frustrated. I let the apple fall from my hand. "No, of course not. This isn't about me and my expectations. This is about Paul and who he was or wasn't. I don't know! I want to know what was real." I took a breath to calm myself down before continuing. "What he let me see of him told me of a loving, generous man. What he hid, on the other hand, spoke of someone else altogether. I don't understand." The tears were coursing down my cheeks again, but for an entirely different reason than before. "Believe it or not, I'm not angry at him anymore. I've forgiven him and let all of that go." I let out a long sigh, "But it would be nice to know the truth."

Martha took me into her arms. "Yes, I know. I hope and pray that you'll figure it out, Brea. I do believe it's out there somewhere, and if it is, you'll find it."

"How can you be so sure?" I whispered into her shoulder.

In response, she just held me until I could hold my own weight again.

INTRODUCTIONS

Days passed by and the forgiveness in me grew stronger. I wavered when I felt tired or vulnerable, but taking a cleansing breath, I would stand tall and firm again, committed to finding beauty despite the thorns. It surprised me that, even with letting go, the question of whether Paul really loved Noah and me lingered in my mind constantly like an unwanted guest. I ached to know, and I didn't know if I ever would.

Time marched on, however, without waiting for me to find that resolution. I soon had to face up to the fact of needing to schedule the visit to see Paul's parents.

Reluctantly, I picked up the phone to call Ava Caste. I was a little flustered when Paul's father answered the phone. It was the first time I had spoken to him, and I wasn't prepared for the sound of his voice, an eerily familiar sound. I never would have remotely questioned the bloodline between this man and my husband. They sounded almost identical on the phone. I wasn't sure I could continue the conversation.

Much to my relief, Paul's mother picked up another phone extension. Righting myself, I concentrated on the reason for my call. "I was just calling to set the dates for my visit. Would two weeks from now be all right?"

We each pulled out our calendars and worked out the details. I could tell they were excited to meet their grandson. Before I hung up, Avalon piped up, "We would like to pay for your plane tickets to come out. Would that be okay with you?"

"Oh, no. I couldn't let you do that. We'll take care of it. We're just fine," and I ended the call as quickly as I could.

I felt the need to be in complete control of my situation. I was not ready to let these people pay for anything. With self-righteous indignation, I picked up Noah and marched over to Martha's house to tell her about the terrible thing Paul's parents had just offered to do.

As soon as she answered the door, the story spilled out of me like an overflowing fountain. "Paul's parents seem like genuinely nice people over the phone, but they don't know who I am. They think I'm some little child that needs to be taken care of. I'm not! They just tried to pay for the plane tickets for Noah and me to visit them. That is so presumptuous of them. That was only the second time I've ever even talked to them."

Martha cut me off. "Brea, come sit down and have some tea."

I looked at her with confusion. Hadn't she heard me?

"Come on in. I've got some cookies for Noah, and I just put a pot of water on for tea."

Stunned into silence, I followed the familiar path to her kitchen table. Noah practically leaped out of my arms toward the waiting cookie jar. I think he believed the cookie jar belonged to him and him alone.

While Noah took turns taking bites out of the cookies in each of his hands, Martha and I settled down, each with a nice cup of herbal tea. My breathing had slowed and I was calmer than I had been.

"Is that better?"

"Yes, thank you Martha. I can't ... "

"Brea, excuse me for interrupting, but I think you should hear me out."

This didn't seem to be going the way I'd planned. "Okay," I tentatively responded.

"These are two people who are hurting. For whatever reason they haven't been in Paul's life for some time, but it's clear they have wanted to be. Now they learn there are two additional people in their family, you and Noah. They are trying to make up for lost time and welcome you at the same time. You are rebuffing those efforts, efforts borne out of love. You're robbing them of that," Martha gently chastised.

Her words surprised me, but I had to admit, even if I didn't want to, that what she said made a lot of sense. "I guess you're right," I finally conceded. "In hindsight, I kind of overreacted." I smiled apologetically. "I think I need to go make a phone call."

"I think that would be a good idea," she agreed. "Let me keep Noah. Then you can come back and talk about it when you're done."

I didn't argue; I just got up and walked thoughtfully back to my house. Paul's mom answered on the first ring.

"Hi, this is Brea again. I need to apologize. I believe I was terribly rude to you a few minutes ago. If the offer is still open, I would love it if you would pay for our plane tickets."

I could hear the joy in her voice as she responded, "We would love that!"

What followed was a back and forth conversation as we both went online and looked at options. A half an hour later, flights were booked, and email confirmations were on their way.

Trust Martha to be right. This was clearly a gesture Paul's parents were happy and eager to make. "Thank you, Ava. I appreciate this."

"Glad to do it," was her simple reply.

Over the simple banter of booking the flights, I had become more comfortable with her over the phone. I was beginning to want to learn more about Avalon Caste. "You know, I still know so little about you and your family, our family now. Have you always lived in Ohio?"

"Fraid so. We like it here. Both of Paul's grandparents were born and raised here as well. We just never considered making our home anywhere else."

"Are his grandparents still alive?" I hadn't thought about there being other family members around.

"No, they had all passed away by the time Paul and Owen were in high school. There are some cousins, but they live all over the country now. We haven't seen any of them for ages."

"Who's Owen?" I asked, curious.

"Paul's younger brother," was her only reply, but I detected something in her voice, sadness or longing maybe.

"Does he live close by?"

I was met with silence. Finally, a small voice responded, "No, he died when he was only sixteen years old."

"Oh, I'm so sorry," was all I knew to say.

"It's okay. They say you never get over losing a child. I think they're right." A chill went through me as the unspoken words passed between us of the death of her other and only remaining child, Paul.

At a loss of what to say, I responded with, "I can't even begin to imagine how hard this is for you." Then to brighten the moment, I quickly added, "We'll bring pictures with us when we come."

"That would be nice." Then with fake bravado, she concluded, "It's been pleasant talking with you. We'll see you in a couple of weeks then."

. . .

After hanging up I sat still, feeling the weight of this woman's grief adding to my own. Assuming Martha wouldn't mind keeping Noah a little bit longer, I turned back to the open computer in front of me.

It only took a short while to find the details of Owen Caste's death. He was driving a car at excessive speed, failed to negotiate a turn, and ran headlong into a tree. He was declared dead at the scene.

I couldn't imagine losing Noah, especially so young with so much life left to live. I turned off the computer and made a beeline for Martha's house to retrieve my little boy.

HEALING

I can't begin to describe the myriad of emotions I felt those next two weeks before visiting my newly discovered in-laws. What I had learned told me that these were three-dimensional people, not just names on a page. They had histories and hopes. They had a whole lifetime full of experiences, both good and bad, and my husband would have been a part of many of those stories. What was he like as a child? What had his growing up in general been like? How did his brother's death affect him?

Despite my growing peace about my own life, I was still nervous about the unknown. I kept telling myself that I wasn't afraid of what they would tell me about Paul, but, if I was honest with myself, I was slightly worried. Worried that I would learn too much and equally concerned that I would learn too little. I tried not to think about it because when I did the butterflies in my stomach felt more like racecars.

Noah was the best salve of all for my angst in so many ways. The attentions he demanded distracted me from my worries and sometimes even allayed them completely.

His crawling became more and more efficient. He could race from room to room at lightning speed. If I wasn't watching closely, or didn't have a baby gate in place, he was gone, making my heart race until I could locate him and reassure myself that he was okay. Finding him, however, was the best of all. He thought it was a game and would giggle and giggle when I came breathlessly around a corner seeking him. Often he would crawl around a corner and turn to a sitting position, just waiting for me to appear. Before long, I let it be the game he wanted it to be.

When I first laughed my carefree laugh, it scared me. It was like a long lost friend, but one I was estranged from. However, Noah reassured me that laughing was good, and soon I welcomed the sound coming out of me as a sign of healing.

Mundane as it may seem, mealtime became a cherished time. Noah was curious about his food. What did it feel like in his hands? How did it taste? What would happen when he threw it on the floor?

A master chewer by now, he loved macaroni and cheese or spaghetti and meatballs. I would make him chicken noodle soup, and when cool, he would reach in to grab the slippery noodles and transfer them to his mouth.

I tried making a ramen one day. Noah could easily grab the curly noodles, but not so easily wrangle them into his mouth. All the time he kept saying, "Noo-noo," for noodle. He ended up with noodles all over his head, like Raggedy Andy hair. I started laughing, and before long, Noah's giggles joined mine. It felt so good to laugh heartily that I laughed until I cried. It was hard to tell if they were tears of sadness or joy. Everything seemed to be a mixture of both these days. I laughed and cried while Noah giggled himself to exhaustion.

When I finally finished cleaning him up from his lunch he laid his head on my shoulder and immediately fell asleep. Rather than lay him down in his crib, I settled in the rocking chair in our great room. He slept in my arms for an hour and a half. It was peaceful and serene.

I admired his beautiful little face and perfectly shaped head. He had sweetheart shaped lips like his father. His ears were small like mine, but the curly strawberry blonde hair was the perfect combination of Paul's auburn hair and my blonde. He was clearly our son, his genes drawing from each of us to make a new little whole.

I couldn't help but think about Paul. The memories came unbidden but not unwelcome, like the pleasant surprise of fireflies lighting up a summer night. I remembered one day Paul coming home from work early to find us just like this, wrapped up together in the rocking chair. He took one look at us and his whole face lit up. "The two of you look as sweet as the apple pie from our wedding," he whispered almost reverently. I don't even think he meant for me to hear him.

I had forgotten that moment, but now I allowed myself to remember his voice, his words. Despite everything, I loved him deeply and knew I always would. I hoped that he had truly loved us, that we had honestly been the apples of his eye.

GRANDMA AND GRANDPA CASTE

I slept fitfully the night before our flight to Ohio. I had dreams that pressed upon me, but when I woke, I could not remember the details; only gray shadowy images flickered through my memory. I shuddered to think of my earlier nighttime scares, worried that this was a premonition of further dilemmas or problems. Out of reflex, I took a gasping breath, as if I were reliving those terrible moments, but I was startled to realize that I was breathing calmly and deeply.

What did that mean? As I sat in bed mulling it over in my mind, only one thing was clear - whatever was coming was the opposite of what came before. Something positive and uplifting was awaiting me. While nervous about the day ahead, I was full of anticipation now as well.

Later that morning, Amy and Martha came by to wish us well. Amy brought snacks and toys to keep Noah entertained, and Martha brought her last-minute advice.

"Brea, can I talk to you for a minute?"

"Sure," was my natural reply.

"You are a kind, strong, courageous woman. If Paul's parents don't immediately fall in love with you, then there is something wrong with them. However, even if that's the case, you can choose to love them. They are the parents of a man who, though imperfect, was a good husband and father. I know how much you love him in spite of everything. I can read it in your eyes. Surely there is much of what was good about Paul that was learned from his dear mother and father. Be grateful to them for that."

I looked at her and nodded my consent, but she was not done. "Good. Now, Brea, know that by making the decision to feel that way, you are playing the game by your own rules. You are choosing your path and not allowing anyone to dictate it for you. You, dear, can do all of that by just being yourself, because that is truly the loving, forgiving kind of person I know you to be."

I was touched by her words and reached to hold her in a long embrace. I turned to hug Amy as well and found her with tears coursing down her face.

"Brea, I wish I could put words together like Martha does. Hey, I'd even settle for putting together cookies like she does. About all I can add is that I love you! And just come back happy, okay?"

I laughed and gave her a big squeeze. "I'll do my best."

Noah had been playing at our feet but started to whine, feeling left out of all the affection. He put up his hands, "Up, up!"

I picked him up and held him close, but he wanted more. "Umum," he said, and Amy responded to Noah's form of her name by snuggling in close. But he wasn't done. "Gaga," his all-purpose grandparent word, summoned Martha into our large group hug. Noah knew what we all needed. I started to cry and then to laugh, filled with joy and wonder.

· · ·

It was only a short flight to Ohio, but it felt like hours as I counted each minute. Keeping Noah entertained occupied some of my attention, but not enough as I still managed to picture the various scenarios I had imagined for meeting Paul's parents. I knew it was a pointless exercise, but I couldn't help but play it out in my mind. I felt like I was a little girl on the merry-go-round, not knowing how to get off.

Martha may have convinced me to accept Paul's parents' hospitality with the plane fare, but even she had understood when I told them there was no need to meet us at the airport. I would rent a car and drive to their house. They seemed to understand too that I needed to maintain some sort of control and have a means of escape, just in case.

The plan was for Noah and me to stay at their home. This made me a little nervous, so I scoped out various nearby hotels and verified that rooms would be available. Having a back-up plan helped me breathe easier.

. . .

We retrieved our luggage and picked up the rental car. I was looking forward to the drive ahead, with time all to ourselves before we would arrive at Paul's childhood home. Noah was quiet in his car seat, watching the world go by. I doubt he noticed, but I could easily tell when we drove out of the big city into a more rural landscape as large buildings were gradually replaced with barns and farmhouses. I felt a relaxing of my muscles, as if stepping out of the hustle and bustle of city life and into a more serene place and time.

It was late summer now, important to me since my seasons seemed to be how I was marking time these days. Was the transition real, I wondered? Paul had died in the spring, late spring. I was meeting my in-laws for the first time in summer. All I could hope was that this meeting was as natural as the shifting of the seasons.

Shimmering, fuzzy waves of heat hung stagnant above the pavement. Was I driving into a fiery furnace? I really wasn't sure what was waiting for me at the end of the road. Ava had seemed polite and kind over the phone, but what did I know about her, really? What about Len? I hoped this trip was not a horrible mistake. I pulled at my collar as I felt the heat rising.

Looking beyond myself, beyond the asphalt outside to the world beyond, I noticed the growing number of trees. Fields of corn and other crops I couldn't identify drifted past my eyes, and it felt as if the heat of summer seemed insignificant. But here, even the heat had purpose, drenching the crops and trees in life giving light.

I rolled down my window and welcomed the weather into the car. It was not an unpleasant feeling. Despite my expectations, it was only mildly warm, and with a breeze born from my highway speed, I found it comforting. It filled me with hope.

. . .

I shouldn't have worried about Ava and Len. They were warm and inviting but also very sensitive to my angst. They invited us in but let every decision be mine. Did I want to sit in the living room or the family room? Would I like the chair or the couch? Would we like something to drink? Or perhaps eat? I assured them I was perfectly comfortable.

We looked at each other, taking stock. My father-in-law was solid compared to my lean father. He was wearing jeans and a plaid button-up shirt. A gold-colored watch was on his left wrist, a short distance from the wedding band on his ring finger. His skin was old and leathery, tanned with a smattering of darker freckles.

My eyes moved to his face. His eyes were blue, just like Paul's. If Paul had inherited his auburn hair from his father, I couldn't tell since Len's hair was now a shining silver, but it had the waves all too familiar to me. His features appeared to me as kind. I could tell he wanted to smile, especially at Noah, but didn't want to appear too eager or pushy. His eyes, however, gave him away. They danced in Noah's direction, just like any new father or grandfather, showing a mixture of love, pride, wonder, and joy. I could deny him no longer.

"Noah, this is your grampy. Can you say hi?"

Noah looked up at me for confirmation then turned to look at the stranger across the room. I smiled at Paul's father, silently giving him permission to do the same. His face beamed and Noah immediately started to laugh. It broke the tension in the room, and suddenly I could see the possibility of being family.

I looked at my mother-in-law, taking her in for the first time. She had eyes only for Noah. While she looked at him, I looked at her. She was a small woman, barely over five feet was my guess, with soft round features. Any hard edges appeared to have been erased over the years with experience and the extra pounds that often come with aging. Her hair was brown with gentle auburn highlights, whether real or from a bottle I couldn't tell, but it was beautiful around her face. She wore no makeup, a woman comfortable with herself. She beckoned to Noah with outstretched hands and a soft, musical voice, "Noah, would you like to come here?"

He turned at her voice, and appearing to trust it, crawled slowly in her direction. Before he reached her arms, she produced a toy, a small, bright red ball. He giggled with delight, moving faster, then plopping down so he could reach for the ball with both hands.

For the next two hours I quietly observed while this newly discovered family interacted with my son, their grandson. Len was gentle in every action. He immediately moved to the floor to be with Noah, using soft words and slow movements so as not to startle or scare his grandson. Avalon was at times soft, at others loud with her contagious laugh.

They all played as if they had never been allowed to play before and might not be allowed again. It was frantic in that urgency, but gentle in its execution. From time to time Noah would search for me with his eyes, to verify I was still there, but then he would return his attention to his new entertainers who seemed to hang on every sound he made. He began to purposely make small noises to catch their delighted reactions. I believe Noah could have played that game alone for the whole two hours had there not been so many other good ones to play.

Ava and Len kept producing new toys, with a sideways look of chagrin at me. I wasn't even sure where the toys had been hidden, but sure enough, every ten or fifteen minutes a new one would appear in one of their hands, and Noah would squeal with delight.

They were clearly enjoying spoiling their grandson, however

prudent their spending normally appeared to be if the surroundings were any indication. Their home was modest, the furnishings neat and clean but old and sometimes worn. They cared for what they had, but were not lavish except when it came to Noah. They must have spent a fortune at the toy store, but I was quite certain, without any regrets.

Len was slowed by age, but Avalon appeared invigorated by it. She was a bundle of nervous energy, playing with Noah, but constantly checking herself to ensure she wasn't stepping on my toes or being too pushy with my little one.

With such intense play, it was no surprise when Noah turned to me and crawled into my lap, nestling his head on my chest. I lifted him with me into a nearby rocking chair. He was asleep before I could even begin to rock.

The three of us went silent, watching the sleeping cherub in my arms, not wanting to disturb him nor break the spell of the moment. But I had not come for only this, even if it was better than I could have hoped.

"Thank you for ... ," I wasn't quite sure how to categorize their treatment of Noah. I didn't want to thank them for the toys; that sounded shallow. I didn't want them to think I only cared about what they would buy for us. I also wasn't ready to thank them for being Noah's grandparents; it was too soon for that. My parents still felt like his "real" grandma and grandpa. These two would become his grandparents, if they chose. I would facilitate it, but a single afternoon was only a beginning. So, not knowing how to end the sentence, I simply nodded towards the sleeping child in my arms.

They nodded silently in return, respectful of my absence of words.

TIME FOR TRUTH

Eager to move to what was weighing on my mind, I asked, "Would you mind telling me about Paul?"

Ava gave me a thoughtful look. I believe she understood the true nature of the question, even expected it. So, she didn't hesitate long before responding, "I have many stories to tell you, and eventually, if you like, I will tell them all to you. But I imagine that what you are really seeking now is something different. You would like answers." She looked at me for confirmation. I simply nodded in reply.

"I think the best place to start is in the middle. Is that all right?"

I appreciated this woman's forthright nature. It wasn't harsh, just honest, and honesty was what I was hoping for. Again, I nodded my assent.

"Paul was an exceptional child, everyone's favorite, as I'm sure you might imagine. He always drew people to him, and for a number of years that was a good thing.

"When he entered high school, it took on a new form. He was learning more about the power he wielded, and it intrigued him. I noticed him experimenting with people around him and what he could get them to do. He was not harming his friends, but he was flirting with danger for himself. His father and I both spoke with him, warning him that his motives were not pure, and his actions would lead to no good if he continued. Unfortunately, where he used to listen, the teenager in him rejected all we said, dismissing us as old-fashioned, meddling parents.

"His behavior escalated, but not right away. For a time we thought maybe he was actually internalizing what we said while rejecting it to our faces. He was doing something good with his power over others. He and his friends, or his following if you will, began to notice the outcasts, the kids who were picked on or bullied on a regular basis. Once they identified these kids, they started to stick up for them and protect them. His group was big enough that they could stand against the worst that high school had to offer. It was quite the thing to watch!" She paused, with a wistful expression on her face. In that moment we were all wishing things had stayed that way.

Avalon was lost for a moment, far away. I hated to pull her back to a far less comfortable place, but I was impatient for the truth. "Then what happened?" I gently prodded.

She was startled back and looked at me as if she didn't know who I was or why I was there. I'm sure she actually knew, but I also represented all that she didn't want to acknowledge. A single tear formed at the corner of her eye and trickled down her cheek. I felt guilty for having brought her back, for having inspired the memories that made her sad.

Len saved us both. "Brea, if you don't mind, I'll continue her story."

I was touched by his kindness, and now at a loss for words myself, just nodded in his direction.

"Brea, Paul was a real piece of work. You know what he did? One day one of the kids he helped offered him some kind of treat. It was a candy bar or cupcake or some such thing. That's all it took. Within a very short period of time, he had turned his kindness into a full-blown protection business! Can you believe that?"

I was learning his frequent questions were all rhetorical, but I nodded or shook my head when the moment was right, making sure not to actually interrupt his train of thought.

He continued, "He and his friends started taking money for their 'services'! It even got bad enough that they started making up invoices! Boy, do you have any idea how we reacted when we found out what was going on? I'll tell you, it wasn't pretty. We tried to help him understand that the only difference between him and the bullies was that the kids were happily giving him money rather than forcibly so, but either way they were victims. Often the nice bully is the worst one of all. He didn't hear a word we said. We informed the school officials about it, and they were none too happy either. He was suspended for a week, along with all his friends." Len shook his head at the memory of it. "He had the further gall to complain to us when we didn't let him hang out with his friends during his suspension! I've never seen such an unrepentant fool."

I dared a glance at Ava, who had pulled herself together again. Her husband was still shaking his head, and she took over, this time to relieve him. "That was, I think, the real turning point for both of us. He became more defiant, and we became more determined than ever not to let him bowl us over as he seemed to be doing with everyone else. He even managed to sweet talk the school into changing his suspension to a private reprimand for his school record. That way it wouldn't affect any possible college admissions. He kept getting away with whatever he wanted, and we warned him that it would catch up to him someday." She stopped with a small gasp, realizing that she could have just been referring to his death. "Oh, I'm sorry, Brea, I didn't mean ..."

"It's okay. I've made peace with all of that. Please, go on, I want to know what happened."

"It's just that Paul didn't know how to back down. Once he chose a course of action, that was it, no turning back. He refused to see any other side to it.

"Well, Paul continued to make his plans. He was intelligent; there was no doubt about that. He set his sights on some of the best colleges in the country. We went over the finances with him and explained that we couldn't afford the pie-in-the-sky places he was looking at. Hard as it was, we told him we would not go to any extraordinary measures to deal with those high costs as long as he was unfeeling and manipulative of the people around him. That did not sit well with him at all, I'll tell you! He was furious!"

Len added, "I didn't know he could get so mad. He finally asked what our bottom line was for money, and could he take it in a lump sum. That seemed an odd request, but we told him what we could pay over time or the smaller amount that he could have right then, if that was his desire. He said he would let us know. After that, he became very secretive and withdrawn from us. The day after graduation he came to us and politely asked for the lump sum of money we had offered."

Ava took over with, "Before he walked out with his bags, he told us this was his inheritance money. He would never ask for more. But, he went on to say, he would show the world how it was really done. He was going to take this 'small pittance', as he called it, and build something out of it. When he was done he would have a real inheritance, one he could be proud of."

"Within a few days he took the money and left," Len concluded sadly.

I'm not sure why it hadn't occurred to me, but I hadn't reconciled how we had bought our house with the inheritance money from his parents, seeing his parents were still alive. The question I had forgotten to even ponder was answered right in front of me. With whatever seed money he had been given, he started college. However, the real breakthrough had come with the app contest he had entered. The half a million dollars was the real inheritance that he created, the one he could be proud of. It felt good, in an odd way, to fill in the holes, putting the pieces together in a puzzle that was part beautiful and part ugly. I realized, with irony, that when he talked about being a "self-made" man, he had been telling the truth all along.

I noticed after their story was complete there was a pause in the conversation, and Len and Ava exchanged odd glances with each other. I didn't doubt what they had just told me, but something was missing; only I wasn't sure what.

I rocked the sleeping Noah in my arms while looking from one to the other of them, trying to understand the unspoken communication passing between them. I posed what seemed to me to be the obvious question. "What about Owen's death? Didn't he die about the time Paul left for college?" I bluntly asked. As soon as the words were out of my mouth, I wanted to take them back. It had been clear that Owen's death was not an easy topic, and I had brought it out into the open without any kind of warning. But as I looked at them in turn, I knew this was the root of what they were leaving out.

My questions were met with silence, but I was not to be deterred, and I returned their silence with an expectant silence of my own. I continued to look from one to the other, but they would not meet my eyes.

Finally, I spoke. "I'm sure this isn't easy for you to talk about. But I need you to understand that I have to start this relationship with complete truth and honesty." I looked at Ava and then Len, but they still would not return my look.

Anger burst over me as I refused to accept the partial story I had been told. Too forcefully, I prodded, "I've had enough of deceit, and I *will* walk out the door without a backward glance if you're not able to give me the whole truth." I was shocked at the threat that had just escaped my lips. Only, I knew I didn't view it as the threat it sounded like. I had learned a lot about myself over the last couple of months, and one thing was clear, I was not going to embrace this extra family without complete transparency.

Avalon looked up at me with shock and hurt, but I was relieved to see no anger. "No, please don't go," Avalon begged. "I just ..." she said before lapsing again into silence.

"Ava, why don't you get us something to eat or maybe a drink? I'm sure we could all use that about now." Len looked at his wife with love and concern. It was clear he was allowing her to leave, to escape the truth hanging heavy in the room. She looked at him with relief and wordlessly got up and moved off in the direction of the kitchen.

"Brea, it's not that we want to hide things from you, but we don't talk about this very much. It's just too painful. We basically lost both of our sons within a few weeks of each other. Dealing with the finality of Paul's death, that no reconciliation will ever happen, has brought back the pain of Owen's passing. It's too much to ask one mother to bear." He looked down at the floor in sadness and regret.

I wasn't sure how to respond. I felt responsible for bringing that grief back, because of Paul's death, but also my insistence on hearing the whole story. *Should I back down?* I wondered. I remembered Martha's counsel to me that I could choose my path. I wanted to get the painful part over with, to not have it hanging unspoken over our heads. Decision made, I turned my attention to the sleeping Noah in my arms. Gently I stroked his sweaty head while waiting patiently for Paul's dad to collect his thoughts.

When he began, he looked me directly in the eye. "Owen idolized his big brother. They were just two years apart and had always been close. Owen would have followed Paul to the ends of the earth. When Paul started extorting money out of his classmates, Owen faltered in that adoration for the first time in his life. But he eventually gave in and became one of Paul's henchmen, at least in part. However, it churned him up inside.

"He confessed all of this to us when the suspensions came down. Owen was given leniency because he walked with the group but never actually demanded money nor accepted it. That seemed to be the middle ground he had found.

"When the suspensions were over, Paul did not seem repentant. We were worried that the behavior would return in one form or another. We started pressing Owen for information about Paul's activities. He didn't want to betray his brother, but he didn't condone what Paul had done either. Initially he talked to us, but soon he clammed up, refusing to talk to us about any of it."

He paused in his retelling while dark shadows crossed his brow. "Then one day, one horrible day, it all came to a head. We confronted Paul about his activities and questioned his intentions. I said, 'Even your younger brother understands that what you did was wrong, but for some reason you don't get it!' He was upset, of course. We argued for some time, back and forth, neither of us budging. His mother brought up Owen again, asking Paul what kind of example he was setting for him."

Len got a faraway look in his eyes. When he continued, his voice was husky. "Owen had been listening from the top of the stairs to the whole conversation. When he had finally had enough, he burst into the room. His words will forever burn in my mind. He said, 'How dare you bring me into this. I do not take sides. I'm just trying to live my life and be a good person. And I will not stay here one minute longer while the people I love tear each other apart.' Then, with that, he grabbed the car keys and stormed out of the house. We heard the car screech out of the driveway, but then we just continued our fight, unaffected by his impassioned speech. It was only a few minutes later when we heard the sirens."

Noah felt hot against my chest as my heart burned with anguish for what this family had been through. However, Len was not done.

"The rest of the story is as we told you except for the words Paul hurled at us. He blamed us for Owen's death. Graduation was only a few weeks later. When it was over, he told us he didn't want to know us, he didn't even want to bear our name and ... and that he would never forgive us."

I didn't know Avalon had returned until I heard her voice behind me. It was wispy and ethereal, as if speaking through a time machine from all those years ago. "With that he left." Then she added in a barely audible whisper, "And that's the last time we saw him."

It was a moment before anyone could speak. I was surprised to hear Avalon's voice break the silence in a calm, serene tone. "He broke our hearts, to be sure. I always hoped that with maturity he would finally learn to back down, to change the direction of his life. Because I knew that if he could learn how to do that, he would come back to me," and then she added, in the tone of voice I expected, "He never did."

I could feel her anguish, and my thoughts ran like wildfire, consuming all that she had told me. I suppose Paul's parents really did die, for him, in a car accident.

Paul's mother finished wiping her eyes with a Kleenex and pulled her head up to look at me. The look was sad and plaintive. There was something I could give this woman, a little piece of hope. "I want you to know something about Paul. He finally learned to back down. It was probably the first time since he left here, but he backed out of the robbery. He even sabotaged the credit card info that the other thieves stole so they couldn't use it. The only reason he was still involved was because they threatened to harm Noah and me. He really had learned to back down!" As I spoke, I realized that I truly believed what I was saying, that Paul was changing his ways, for real. With that understanding came a desire for Avalon to understand as well. I desperately wanted this woman to have the hope that her son was on his way back to her. It was true; I was sure of it. I just didn't know if I was successful in convincing his mother of that. I waited expectantly for her speak. She didn't respond right away, so I added another memory I had stored away, without realizing its significance. "One time, when Paul was putting Noah down, I heard him through the baby monitor. He said, 'I wish your other grandma were here.' He did want you back in his life."

"Brea, thank you. I hope that was so. I guess after so many years it's hard to know. How do you do that to a mother? How can you leave her hanging for so long? It makes me wonder if he had any love left in his heart for me, for us. I understand things can be rough at times with kids, but it would mean the world to me if I knew he still loved me somewhere under it all. That is my biggest regret, not knowing that, and now he's dead and I can't ask him, and he can't tell me."

Chills ran through my body. I knew exactly what she was feeling. And at that moment my sweet little boy woke up in my arms.

PLANTED SEEDS

Noah roused then gazed at the somber gathering around him. Apparently, he felt it his responsibility to change the mood. He looked around and smiled at everyone, then climbed down from my lap ready to be the center of attention again.

Ava stood up, grateful for a change. "Why don't I get us that food we had talked about? Is anyone hungry?"

I had to admit that I was, and I'm sure Noah was ready for a snack. "Would you like any help?"

"No, Brea. You just sit and visit. But I'll take Noah with me, if he's willing," and she quickly added, "If that's okay with you?"

"Of course," I replied, realizing that despite the tension of what we had discussed, I was at ease with this woman I had just met. Ava reached down with her arms, beckoning Noah to her. He reached up his hands to meet hers, and she beamed in response. She scooped him up and held him close before turning towards the kitchen.

Len was a gentle creature to be sure, but it was Ava who radiated love and acceptance. It was not a surprise to me that Noah willingly left my side to go with his new grandma into the kitchen. Her warmth was palpable.

I didn't begin another conversation with my father-in-law, leaving the quiet of the moment alone. I perked up my ears to the sounds coming from the kitchen, plates and cups, the refrigerator door, running water, and the running chatter of grandma to grandson. "Noah, you are such a big boy. Would you like a drink of water? Grandma and Grandpa went out and bought brand new sippy cups just for you. Which one would you like?"

The noises became indistinct, but I gathered they summed up to Noah's now drinking out of his new sippy cup. It made me smile, the gentle hand of Noah's new grandma.

The words came clear again. "Noah, would you like a snack? Do you like apples? Noah, you are the apple of my eye!"

I bolted upright. Had I heard right? Again, the sound came from the kitchen, "Noah, you little apple of my eye, I love you."

Len startled at my sudden movement as I leapt up and nearly ran into the kitchen. My sudden entrance startled my mother-in-law. She saw the shocked look on my face and searched to understand it. Following my gaze, her eyes rested on the apple piece in Noah's fingers.

"Oh, Brea, I hope it's okay I gave him an apple. It's a very soft one. I didn't think he'd have any trouble chewing it," she said apologetically.

"No, that's okay. What did you just call him?"

She seemed a little intimidated by my intensity. "The apple of my eye?" It was a question, as if searching for something because of the sound of my voice, but not sure exactly what she was searching for or even why.

"Why did you call him that?" I tried not to sound accusatory, but I wasn't succeeding very well.

Again taken aback, she responded, "It's what I used to call Paul and Owen all the time. They were the apples of my eye." Then she grew silent, not knowing if she needed to apologize for something.

I could say nothing in response, but tears started to bud at the corners of my eyes. Soon they were coursing down my cheeks, and I was powerless to stop them. Ava looked distressed, fearing she had caused me anguish but not sure how.

It was some time before I could speak, but when Ava started to apologize, for what she knew not, I waved the apology away. "No, no, you don't understand. It's actually okay. Everything is okay. Paul loved you more than you know, and that means he loved me and Noah, too." I could not explain further as all my emotions broke out in joyful sobs. Paul's mother did not fully understand, but she caught the significance of the moment and wrapped her arms around me, joining her tears with mine.

When my tears subsided enough that I could speak, I took my turn to explain to Paul's mother the things she had not known. "Mother Caste," somehow the name felt more sincere, "when I first met Paul he gave me an apple. Then when he first asked me out, he said I was the apple of his eye. It is something he said to me in one form or another ever after that. Once Noah was born, he referred to him the same way." She still looked slightly puzzled.

"Don't you see? He never forgot you! He remembered everything you taught him. He loved you; he never stopped loving you. He just didn't know how to back down and come back. I already told you how he finally learned to back down when he decided not to go through with the credit card fraud. I'm certain if he had lived, he would have come back to you.

"But even though he didn't have the time to bring you personally back into his life, you were always there in spirit. He always remembered and honored you by simply modeling your love, by telling me and by telling Noah that we were each the apple of his eye."

As I saw truth dawn on Ava's face and encompass her whole frame, it more fully embraced me as well. I suppose in that moment I got my Paul back. He had still been a thief and a manipulator for a time. He was still guilty of far too many indiscretions, but I knew, with a clarity that had been missing since the very first phone call in the middle of the night, that he had loved me, that my memories owned the one true and honest part of him. Here was something that I could tell Noah as he grew, that his father loved him with all his heart and soul. While I would not lie to him about the other choices his father had made in life, we could choose to focus on this better part. Together we could and would always be the apple of his eye.

. . .

It was quiet while we both let all that had passed between us sink in. It was with a warmth and peace that we smiled at each other and then fell again into a natural embrace. I felt, wrapped in her arms as she was in mine, a kinship that was more than blood. We had both been through the same emotional turmoil and had both come out the other side, if not triumphant at least secure. We both loved Paul deeply, faults and all, and we especially knew, without a doubt anymore, that he loved us deeply too.

As we let our arms loosen and eventually fall to our sides, we stepped back and took a new stock of each other. We had just become more than blood relations; we had become friends.

I looked at this woman who I now knew would be a part of my life to her dying day. I thought of her not as a mother-in-law, but as an equal. I wanted to learn everything I could about her. What were her likes and dislikes? Did she have a favorite color or favorite food? What was her childhood like, and who were her parents? I wanted to get to know Avalon Caste.

There was so much to ask. I wanted to know these things about her, but I also wanted to know all about Paul. From her would flow stories, one after another, I was certain. She contained within herself the tidbits missing from my knowledge of Paul, answers to all those questions I hadn't had the time to ask. From those stories, good and bad, my love for my husband would grow. I suppose *The Princess Bride* had been right all along, "Death cannot stop true love."

Where should I start asking questions? I asked the one thing I had already wondered. "Avalon is such an interesting name. I like it. Where is it from?"

She looked me straight in the eye and her whole face smiled at me with love. "It's Welsh, dear. It means 'apple tree.'"

241

EPILOGUE

We celebrated Noah's first birthday on a bright, sunny day with our typical gathering plus two. Martha, Amy, and the Professor all came loaded down with food like normal. Mom and Dad had flown in and Paul's parents came in as well.

It was the first time that my friends and parents met Len and Ava, or Grandma and Grandpa Caste. I thought it might be a little awkward at first, but I shouldn't have worried. Despite what we had all learned about Paul, everyone in my gathering loved him. It was easy for them to extend that love to his parents. In turn, his parents were grateful to all who were present for loving and caring for their son during a time when they weren't allowed to do so.

Gifts in abundance were produced to match the amount of food we couldn't possibly all eat. I sat back and watched the happy gathering, content with my life.

Part way through the party, by prior arrangement, Noah and I slipped out the back door. Noah had begun to toddle in the last month, and we slowly made our way to the edge of the backyard. A hole had been prepared ahead of time by the gathering that was now inside, even primed with fertilizer. Beside it stood an apple tree and a pile of removed dirt.

I lowered the tree into the waiting ground, and then Noah and I packed earth around it, me with big shovelfuls and Noah by the fistful, adding water periodically as we went. He viewed it as a charming new game. Before long, I joined him, getting down on my knees to move the dirt all around the roots of our new apple tree. There was more dirt than we needed, as the tree's root ball had taken up a lot of space. We mounded the remaining soil around the tree until even Noah said, "Done."

We stood back to examine our handiwork and knew that it was good. After cleaning off in the hose, we stepped back into the house.

A wave of quiet reverence greeted us, broken only by the sound of an occasional sniffle. My mother and Paul's mother were locked in an embrace; I couldn't be sure who was comforting whom. Even Len and Dad sat close together in some conspiratorial fashion. Clearly all eyes had been watching our labors, and there was not a dry eye among them.

I surprised myself by not joining them. I had left tears behind, replacing them with a sense of peace and wonder. I had been married to a wonderful man. I didn't know what the future held for me, but I was certain that wherever it led, Paul would be watching over me from above. We would come through just fine.

We had one more birthday stop to make, and this time everyone was invited. We all piled into a couple of cars and drove to the chapel where Paul's funeral had been held. Only we passed the church parking lot, instead turning into the drive for the apple orchard next door.

After we had all spilled out, the orchard owner, Mr. Charles, greeted us. I had visited with him over the phone a few weeks back. He didn't normally sell apples on a pick-your-own basis, but when I told him my story, he gladly consented.

"This way folks," Mr. Charles motioned, as we all obediently followed. He led us past different varieties of apples until we got to the back of his orchard. He finally stopped under a charming, little apple tree. Its limbs twisted and turned before finally pointing heavenward. It was laden with rosy colored fruit. "This tree is yours. I've placed a couple ladders for ya', and there's buckets here at the base of the tree." Everything was in order as he indicated. "Picking apples is easy, just give 'em a firm, hard pull and they'll come off for ya'," he instructed. "Use the ladders only if you want, 'cause there's plenty you can reach from the ground. I'll leave you be, now. You can come find me when you're done." Then silently he disappeared into his trees.

Everyone wanted to help Noah pick an apple, and so with a smile, I turned to pick apples on my own. I spied a perfectly shaped apple just above my head. It was without blemish. Eagerly, I reached for it. Just before my fingers could touch the apple, it dropped from the tree into my waiting palm. I stared at the beautiful apple that had been placed in my hand. Slowly I lifted my eyes to the sky and whispered, "I love you, too."

Thank you so much for reading one of Mary Ellen Bramwell's novels.
If you enjoyed the experience, please check out our
recommended title for your next great read!

Dandelion Summer by Mary Ellen Bramwell

2019 PenCraft Award Winner - Mystery/Sleuth

Made in the USA
Monee, IL
26 June 2024

60658683R00136